FANG GIRL

FANG GIRL

HELEN KEEBLE

HARPER TEEN

An Imprint of HarperCollinsPublishers

HarperTeen is an imprint of HarperCollins Publishers.

Fang Girl
Copyright © 2012 by Helen Keeble
www.epicreads.com

Library of Congress Cataloging-in-Publication Data
Keeble, Helen.
Fang girl / Helen Keeble. — 1st ed.
p. cm.
Summary: Although fifteen-year-old Jane has always loved vampire lore, she
is surprised to awaken in her coffin with fangs, and she goes to her parents
and younger brother for help in figuring out why undead factions are vying
for her eternal allegiance.
ISBN 978-0-06-208225-1 (pbk. bdg.)
[1. Vampires—Fiction. 2. Supernatural—Fiction. 3. Loyalty—Fiction.
4. Family life—England—Fiction. 5. England—Fiction. 6. Humorous stories.]
I. Title.
PZ7.K22549Fan 2012   2011042306
[Fic]—dc23   CIP
                                                                              AC

Typography Alison Klapthor
12 13 14 15 16 CG/RRDH 10 9 8 7 6 5 4 3 2 1

First Edition

To Eljas Oksanen, who read every draft

Chapter 1

Just because I like vampires doesn't mean I'm stupid. Okay, so my bookcase groans under the weight of paperbacks with moody black-and-red covers. So I've seen every episode of *Buffy* and *The Vampire Diaries* three times over. So I hang out a lot at Fang-Girls.net—*the* fansite for all things vampire. But despite all that, I don't mistake fantasy for reality. I never, not once in all my fifteen years, thought vampires were actually real.

Until, of course, I woke up dead, six feet underground, in my coffin. That'll convince pretty much anyone.

"Oh, crap," I said, rubbing my forehead where I'd banged it against the lid while trying to sit up. I performed a quick inventory. Yep—coffin, churning thirst, not breathing, fangs. I could practically hear the ominous music swelling as I reached the inevitable conclusion. I was a vampire, a creature of the night—

Hang on. I *could* hear ominous music swelling. At least, slightly tinny and rather repetitive ominous music, reverberating in the close confines of the coffin. From my vast store of vampire-related trivia, I identified it as the opening theme from Francis Ford Coppola's *Dracula* movie, as interpreted by ringtone.

I was a vampire, and . . . someone was trying to call me?

When my parents had said that not even death could pry me from my mobile phone, I'd thought they were joking. I wriggled around in the narrow coffin until I could reach the ringing handset. I instantly knew it wasn't mine—my phone was small and sleek, with a USB stick dangling on the charm strap. This felt like a brick, bristling with extra battery packs. The glow of the screen seemed dazzlingly bright in the darkness, making my eyes water. UNKNOWN CALLER, it said. I stabbed the CALL button. "Uh . . ." How did you start a conversation when you were dead? "Hello?"

"Xanthe Jane Greene," said a woman's voice, under-cut by the crackle of interference. "At last."

So she knew me. I, on the other hand, had never heard her before. "Who are you? What's going on? Why——?"

"Time enough for all that, my darling!" She laughed—an amazing laugh, soft and supple, like a cat arching into my hand. "We have all the time in the world. And as for who I am . . . I'm your dearest friend, of course." Somewhere above my head came the scrape of a shovel biting into earth. "Don't worry, darling. I'll soon have you out."

In my books, only two sorts of people ever dug up vampires . . . and I was pretty certain that someone looking to plant a stake through my chest wouldn't phone to chat first. Which meant— "You're my sire, right?"

"Indeed." The sounds of digging were getting closer. Her voice dropped into a low purr. "And you are my masterpiece. I've been looking forward to this day for— oh, blast. Not *now!*" There was a clatter, as though she'd dropped the shovel. The phone went dead.

"What? What?" My dry voice cracked. I hammered at the lid. There was a bit of give to it now, but before I could brace my legs to push properly, the whole coffin shook under the weight of someone jumping down onto it.

"Listen, darling." The woman's voice was clearer now, with nothing between us but the coffin lid and a thin layer of dirt. "I've got to lead this idiot off. Find somewhere to hide, and I'll contact you as soon as I can. Wait for me!"

"But—" The coffin lid rattled as she sprang back out of my grave. I heard the muffled sound of running footsteps—two pairs—followed by the unmistakable crack of gunfire. I froze, huddled in a ball with the phone clutched between my hands.

Then—silence.

If there were two sorts of people who came to dig up vampires, I was guessing that the other sort had just turned up. Vampire hunters. There were *always* vampire hunters. And even now one of them could be dusting my sire.

I squirmed until my feet were planted solidly against the top of the coffin. It creaked, resisting me—then, it flew open, and a whole load of earth fell right into my mouth. I'd intended to burst forth with a dramatic cry and fangs agleam, but it ended up being more of a splutter and a stagger.

Coughing and spitting, I struggled out of my grave. I did not immediately catch fire, turn to dust, or have an acrobatic blonde Buffy-wannabe put a stake through my chest. So far, the first day—night—of my unlife was off to a good start.

Blinking watering eyes, I risked a quick glance around, expecting a crossbow bolt or a silver bullet to come whizzing toward me at any second. The ground rolled away before me, covered with close-cropped grass and sheep droppings. A couple of small trees overhung the collapsed pit of my grave. A full harvest moon rode high among thin streaks of cloud, casting a fine bright light that let me see for miles across the low, gentle slopes of the South Downs.

Both vampire hunters and other vampires were conspicuous by their absence.

"Baa," said something behind me. I was running before I'd even properly registered the sound. And by running, I mean *running*. I shot down the hill as if rocket propelled. Wind roared past my face, carrying with it the sharp, rich scents of earth and grass. A wonderful sensation of warmth spread outward through my chest from my silent heart. No hunger, no thirst; no lungs heaving; no ache of muscles or burn in my joints. I was barely making an effort.

Ah yes. Vampiric superspeed. Of course.

Awesome.

Some little part of my brain was leaping up and down, trying to point out that not many vampire hunters said "baa," but I was having too much fun running to stop now. I quickened my pace, and it was as easy as shifting gears on a bicycle. When I looked down at my feet, they were flickering over the ground almost too fast to see, and—

I ran straight into the wooden fence at the foot of the field.

It didn't knock the breath out of me, seeing as how I wasn't breathing to start with, but I did have to spend a few minutes lying flat on my back, convincing myself that I wasn't dead. Or rather, deader. Sitting up, I prodded at my ribs, but nothing seemed broken. I was lucky that it had been a rail fence, rather than barbed wire, or I would have shredded myself into vampire linguine. I was even luckier to have caught myself across one of the horizontal rails—a foot to the left, and I would have hurled myself onto an upright support. Staking myself on my first night as a vampire would have been terminally embarrassing.

"Baa," said the sheep again. It had ambled down the hill after me, and was now regarding me from some way off as if waiting to see what entertaining thing I would do next. I could make out every detail about it, down to the fine hairs on its ears.

I stared hard at the sheep, trying to see if I could view the movement of its blood through its skin, or sense the beating of its heart, or see the aura of its warmth glowing against the night. It stared back at me, looking resolutely like an ordinary sheep. I guess I wasn't that sort of vampire. Or maybe sheep didn't have auras.

I ran my dry tongue over my weird teeth. Sheep *did* have blood, and I was suddenly very, very thirsty.

That's when it truly hit me: I was a vampire. A real, live—well, actually not—bloodsucking vampire.

Holy *crap*. I put my head between my knees—I wasn't sure if that could help with shock if you weren't alive, but it was worth a try—and tried to sift back through my memories. I was pretty sure I would have remembered being bitten by a vampire, but the last thing I could recall before waking up in the grave was . . . sitting in the backseat of Alice's mum's Volvo. I wasn't really friends with Alice—I wasn't really friends with anyone down here yet, as my family had only moved in two weeks ago—but we both played the violin and sat next to each other in the orchestra, and her family lived down the road from mine, so her mum had offered to give me a lift back from practice. We'd been coming up one of the twisty little country lanes, and I was trying to make Alice like me by laughing at all her jokes and agreeing that the boy she liked probably fancied her back, and then—a sudden lurch, my seat belt abruptly strangling me, and—nothing.

I must have died in a car crash.

In all my books, movies, and TV shows, I'd never heard of someone becoming undead through being hit by a vampire's *car*. Not even in fanfic.

But however it had happened, I was definitely a vampire. I stood up and dusted myself off, then looked around. On the other side of the fence, a narrow country lane snaked away, leading from the Downs toward the south coast. I could hear the distant roar of cars on the main road. Lacking any better option, I started to walk toward the sound. Vampires were urban creatures, after all, and the nearest thing to urban around here was the grubby seaside town of Worthing. It wasn't much, but it was better than an open sheep field. I could go and hide in . . . in the sewers, I guessed, since there were only two places feral vampires tended to hang out, and Worthing was really, really short on decadent Goth nightclubs. I'd hole up and wait for my sire, and then . . . then . . .

Then I guessed I'd have to start my new life. Unlife. On the plus side, there would probably be stylish clothes and amazing psychic abilities and really hot guys in leather trousers. On the negative side, I'd probably never see sunlight again, or eat chocolate, and I might slowly spiral into a sinkhole of angst and despair until someone staked me. And I didn't have any money. Or a change of underwear. Or a way to have a shower. And—my stomach rumbled—it was looking increasingly likely that I was going to have to eat raw sheep.

And I wasn't going to be able to see my family ever again.

My vision went a bit misty, and my lower lip started to tremble. I blinked the tears back. Vampires didn't cry. Vampires were *cool*. Deliberately, I thought of all the things I'd be leaving behind. No more constant moving. No more always being the new girl, trying to break into social cliques. As a vampire, *I'd* be the queen bee with a constant circle of admirers. No more worrying that my exam results wouldn't be good enough to get into university, or whether I was getting fat. I was going to be slender and gothically beautiful *forever*.

Well, I was going to be fifteen forever. That kind of sucked. Why couldn't I have been turned next year?

Never mind, I told myself firmly. I was a vampire. This was going to be great. I'd get to hang out with other vampires, who would be effortlessly elegant and would treat me like an adult. No more fights with my mother over my spending habits. No more annoying little brother stealing my eyeliner. No more embarrassing dad wearing yellow spandex in public and making me go out with him on bike rides. No more, no more.

I stopped, tears streaking my face.

"Well, screw *that*," I said, and punched my home number into the mobile phone.

Chapter 2

The phone rang eight times, which was just long enough for me to have second thoughts. I was a *vampire*. What was I doing? But even as my thumb hovered over the END CALL button, there was a click on the other end. My dad's mumbling, sleep-slurred voice said, "Mmfgh?"

"Daddy?" Despite myself, the words came out high and trembling, a little-girl voice.

"Wha?" I could picture my dad flopped face-first into his pillow, phone mashed against one cheek. It usually took four cups of tea or two espressos to haul him up to full consciousness. "Whozit?"

I swallowed hard, forcing my voice back down into

its usual register. "Dad, it's me." Silence, so long that I wondered if he'd fallen asleep again. "Dad?"

"I'm asleep," he said, sounding wide-awake. "I'm dreaming."

"Um, no, Dad, it's really me. Look, I know this is going to sound really crazy, but I don't have time for long explanations, so please just bear with me. See, the thing is—" I stopped. There was a strange sound, like broken static, coming from the phone. I took it away from my ear to glare at the screen, but the signal bar showed full strength. "Dad? Can you hear me? There's some sort of interference—"

"Who is this?" My mother's familiar sharp tone made my stomach flip with habitual guilt, even though I hadn't done anything wrong (rising from the dead didn't count, in my opinion). Her voice came through crystal clear, though that weird sound was still in the background. "What did you say to my husband, arse-hole?"

"Mummy?" Again, the little-girl squeak. God, I sounded so pathetic. I was glad there weren't any other vampires around.

For the first time in my life, I witnessed my mother at a complete loss for words. Figured that I'd have to be dead to experience it. In the pause, I realized that the dry, harsh sound in the background had to be Dad, crying. Another first—but a much less pleasant one.

"Xanthe?" whispered my mum.

For once, my stupid first name didn't make me wince. "Hi," I said, unable to come up with anything less inane. "Um."

When my mother spoke again, she sounded as calm as a frozen river. "You are a sick, sick person, and I am phoning the police."

"No, wait—crap!" I stared at the phone in disbelief. She hung up on me! My own mother! I tried redialing, but all I got was the shrill beep of the busy tone. I started entering Dad's mobile number—but then a much better idea occurred to me.

This time the phone barely managed one ring before it was picked up at the other end. All the commotion down the hallway must have woken him up. "Hey," I said in greeting.

There was only the briefest of pauses before "Hey, Janie."

I grinned. *Nothing* fazed my little brother. "Hi, Zack." Perhaps my parents had subconsciously had to admit that "Xanthe Jane Greene" might have been a mistake, because when it came to naming their next child, they'd gone for the slightly more normal "James Zachariah Greene." Unfortunately, this had turned out to be the wrong way round again. "Look, first of all, if Mum catches you and makes you hang up, you gotta ring me back, okay? She threw an absolute fit when I tried to talk to her."

"Well, you are meant to be dead," he pointed out reasonably. "Are you, by the way?"

"Sort of. It's complicated." I hesitated, trying to find a good way to put it, but in the end I just blurted out, "I think I'm a vampire."

Another fractional pause. "Awesome."

"Well, yeah. But I nearly got stuck in my grave, and I only escaped because a woman who I think is another vampire came to dig me up, only she seems to have been chased off by vampire hunters, and now I'm in a sheep field. Where the heck did you guys bury me?"

"It's not a sheep field," Zack said, sounding rather wounded. "It's a real pretty countryside spot, with views and song sparrows and—and, you know, all that ecological stuff. We thought you'd like it."

"I'm sure it's very attractive. Just not from six feet under." I swiveled on my heels, scanning the dark countryside. "To be honest, it would have been more useful if you'd buried me somewhere near a bus stop. Can you get Mum or Dad to come pick me up?"

"Hang on, I'll go look." I heard the creak of his bedroom door. "Um, I'm not sure they should be driving right now, actually."

"Great. Now what?" I rubbed my forehead with one muddy hand, trying to think. It was a good thing Zack was taking this so well. . . . "Hang on. You and your weird Goth friends wouldn't have had anything to do with this, would you?"

"*Steampunk,*" he corrected me, indignant. "It's totally different!"

"Zack," I said warningly. "Did you feed me to a vampire?"

"No!"

"It's just that you don't seem to be surprised by the whole coming-back-from-the-dead thing."

"You're my big sister. I knew you couldn't really be gone forever," he said, with a twelve-year-old's utter, simple certainty in the order of the world. "Uh, hang on a sec." An earsplitting burst of static made me wince. Evidently a scuffle was going on—I could hear Zack whining, "But, Muuuum!"

"James, you give that here right now!" My mother's voice got louder as she claimed possession of the phone. "Right. Now listen here," she snarled in my ear. "I don't know what kind of sick—"

"In January you were home sick for nine days and I made you a special playlist and lent you my iPod," I said, speaking as fast as I could. "Your favorite soup is parsnip and Stilton. Um, um." I grasped for something else that only I would know. "And behind the set of old *Good Housekeeping* cookbooks you have a collection of erotic bondage novels that I'm not supposed to know about—" I heard a crash. "Mum? *Mum?*"

"Hi," said Zack's voice cheerfully. "She's out cold. What did you tell her?"

"Nothing. Is Dad there?"

There was a rustle, then, "Xanthe? Baby?" said Dad. He sounded quavery, lost.

"It's really me, Dad. Um, I don't know how to break this to you gently, but I seem to be a vampire."

"Okay," said Dad quite calmly. I guessed that he'd gone into shock. "I'm going to come and pick you up. Where are you?"

"At my grave, where else?"

"I'm coming right over."

"Gre—*no, wait!*" Crap, how could I have forgotten? "Dad, listen, you can't come! I probably have bloodlust!"

"What?" he said, utterly bewildered.

"I'm a brand-new vampire, remember? I might flip out and eat you if I smell your tasty blood."

A pause. "Should I phone for a taxi?"

"I don't want to eat a taxi driver either!" Accidentally eating my own dad on my first night as a vampire would be a spectacularly gothic start to my undead career, but I really didn't need to cope with *that* much angst straight off. "Anyway, I can run over to you. I've got amazing vampire superpowers now, of course. I don't need a lift." But that didn't solve the bloodlust problem. I frowned, thinking . . . and it hit me.

"Hey, Dad? Can you put Zack back on?" There were some things that you couldn't ask a parent, and this was one of them. "Hi, Zack. I need you to look something up for me."

Chapter 3

When your parents move around as much as mine do, you get a hands-on practical in Darwinian theory: adapt or die. I'd never attended the same school for more than two years at a time, as my mum chased research grants around the country, so I'd had to get used to being the perpetual newcomer. There're only two ways to survive that, and I'd long ago learned which one was preferable—shut up, keep your eyes open, and blend in like a chameleon on speed.

Starting at a new school was like diving down into a vast coral reef, with thousands of different creatures going about their business in an intricate network of relationships. The trick was not to make a splash when you entered, to approach without attracting too much attention. That way you could study the situation, see who went where and what they ate and how they interacted. If you did it right, you could fit yourself right in, and all the life would carry on around you with barely a ripple.

If you did it wrong, of course, you got sharks.

Lorraine was a shark. The skinny, mean sort that makes everything else on the reef creep around in terror, because you could never tell if she was going to ignore you or bite your head off. I'd managed to piss her off on my very first day—three different teachers had made Lorraine sit next to me instead of her best friend, which from my point of view was about as helpful as your diving instructors handing you a couple of raw steaks before pushing you into the water. After that, it wouldn't have mattered if I'd bought Lorraine a naked boy toy and her own Porsche; she hated me, and the rest of the school avoided me like the freshly bleeding sacrificial goat I was.

Which was why I was clinging to the wall outside her window, trying to break into her bedroom. I reckoned that if I did turn out to have bloodlust, I'd be doing the world a favor.

I'd been worried about mystic barriers blocking my way—I had no idea how to convince Lorraine to invite me in, seeing as how I wasn't a brooding stud-muffin in a leather coat—but it turned out that I should have been more concerned about the double glazing. The window was slightly open, but locked in position. I squeezed my hand through the gap, my wrist twisting as I scrabbled for the catch. My fingernails brushed the plastic; I stretched as far as I could, flattening myself as if I could slip my whole body sideways through the crack.

And somehow I *did*. One second I was straining to reach the handle; there was a weird sensation like a whole-body sneeze, and then I found myself teetering on the sill on the other side of the window. I nearly face-planted straight onto Lorraine's sleeping form. Grabbing the wall for support, I cast a wild glance backward. Sure enough, the window was still only cracked open two inches.

Ah. So my secret vampire power was teleportation. Win!

Lorraine was curled into a tight ball under her purple satin duvet. Without her makeup, she looked pale and weirdly young, like a little sister version of herself. She did not, I had to admit, seem at all delicious. I stared at her neck until my eyes started to water, but it did not become a luscious, peach-skinned column, or an inviting white satin veil over sensual red delights. It was, well, a neck. No more enthralling than I would have found it when alive. I leaned in close, until my face was only centimeters from her skin. Feeling a little dumb, I opened my mouth, trying to work out how to extend any retractable fangs I might be hiding. Closer . . . closer . . .

"MWA-HA-HA-HA-HA-HA!" announced the mobile phone from my pocket.

I hurled myself down onto Lorraine as she opened her mouth to scream. "Shut up, shut up!" She went deathly still underneath me, her eyes fixed on my teeth. "I'm not going to . . ." I paused. It was true: I really didn't want to hurt her. Even with my nose practically pressed into her skin, she just smelled of kiwi shampoo and tea-tree oil face wash, with a slight undertone of sweaty socks. It would have taken a truly sick vampire to be provoked into an animalistic hunger by *that* scent.

Still, I had to be sure.

Our biology lessons hadn't included anything as practical as how to locate the jugular vein. Besides which, even if I did manage to find it, chowing down on a major vein sounded like a great way to kill her, or at least make a terrible mess.

So I bit her ear. She already had four piercings; one more couldn't hurt.

Lorraine bucked, writhing against my hand, but I held her down with little effort. Feeling terribly perverted, I sucked on her earlobe. A tiny trickle of blood dripped down my throat. It tasted different from how it had when I'd been alive. Not that I'd gone around drinking blood on a regular basis, but I'd done my share of sucking on scraped fingertips as a kid and never really noticed anything much. But this . . . this was a rich, salty taste, like bacon. My taste buds were definitely registering it as food—but it wasn't like an angelic orgasm on my tongue or anything. At least, not more than bacon.

I didn't have bloodlust! Great!

Now what?

I stared deep into Lorraine's wide eyes, desperately hoping that I was the sort of vampire that could glamour mortals. "You never saw me," I whispered, trying to imbue my tone with psychic force. "I'm going to get out of here, and you're going to go back to sleep, and in the morning you *aren't going to remember a thing*. Understand?"

She nodded vigorous agreement, still muffled by my hand.

"All right then." I tensed my muscles in preparation. "One. Two. Three."

If I did have psychic powers, I hadn't managed to activate them, because Lorraine's scream split the air seconds later. By that time, though, I was already four gardens over. I'd thought I'd been running fast before, but it was nothing compared to what I could do with a little motivation. A tingly heat spread out from my chest to fill my whole body with liquid strength. I shot out down the main road, heading for home.

I probably would have kept on going until I reached my own doorstep, except that my feet caught fire.

"Augh!" I beat out the flames, knocking away charred remnants of leather. Friction had entirely eaten away the bottom of my shoes, and my feet were raw lumps of gravel-studded flesh. I should have been in utter agony. But I couldn't feel anything at all, other than a vague sense of warmth flowing through my veins . . . and, even as I watched, my skin started to knit back together.

Superspeed, teleportation, and now superfast healing. I could live with that. Pity about the psychic powers, though. Maybe I'd learn those later.

"MWA-HA-HA-HA-HA-HA!" said the phone again.

With a sigh, I pulled it out. Sure enough, two new text messages. I spent a couple of minutes navigating menu options until I discovered that the ringtone was set to Gothic Overture, and the message alert to Maniacal Laughter. Evidently, my sire had a terrible sense of humor. Shaking my head, I set the phone to vibrate, then flipped back to new messages. They were both from the same number as the last call.

The first message read:

X—CANT GET RID OF HIM 2NITE :-(U HIDE, I WILL FIND U L8R. XXX, L.

And the one from just now was:

X—V V IMPORTANT U DONT CALL BACK TILL AFTER 5:08 AM. DONT TALK TILL THEN & B CAREFUL XXX, L.

I blinked at them both. "Huh?" I flipped back from one to the other, but no new meaning became apparent. "What's wrong with phoning now—?"

The phone vibrated in my hand. A new message flashed up, from the same number as the previous ones.

BECAUSE U R BEING WATCHED

Chapter 4

The moon was balanced on top of the Downs by the time my bare feet touched our house's paved driveway. The sky was fading like drying paint; not yet dawn, but no longer full night. It made me feel edgy and uncomfortable, though I didn't know whether it was just my anxiety or a real physical reaction.

I could have covered the distance between Lorraine's house and mine much faster, but I'd spent half the night doubling back on my tracks. I hadn't seen anyone apart from late-night traffic and a few drunks outside pubs, but nonetheless I'd gone far enough east to hit the outskirts of Brighton, then turned north to range into the hills of the Downs, and finally headed straight south to spend an hour splashing back along the coast, through the sea. If there were any vampire hunters following me, at least I'd given them a good workout.

Now, at last, I was back in Lancing—home, at least theoretically. The village still felt foreign to me, with its sprawl of low bungalow retirement homes and rigidly identical houses marching from farmland down to the sea. I'd felt out of place enough as a normal, urban teenager here, what with all the retired oldies and farmers. Being dead didn't improve matters.

I cast a last glance around as I approached our house. Streetlamps cast empty pools of light on the deserted road. It was hard to imagine vampire hunters lurking amid the recycling bins and neatly tended front gardens, but the skin between my shoulder blades still itched, expecting a bolt from a crossbow at any moment.

The neighbor's windows were dark, but lights were on in my own house. I skittered through the shadows toward the welcoming glow, ducking down behind the cover of parked cars. Thanks to my mother's latest research spin-off and some unexpected royalties from one of my dad's picture books, we'd finally been able to afford a proper detached house. Its vampire-hiding potential hadn't been one of its selling points, but it was actually pretty good—set back from the other houses on a larger-than-average corner plot, and entirely surrounded by high, dense bushes. A weight eased off my chest as I passed into their welcome cover.

I searched my pockets as I headed up the driveway, but my parents had thoughtlessly failed to bury me with my house key. Figured. I tapped on the door.

My knuckles had barely brushed the painted wood before it slammed open, and Zack barreled into me. "Janie!" he wailed, somewhere between a sob and a delighted shout. My throat suddenly too tight for words, I buried my face in his spiky brown hair and hugged him back. His cry changed into a squeak. "Wow, you're—really, *really* strong."

"Sorry. Zack!" I held him out at arm's length to savor the sight of him. Funny how he could look so different to me, when he hadn't changed a bit. He was still just my scrawny kid brother, barely up to my shoulder. He was wearing a green velvet frock coat over white silk pajamas, accessorized with brocade slippers, a braided leather collar, and black nail varnish.

There are two ways to cope with being the perpetual new kid at school. Zack had chosen the other one.

"Xanthe?" said a tremulous, wondering voice. My

dad was standing in the hallway, clutching at the banister as though it was the only thing holding him up. He looked more dead than I felt, with huge, dark rings under his eyes and deep lines in his forehead that hadn't been there the last time I'd seen him. For a moment we simply gazed at each other without speaking. Slowly, as if I were some wild animal that might spook if he moved too fast, he unfolded one long arm, his hand shaking, and touched my shoulder. Then I was enfolded in the familiar comfort of his embrace. I could feel the rapid beating of his heart against my cheek. It was all going to be all right. My dad would fix everything.

"Keith!" my mother's voice barked, and we both jumped guiltily. I turned in his arms to see her standing in the doorway to the kitchen, her short, curly hair bristling like the fur of a frightened cat. Her face held the same gray gauntness as Dad's, but her brown eyes were as sharp as ever as she strode toward us. "Be careful, she might have internal injuries!" She inspected me from head to toe as though I were a malfunctioning piece of lab equipment that might explode at any moment. "James." She turned to my brother. "Don't stand there gawping, run! Call for an ambulance—"

"No, don't!" I yelped as Zack obediently pulled his

mobile phone out of his pocket. "Mum, I don't need an ambulance. I'm not sick. I'm a vampire!"

"Don't be silly, Xanthe," she said, though her gaze flickered uncertainly to my mouth. "There's a—a perfectly rational explanation—"

Dad cleared his throat. "Janet, she's cold."

"It's probably shock." I wasn't quite sure whether Mum meant me, Dad, or even herself. She took my wrist to check my pulse. "She's freezing! James, get upstairs and run a hot bath! Keith, quick, we need—"

"Mum!" I shouted, pulling away from her. "You're not listening to me!" Of course, she generally hadn't when I was alive, so I don't know why I'd expected things to be different just because I was dead. "I'm cold because I'm a vampire. I'm supposed to be cold!"

I was still leaning against Dad, his arms around me, and now I felt a shiver pass through him. I twisted to look up at his face, into his clear blue eyes. Artist's eyes, Dad had, that saw what was there, not what the brain thought should be there. He looked down at me now, and wonder crept across his face. "You're not breathing," he said. "And I can't feel your heartbeat."

I squeezed his hand. "It's going to be all right, Dad."

"Hypothermia," Mum stated. "That's all it is. It

slows the brain down and makes people say nonsense."

"Does it give them fangs too?" asked Zack.

"That will be due to—to—" The gears in Mum's head jarred to a halt. She struggled for a moment, then shook herself and snapped, "James, do as I said! Do you want your sister to drop dead?"

"I'm already dead!" In a blur of superspeed, I wriggled out of my dad's arms and grabbed hold of her shoulders. "Look at me." I bared my teeth, then lifted her unresisting hand to rest over my still, silent heart. "I'm only breathing in order to talk. I'm a vampire!"

She stared at me.

"Um. Sorry," I added.

She stood there motionless for a breath more. Then, her hands closing on mine, she said, quite calmly, "James, go and fetch a clean glass. Keith, I'll need the first aid kit, please."

I rolled my eyes. "Mum, I don't need first aid."

"Not for you, for me." She dropped my hands and bustled up the stairs, abruptly all business. "Quickly!" she shouted over her shoulder as she disappeared.

We all looked at one another. Dad spread his hands, obviously as lost as I was. A crash drifted down from above, as Mum flung things around the bathroom. Zack shrugged and wandered off toward the kitchen.

"Baby Jane," Dad said, and my unbeating heart melted at the old nickname. "Is this . . . are you . . ."

I shook my head. "Honestly, Dad, I have no idea. I'm still trying to figure this out."

"Do you think there could be other—you know?" He made a small gesture in the vague direction of my teeth.

"There must be. I mean, that's how you become a vamp—" He flinched, and I changed it to "Er, like me, isn't it? And . . . well, I didn't get out of my gr—uh, predicament, by myself. Someone came and dug me out. She said she's my sire."

He looked confused. "Sire? A woman?"

Of course, Dad didn't read vampire novels. "*Sire* is a word for the parent vampire, Dad. She turned me into one. Anyway, she got chased off, and—"

"Right," Mum interrupted, thumping back down the stairs. She had her laptop balanced in one hand and was clutching a pink lady's razor and a screwdriver in the other. "In there, now." She shooed us both through into the kitchen, where Zack was still hunting through cupboards. "James, where's that glass? Good. Now . . ." She handed the laptop to Dad and started disassembling the

31

razor with the screwdriver.

"Uh," Dad said, looking down at the screen. "Honey? This is a Wikipedia article on phlebotomy."

"Exactly." Mum dropped the freed razor blade onto the table and rolled up her sleeve. "Where's the first aid kit?"

"Mum, what are you doing?" I asked suspiciously.

"Making dinner," she replied as though it should be self-evident.

"Making—EW!" I snatched up the razor, holding it at arm's length above my head. "Mum, I don't want to drink *your* blood!"

"Honey," Dad said, scanning the laptop screen in fascinated horror, "I really don't think you've thought this through."

Mum put her hands on her hips, regarding us all sternly. "If Xanthe has indeed become a vampire"—she didn't falter on the word at all—"then she will need to take in sustenance. Our first hypothesis must be that the traditional legends are correct. In which case, she will require fresh human blood."

"I'm not going to drink my own mother's blood!" I yelled. "That's disgusting!"

"You can drink my blood if you want," Zack chimed

in. "I'll even let you bite me."

"No biting," Mum said. "It wouldn't be sanitary."

"What do you think I've got, rabies?" I said to her in indignation, then turned to Zack. "And, no!"

"Why not?" He looked vaguely offended. "I bet my blood is tasty!"

"You're too young, anyway," Mum said to him. "You have to be at least eighteen to give blood at a clinic, so twelve-year-olds certainly shouldn't feed vampires. You don't have enough body mass."

"I'm much larger than either of you," Dad pointed out. "It would be better if *I* donated the blood."

"Stop it, all of you!" I dropped the razor into the garbage, letting the lid slam shut with an emphatic thump. "I'm not going to drink blood from *family*. That would be like incest." They all stared at me with uncomprehending expressions, and I remembered too late that none of them had my experience with vampire erotica.

"Hey, vampires can blush!" Zack said, examining my face with interest. "How can that work?"

"Capillary . . . action?" To my relief, this problem distracted Mum from her unwholesome interest in me sucking her blood—she was professor of fluid dynamics at Sussex University, and equations must have started spinning in her head. "No, wait. Hmmm . . ."

"Xanthe, you've got to eat," Dad said earnestly. "At least try a little."

"Daaaaad! Honestly, I'm not hungry." It was true—I wasn't. But I *was* abruptly exhausted, as though all the muscle pain I should have experienced while running had finally caught up with me. I dragged my leaden gaze over to the microwave clock.

5:46 A.M. Dawn.

"It's . . . sunrise," I slurred. My knees gave way underneath me, and I slumped against the kitchen cabinets. I'd missed my chance to call Lily . . . but there was still something terribly important I had to say now, something my clueless family needed to know. . . . "Gotta sleep." I struggled to scrape my thoughts together; I could feel my brain cells switching off. "Sunlight . . . hide . . ."

My eyelids clanged down like steel shutters, and I was dead to the world.

Chapter 5

I woke up in pitch blackness, lying on my back and utterly convinced that I was still six feet underground in my coffin and had hallucinated the entire previous night due to oxygen deprivation.

"Aaaaaaaaaugh!"

I flailed for a moment before my brain kicked in with three simple observations: first, I was wrapped in a fluffy fleece blanket that certainly had not been included in my grave goods; second, I'd just sat up, which I wouldn't have been able to do in a coffin; and finally, the air reeked of hay.

The first two let me deduce that I was not, in fact, buried alive. The third made my brain stall.

A knock came from the other side of the—door? wall?—to my left. "Janie?" Zack called. "Are you alive again?"

"Yeah." I struggled out of the clinging blanket, banging my elbows against the walls on each side in the process. Something light and metallic clinked against the top of my head when I tried to stand up, making me duck again. I reached up and found—coat hangers? "You guys put me in a closet?"

"Well, it's not like we have a convenient crypt, you know. It was the only place we could think of where you would be totally out of the sun." He paused. "Um, by the way, you haven't gone insane with bloodlust, have you?"

"Uh . . ." Actually, I was feeling rather light-headed. My stomach was one big, growling void. "Give me a minute here, okay?" I closed my eyes, trying to make the hunger go away. It was only a signal from my body, that's all. . . . I could tune it out.

Warmth spread outward from my chest and down into my stomach. The cramping ebbed away. I opened my eyes. "I'm fine now." I pushed at the closet door; it flexed, but didn't open. "Hey, what's up with this?"

"Oh, we duct-taped you in," Zack said cheerfully.

"To make sure all the light was blocked out. Hang on."

Something sneezed on my foot.

"There'ssomethingaliveinhere," I observed with all possible calm and flung myself forward shoulder-first with full vampiric strength. Plywood burst under the impact, sending me sprawling onto the horrible floral-patterned carpet in my parents' bedroom.

"Yes," said Zack. He was wearing pajamas, with a long strip of tape stuck to one leg. "That would be toast."

"Toast," I repeated. "Sneezing toast."

"Not toast, *Toast!*" He ducked into the closet, and reemerged clutching a large wire cage. "I named her myself. Isn't she the greatest?"

I got to my feet, gathering up the shredded remains of my dignity, and peered through the bars. A fuzzy brown-and-white ball of fur looked back at me with round, black eyes. Its pink velvet ears quivered. "It's a guinea pig," I concluded in the face of the evidence before me. Well, that explained why the closet had smelled of hay. "Zack, why is it a guinea pig?"

"Dad got her for you." Zack gazed fondly down at the little fluffball. "I guess if you aren't going to eat her, I can keep her!"

I rubbed at my forehead. It was way too early in the night for this conversation, and the terrible clashing colors of the room decor were giving me a migraine. "Dad got me a . . . guinea pig?"

"For breakfast," Zack said. "That's why I named her Toast. You aren't going to eat her, are you?"

"No!"

"Woot!" Zack hugged the cage to his chest, carrying it off in the direction of his bedroom. "I hope you don't want to eat Marmalade or Sugar Puff either!"

"Marma—oh, never mind." Shaking my head, I sought refuge from the weirdness by retreating to the bathroom. My headache eased in the plain, white-tiled room, vanishing to nothing as I sorted through toiletries in search of something that would wash away grave dirt. After forty-five minutes of scalding water and an entire bottle of shampoo, I felt halfway human again. Or, to be more accurate, totally vampire.

The mirror had fogged up; I wiped it clean and squinted at my blurred reflection. My first reaction was relief that I *had* a reflection—I'd been worrying about how vampires applied eyeliner. My second reaction was . . . disappointment. My skin, though slightly paler, hadn't turned a shimmering alabaster. My brown eyes had not become exotically golden or blood-scarlet. My face looked a little gaunter, but I hadn't magically acquired elegant cheekbones and an aristocratic nose. My nondescript hair was still, well, nondescript.

I looked, all in all, the way I always had. Perfectly normal.

Except my acne was gone. That counted as a miraculous transformation into astounding inhuman beauty, as far as I was concerned.

My mouth seemed ordinary enough when it was closed. I drew my lips back from my teeth, leaning close to the mirror. The canines were definitely bigger and sharper. They crowded together, slightly askew, with the top set overlapping the lower. When I tried opening and closing my mouth, I could feel the edges of them sliding against each other like chisel blades. But they certainly weren't monster-movie fangs. Anyone looking at my teeth wouldn't immediately think "vampire," just "typically awful British dentistry."

Crap. Three years of braces down the drain.

Someone knocked softly on the bathroom door. "Xanthe?" Dad said. "Are you okay in there?"

"Fine." I tied my robe shut and went out. "I don't look all that different, do I?"

He pulled me into a brief hug. "You're still my girl. Are you hungry? We got, um—"

"Yes, I already met Toast." I sighed. "Please tell me that Marmalade and Sugar Puff aren't a rabbit and a hamster."

He dropped his gaze sheepishly and mumbled, "Chinchilla."

I shook my head. "I hope the pet store gives refunds."

"We got some other things to try as well." He trailed after me as I headed toward my room. "We'll work something out."

"What, did you rob a blood bank or something?" I opened the door to my room. "Let me get some clothes and—*Jesus Christ, what did you people do in here?!*"

My bedroom—my private sanctuary, my castle, *my room*—was a complete mess. Incredible, utter chaos. Stuff was strewn everywhere. Books were stuffed willy-nilly on the shelves, in a shrieking clash of sizes and colors. Papers were scattered all over the desk, my bed was askew, and my sheets were as wrinkled as an elephant's backside. Even the walls were wrong, my movie posters hanging drunkenly at odd angles. The sight made me feel like I was being stabbed in the eyeballs.

Dad looked utterly bemused. "We haven't touched it, sweetie."

"It never looked like this before! Did you let Zack in here?"

He backed up, putting his hands into the air. "Honestly, it's exactly as you left it! I'll, er, I'll go see about breakfast, shall I?" He fled downstairs.

I glared around the room in disgust. It was obvious that *someone* had messed things up. "I'm going to kill you, little brother," I muttered. Savagely, I tugged my bedclothes straight, then folded the sheets back with surgical precision. I threw everything from my shelves onto the floor, and started sorting them into categorized piles. Holiday souvenirs and various trinkets went back on first, in straight rows from smallest to largest. Books on the next shelf, arranged first by genre, then by author within genre—but that looked wrong, so I re-sorted them by size. Much better. Next the underwear drawer.

I was busily rearranging my socks in neat rows ordered by color when it occurred to me that what I was doing was just possibly, slightly, rather unusual.

I looked around. My room looked as though it had been cleaned by an extreme OCD sufferer who'd been flushing her medication for the past month.

Okaaaaay.

I had a pair of black socks in my hand. I stared down into the drawer, seeing the empty space where it should go, next to all the other black socks. The space called out to me, begging me to put the socks there. They *wanted* to go there. The laws of space and time and the entire universe *demanded* that they go there.

My hand trembled. I threw the black socks down amid the row of pink ones, slammed the drawer shut, and leaned against it. After a moment, I moved cautiously away, and sat down on the edge of my bed, knotting my hands together. I started counting.

I held out until "eight" before leaping off the bed, yanking open the drawer, and moving the black socks into the right place.

Right. Possibly, I might have a small problem here.

"Janie?" Zack called from the other side of the closed door. "Dad says breakfast's ready."

"Coming!" With a last disconcerted glance around my unnaturally neat room, I hastily got dressed. My wardrobe was somewhat lacking in leather catsuits or velvet evening wear, so I made do with a pair of black jeans and a black tank top. I reckoned black was *always* acceptable.

Zack met me on the landing. "You look very vampiric," he said brightly.

"Thanks. You look . . ." Zack also seemed to have made an attempt at "vampire"—or at least, "vampire's brother"—from his eclectic wardrobe. In his case, this meant boots with two-inch soles, baggy black trousers mostly made out of zippers, a white shirt with enough ruffles to furnish six brides, a black brocade vest that was probably older than the two of us combined, and a pair of heavy brass goggles pushed high up on his forehead. "You look very you," I concluded. We started down the stairs together. "Listen, has there been anyone lurking around here during the day? I think there are guys after me."

"Vampire hunters? Awesome!" He deflated at my glare. "Um, no. Haven't seen anyone, and Dad and I were here all day—I called in sick to school. Mum went to work."

"Work? She went to work the day after I *rose from the dead*?"

"It was important," Mum said, coming out of the living room. "We needed research materials." Her eyes were bloodshot, but she regarded me critically. "Why do you look so funereal?"

"Mum, I'm a vampire. I have to be Goth now."

She gave me her familiar disapproving, why-must-you-always-follow-the-herd look. "If the other vampires

43

turn out to be man-eating killers, will you do that too?"

Yep, I'd only been animate again for twenty-four hours, and I'd already managed to disappoint my mother. Business as usual, then. From the kitchen, I heard the clatter of pots and pans and muffled swearing. "Dad had better not be boiling a bunny in there."

"I heard that!" he yelled. "Come and look."

"We have to deduce your diet," Mum said seriously, taking my hand. She paused, glancing down at it. "At least you're warmer now. That has to be a good sign."

I didn't feel either warm or cold and hadn't since I'd woken up in my coffin. "I think I've finally reached room temperature," I said as she dragged me into the kitchen. "It's—whoa."

The table was covered in food. There were three thick steaks, ranging from totally raw to well done. A raw chicken sat next to a cold, cooked one. The halogen light gleamed off silver mackerel scales—*raw* mackerel, with the heads and fins still on. There were sausages, eggs, and bacon; a couple of hamburgers in freshly toasted buns; cakes, muffins, cookies, raw and cooked carrots, spinach, shepherd's pie, a pepperoni pizza, a goldfish in a small tank, chips, salad, bread, raw ground beef, oatmeal, cornflakes, and, amid it all, a very nervous-looking rabbit in a cage.

"Try what looks good," Dad said anxiously, watching my face.

"Okay," I said, pulling out a chair and sitting down in front of the mound of edibles. My eye was caught by the steaks, and my mouth started to water. "First of all, can we please get rid of the bunny and the fish? No," I said as Zack started to lift the platter of mackerel, "the live fish. Good grief, what were you thinking, Dad?"

"That shouldn't be there anyway," Mum said, dropping a tea towel over the tank to hide it from view. "That's a different experiment. Now, Xanthe . . ." Her voice fell into the same sort of tone she used with new undergraduates in their very first lab session. "Take small bites to start with. We have no idea how your digestive system works now, so we don't want—*Xanthe!*"

"Buf ish tastgh sho *ghud*," I said around a huge mouthful of meat. It really was the most delicious thing I'd ever eaten—so fresh and sweet with an amazing juicy tang.

"But what if you're allergic?" Mum dived for my plate. We spent a moment wrestling over the remaining half of the steak, but I had vampiric strength and twenty-four hours of hunger on my side. I stuffed the rest frantically into my mouth, chewing at superspeed to wolf it all down.

"Neat," my brother observed. "You went straight for the raw one."

I paused on the last mouthful, looking down at the remaining two steaks.

Oh. Ew.

"I've got a theory," Zack said, pulling up a chair for himself and selecting a jam tart. "I think we're completely wrong. You're obviously not a vampire."

We all looked at him.

My brother pointed at me. "You," he said in tones of utter certainty, "are a *zombie*."

Chapter 6

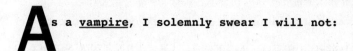

As a <u>vampire</u>, I solemnly swear I will not:

1) Angst

2) Suck

3) Summon a dark goddess

4) Fall in love with a vampire hunter

  a) Or a werewolf

  b) Or anyone evil, no matter how hot

  c) Or anyone of a species not approved of by my vampire elders, because no one is worth that sort of stress

5) Accept any gifts, give any gifts, carry any messages, take part in any mysterious rituals, etc. etc.

"Here's another one," said Mum, sticking a Post-It into the massive tome in her lap. "Running backward while carrying a lit candle in one hand and a live tortoise in the other. Makes vampires flee in terror."

"Thanks, Mum." I didn't bother to look up from my laptop. I'd given up making notes on any of her findings over an hour ago—Eastern European vampire folklore was turning out to be utterly cracktastic. "Can I remind you that we're looking for ways to stop vampire *hunters*, not vampires?"

When Mum had said she'd gone to work to get research materials, she wasn't kidding. Every surface in the living room was piled high with books. This was not unusual, but the familiar physics journals and academic monographs had vanished. In their place: *Interview with the Vampire, Dracula, The Vampire in Romanian Legend, Vampire Nation, The Encyclopedia of the Undead, Love Bites, Fourteen Essays on Vampirism, Twilight, Undead and Unwed, Vampires of Stage and Screen, In Search of Dracula* . . . everything from huge, leather-bound library reference volumes with cracked spines to shiny new paperbacks with luridly embossed covers. Mum must have checked out every book about vampirism from every library in a thirty-mile radius. I wasn't quite sure what she was expecting to learn from texts like *Marxism and the Vampire*, but at least it was keeping her occupied. Even if I did have to keep surreptitiously straightening the piles.

"Um, Baby Jane?" Dad said from his cross-legged position in front of the TV. He paused the DVD on a close-up of Angel's game face, bumpy forehead and demonic eyes frozen in an expression of insane blood-lust. "Are you going to do this?"

"I don't think so, Dad." But that reminded me . . .

6) Lose my soul, no matter how much of a good idea it seems like at the time

I tapped my fingers against the laptop, my gaze skittering back to the closed curtains hiding the living room windows. Despite my best efforts to distract myself, I kept imagining sinister silhouettes moving behind them, stalking toward me with stakes raised high. . . .

Mum turned a page. "Apparently, a virgin boy riding a pure-white virgin stallion can track down a vampire's lair. Maybe we should phone local riding stables."

"Mum, I think we need to be more worried about vampire hunters tracking me back from the name on my headstone." My head snapped up. "Or anyone else! My grave's lying there wide open—"

"No, it isn't," Dad interrupted. "I went back and filled it while you were asleep. I took the plastic grave marker away too."

"Hey, thanks—hang on, plastic?" Indignation filled me as I double-checked today's date on the laptop clock. "You haven't even bothered to get me a proper headstone? I was dead for nearly four months!"

Even I felt the temperature in the room drop. Mum bent her head over her book. Dad's shoulders hunched. "Three weeks," he said, his voice going oddly thick. "You were . . . it's been three weeks. The rest of the time . . . you were in a hospital. In a coma."

"Well, why didn't you say so!" I yelled. They both jumped, twisting in my direction. I waved my hands in exasperation. "I've been going nuts trying to work out how I got vamped in a car crash, and now you tell me I was in the hospital?" My parents were staring at me. "Hospital," I repeated as patiently as I could. "Where there's blood. And needles."

Dad's eyebrows shot up. "You think you got vampirism in the hospital, like an infection?"

"It would make sense, right? All my sire would have to do is sneak in and drip some blood down my throat."

"The question is," said Mum, "why?"

Our eyes all went to the mobile phone, sitting innocently on top of *The Lust of the Vampire*. It continued to not ring.

"How long until 5:08?" Mum asked.

"Hours still," I replied with a sigh. I'd tried calling back anyway, but had only got voice mail.

"Well," Dad said, turning back to *Buffy*. "At least it gives us time to research vampires."

"Zombies," corrected Zack, wandering into the room with Toast in his arms. I aimed a glare at him, which he totally ignored as usual. "I'm telling you, we're looking in the wrong place. We need to rent *Day of the Dead* and *My Name Is Legend*."

"Actually, I thought of a way to test that hypothesis," Mum said, tipping the books off her lap as she stood. I twitched as they hit the floor in a jumbled heap, fighting off a weird desire to pick them up and stack them neatly. She started hunting among the piles of books on the crowded coffee table. "I need you to do something for me, Xanthe."

I eyed her warily. "What?"

She flashed a wry grin at me, brandishing aloft a sterile lancet. "I vant to suck your blooooood."

"What? No!" I jumped out of my chair as she advanced on me.

"Come on," she cajoled, chasing me round the sofa. "For science!"

"Your mother knows what she's doing," said Dad with what I felt was unwarranted optimism. "She just needs a few drops, that's all."

"Well . . . all right." I submitted to the needle, looking away squeamishly as it stabbed into my skin—though, actually, I didn't even feel it. In a few seconds, it was all done. "What are you going to do, take that into the university and get a colleague to run tests on it?"

"No," Mum said over her shoulder as she swept out of the room. "I'm going to perform animal experiments."

Zack and I looked at each other. Then, with a cry of *"Not the bunny!"* we pelted after her. We got tangled up with each other in the doorway; by the time we burst into the kitchen, my mother was standing by the table with a calm expression and a clean needle.

"Marmalade!" Zack snatched the rabbit up and clutched it to his chest, probably causing it more distress than Mum had. "Mum, how could you try to turn my bunny into a zombie?"

"Vampire," I snarled. "And, yeah!"

"I haven't touched the rabbit," Mum said. "That would probably have required more blood. I thought it was best to start small." She moved to one side.

The goldfish lurked sullenly at the bottom of the tank, looking distinctly peeved.

"You mean," I said, "if this works, I'm going to be the sire to a vampire goldfish?" I shook my head in despair. "Thanks, Mum. You do realize you've probably ruined my undead social life?"

"I've decided what to name the fish." Zack was hunched over, peering through the glass in fascination. *"Braaaaaaains."*

After he'd fled to his room to avoid a painful demise, I turned back to Mum. She was staring bleary-eyed at the coffee machine, waiting for it to percolate. "Mum, you've had, like, six cups tonight already. You know that stuff's not good for you." Or the rest of us. Mum got more focused and less practical with each caffeine hit.

"I need it." She rubbed at the bridge of her nose. "Your father and I have been awake since the middle of last night."

"Go to bed, then." I cut across her as she started to protest. "Look, I'm a solitary creature of darkness, remember? I need you to watch over things during the day—you can't do that and stay awake all night too." I herded her out. "I'll wake you up if my sire calls. Or if a howling mob brandishing torches storms the house."

As my parents got ready for bed, I wandered around, turning off lights and double-checking that all the windows and doors were locked. Still no sign of vampire hunters. I fetched myself a snack of—sigh—raw ground beef, resisting the urge to check all the windows again. I had to find something to take my mind off the possible assassins closing in on me, but what did a vampire *do* all night?

When Dad poked his head into my room to check on me, I was sitting at my desk, spooning raw ground beef with one hand while I flicked through my favorite websites on my laptop. Well, there was only so much melancholic lounging a girl could do.

Dad peered over my shoulder. "You're Googling your own obituaries?"

"I meant to look for vampire hunter organizations, but I got distracted. This is awesome!" I eagerly scrolled down the forum thread. "Look, Fang-Girls.net held an online fan auction in my memory—see, 'The JaneX Memorial Fund.' They're raising loads for charity! And look at all these tributes on my profile page!"

I yanked my fingers back as Dad firmly shut the

laptop lid. "This can't be psychologically healthy, Baby Jane. Why don't you go and read a nice wholesome vampire novel instead?"

"I don't need to research vampires, Dad. I've been reading about them all my life." I looked out at the dark garden. Apart from the breeze ruffling the leaves of the big oak tree outside my window, all was still. I stared hard into the shadowed branches. Just the place for a stalker to lurk, clutching a stake and a cross. . . .

"You sure you're going to be okay by yourself?" Dad said, breaking my train of thought. "I could stay up."

"You look deader than I do, Dad." I shooed him away, opening the lid of my laptop again. "Go to bed."

He cast me a stern backward glance from the doorway. "No more morbid Googling, Xanthe Jane. Promise?"

"Yeah, whatever." Making sure he could see the screen, I pulled up the BBC News website. The state of the world hadn't changed much while I'd been dead. Blah, blah, riots somewhere, economy crashing, political scandal, blah, blah, blah. I clicked randomly through headlines without reading, and after a second I heard my dad's footsteps moving down the hall. My hearing sharpened as I concentrated; I could hear the rustle of the sheets being pulled back, and the creak of the springs as my parents got into bed. Straining my senses to the utmost, I could even catch the soft sound of their breathing. I waited until they'd both slipped into a deep, easy rhythm.

Then, of course, I went straight back to Fang-Girls.net.

I'd never thought of myself as a Big Name Fan or anything, but literally hundreds of people had posted messages about how great I'd been as a moderator, and how insightful my commentaries had always been, and how much fun I'd been in the role-playing chat-room, and what a tragedy it was that I'd never finish my epic, multi-fandom, crossover crackfic saga (though there were not, in my opinion, nearly enough comments expressing this latter regret). With the number of times my family had moved, I'd always found it easier to maintain friendships online than in person; I'd never even met most of these people, but I'd still been a part of their lives. And they'd missed me when I went away.

For a while, at least.

People may have been sad about my accident, but . . . fandom went on. My smug glow evaporated as I realized just how *much* it had gone on in my absence. Four months was like a year, in internet terms. While I'd been in my coma, whole flamewars had broken out and died down again; at least three new fangroups had formed, mainly over characters I'd never even heard of; several prominent bloggers had flounced off the site over some imagined insult, only to come creeping back again a couple of weeks later. There were masses of squee over a trailer for a new vampire film; twenty-eight of my favorite fanfic authors had new stories up; there had been six vampire-related conventions in various parts of the world, dutifully blogged about by hundreds of fans; new pictures, new book announcements, new reviews, new arguments, all new, new, new. . . .

It was a good thing I was an immortal vampire (*not* a zombie), because it was going to take me at least two years to catch up with all the gossip. My fingers automatically hovered over the keyboard . . . then hesitated. Normally—if I'd been on holiday or something—I would simply post asking people to let me know the juiciest happenings, but I could hardly do that now. Sure, I could make a new account, a new user name . . . but then it wouldn't feel like being *me*. I was dead to all these people. All my friends.

Great. Now my mood was hovering dangerously close to angst. I determinedly clicked over to the fanfic forum. Nothing like some imaginary angsty vampires to distract you from your problems, even when you're a *real*, angsty vampire.

I was settling down to the latest installment of my favorite long-running fanfic novel (thirty-four chapters, and still going strong) when there was a bing. I nearly fell off my chair in my haste to grab the phone—but it was still dark. My laptop beeped again. A chat window had popped up.

Superluminal: JaneX

Superluminal: I see you

"Crap!" Leaping out of my chair, I flung the window open. The garden lay calm and deserted under the stars, and the tree was still devoid of anything but shadows. Sanity seeped back through my panic. I sat down at my desk again, staring at the name in the chat window.

I knew *of* Superluminal—probably everyone on Fang-Girls.net did—but my interactions with her (if she *was* a her) had been limited to downloading her vids. She was famous online for her fantastic vidding, mixing DVD clips and music seamlessly to make vampire-themed music videos that you'd swear could have come out of major record studios. She was also notoriously reclusive. Unlike most fans, she never commented on other people's work, never hung out in the forums.

So what was she doing messaging a dead girl?

The laptop binged.

Superluminal had sent me a URL, apparently to a blog. My eye went to the browser window in the background, still open to one of the Fang-Girls.net forums, and fell on one of the headings in the sidebar: FANS ONLINE NOW.

"Oh, *crap!*" I'd forgotten that my settings automatically logged me into the site. There at the top of the list was my internet name: JANEX. Which, thanks to the outpouring of grief over my death, had now been linked to my real name.

Fang-Girls.net was *the* central fan-run site for all things fanged. The ideal hangout for vampire-obsessed fangirls . . . or vampire hunters.

I thought fast.

JaneX: Hello!!! A/S/L?

Superluminal: ??

JaneX: Im 18 blonde model! who lieks to party!!

If u wanna watch me and my sexxy freinds,

CLICK HERE NOW!!!!

[Superluminal has gone Offline]

I sat back with a sigh. Hopefully, Superluminal, whether a real fan or a hunter, was now thinking my account had been hacked by a spambot. Out of curiosity, I clicked the link she'd sent me. It was a blog, by someone who really loved the color purple. Squinting past the clashing typography, I read the title of the latest entry:

VAMPIRE IN SUSSEX???

"Oh, craaaaaap," I said for a third time with three times as much feeling. I scrolled down, my unbeating heart sinking with each click. Yep. Lorraine had a blog, and she'd used it to tell the world—or at least, her friendlist—about the really weird thing that had happened to her last night. And she'd said how much her mysterious assailant had looked like one Xanthe Jane Greene. . . .

"Well, great," I muttered. "I'm sure the Elder vampires are going to love this. . . ."

The phone buzzed, vibrating across the desk like a deranged mechanical spider. I caught it as it hurled itself off the edge, nearly putting it to my ear upside down in my haste. "Hello? *Hello?*" As I spoke, I glanced at the clock.

5:09 A.M.

"Xanthe darling," purred my sire. "You shouldn't worry about what they think."

Chapter 7

Once was coincidence, but twice . . . "You've got some kind of psychic bond to me, right?" I said.

There was a tiny pause from the other end of the line, filled with the background rumble of a car engine. "Goodness," said my sire eventually. "And I had a nice, soothing speech prepared to break it to you gently."

"Well, you're my sire. I was kinda, um, expecting there to be a connection of some kind. You know, my blood is your blood and all that stuff. It always is, you know?" Was I babbling? Oh God, I was babbling. I wanted to seem cool, poised, but just listening to her voice made my stomach flutter as if I were about to take an exam.

Oh.

Uh-oh.

"This isn't going to be a master-slave sort of thing, is it?" I asked without much hope.

She laughed—a rich, throaty sound that would have set my pulse racing, if I'd had one. "Poor darling. I certainly hope not. In any event, I do indeed have a connection to you, like all vampires have to their descendants. It's called the Bloodline. It means I can see what you see and hear what you hear."

"Uh." I was *really* glad I hadn't yet visited my favorite fan-art forum, which tended to feature a lot of drawings of hot, shirtless vampires. "Exactly how much?"

"Everything, I'm afraid. And I can feel where you are, as well. Which, by the way, is a terrible place for you to be. Honestly, Xanthe—your parents' house? What sort of a hiding place is that?"

"A warm, dry one," I said, wrestling down my instinctive urge to whimper and grovel. "And it's Jane, actually."

Another fractional pause. "Your name is Xanthe Jane Greene . . . and you prefer *Jane*?" my sire inquired in the tones of one suddenly suspecting the other person of being a bit Special Needs.

"If you had to go to my schools, so would you," I muttered. "Um, sorry for being rude, but who the heck are you?"

"You may call me Lily. And, my Xanthe, you do not have to concern yourself with being plain Jane anymore." For the first time, all traces of amusement were gone, her voice as dark and solemn as night itself. "No one is ever going to laugh at you, or belittle you, or order you around, ever again."

"Guh" was all I could manage in response to this. Lily's voice reached straight through my ears and shut down my brain.

"Oh dear," Lily said, sounding apologetic. "That came on rather too thick, didn't it. Sorry, my darling." The light archness was back, and I found I could move again. "I've never sired anyone before now, so all this is as new to me as it is to you."

"Um, speaking of which, and not meaning to sound ungrateful . . . why me?"

"Darling, I may have fangs, but I'm not a heartless monster. I could hardly let a young girl die, could I? But we haven't got the leisure to talk history now, I'm afraid. We're both in terrible danger."

"Yeah, I got your text." I once again scrutinized the

garden for any hint of movement. "What's going on?"

Lily hissed between her teeth. "I don't yet know fully myself. I didn't intend us to get separated, but Hakon sprung a trap on me."

"Hakon," I repeated, my brain conjuring up an image of a huge, scowling Scandinavian. "I'm guessing he's a vampire hunter."

"Hunter?" Lily sounded startled. "Goodness, darling, no. Those buffoons are the least of our worries. Hakon's a vampire. A very old, very powerful, Scandinavian vampire, who's spent a thousand years becoming the most feared Elder in Europe."

I wasn't liking this. I wasn't liking this at all. "And . . . he's your enemy?"

"More like I'm his. My word, he holds a grudge. Let's just say that I managed to escape from the horrible little feudal system he's got set up, and he can't let that sort of challenge to his authority go unpunished." Lily clicked her tongue in dismissal. "Tell you the whole story over cocktails sometime, darling. We're running out of night, and Hakon's vampires could be right on your doorstep. You've got to get out of there."

I stared out my window. Now I was seeing evil vampires lurking in every shadow, rather than zealous hunters.

It wasn't an improvement. "He knows where I am?"

"Darling, I'm afraid he must, thanks to your naive return to your roost," Lily said with a touch of asperity. "As well as being an utter prig, Hakon is, very inconveniently, my sire's sire. Your great-grandsire. Which means he's got a direct Bloodline to both of us. He can piggyback our senses, and there's not a thing we can do to stop him."

"What?" One of my parents stirred in their bedroom; I cut off my shriek. "You mean more people can stare at me whenever they want?"

"Only those in your direct line, which means we just have to worry about Hakon at the moment. And not quite whenever he wants—it's tiring to reach more-distant descendants. I can stay in contact with you near enough indefinitely, as your direct sire, but Hakon, as your great-grandsire, is a bit more limited. He can probably only manage to look through your eyes and ears for about a quarter of any given hour. The catch, unfortunately, is that we can't tell when he's peeping in and when he's not."

Oh God. I was never getting undressed *ever again*.

"As your distant ancestor, he can't directly sense your location like I can, but he must have picked up enough clues as to your whereabouts by now," Lily continued over my appalled silence. "He's probably been riding along with you intermittently all night—but being so much older than us, he has to return to rest an hour earlier than we do. So now we can arrange our rendezvous without him being any the wiser. Any suggestions?"

"Uh . . ." Even though my blood leaped at the thought of meeting Lily in the flesh, growing up on the internet meant I was well trained in never agreeing to private meetings with strangers. "Could you come here?"

"Darling, if I could, I'd already *be* there. Hakon's goons are practically crawling up my tailpipe to herd me away from you. I've dispatched someone to help you, but he's a bit of a dark horse—we shouldn't rely on him being able to keep you safe at your house. So I think our best chance is for you to get on the road, present a moving target. With a bit of luck, we should be able to outrace Hakon and meet up." Her voice warmed. "I can't wait to see you again, darling. We'll be so much safer once we're reunited."

The phone slipped in my sweating palm. Eight different schools had taught me—brutally—how to read the social battlefield. I'd found out the hard way that the girl who wanted most desperately to be your friend . . . was the girl you could least afford to be friends with.

And Lily was being very, *very* friendly.

On the other hand, at school the popular kids hadn't also been thousand-year-old evil vampires. "Look, um . . ." I said. "Don't take this the wrong way, but you seem to be seriously outgunned. Even if we meet up, I don't see how you're going to be able to protect me from some sort of vampire Godfather."

"Oh, I'm not," Lily said, quite cheerfully. "I'm counting on you to protect me."

Alarm bells went off in my head so loudly, they drowned out Lily's glamour. "Say what now?"

Her laugh echoed from the phone's speaker. "Ah, my Xanthe. You don't yet realize how special you are."

"Oh no," I said in dismay. "There isn't a prophecy, is there?" That never ended well.

"Darling, I can tell we're going to get on simply famously." Amusement still threaded through Lily's voice. "No. No prophecies, no destinies—nothing shaping the future but our own determination, I promise. But you *are* unique."

"I don't want to be unique!" I'd always worked so hard to fit in, and now I was going to have to spend eternity as some sort of freak? "I want to be a normal vampire!"

"But your Bloodline isn't normal. And we can be

grateful that Hakon hasn't been able to sense that, or you'd already be dead."

I froze.

Not because of anything that Lily had said. Because a patch of shadows and leaves—that I'd spent the past hour convincing myself were only producing the *illusion* of an evil, lurking assassin—had just moved.

There was a tall man in black clothing stretched out along a branch outside my window . . . my open window. He'd overheard every word.

Lily must have been looking through my eyes. "Hell-fire," she murmured, very softly.

"Call you later," I whispered back, barely moving my lips. Then, more loudly, "I dunno, Lily. I don't like the sound of all of this." I thumbed the phone off, but kept it pressed against my ear. The man outside didn't react. "Uh, um, I mean," I continued somewhat randomly, edging toward my bookcase as I spoke, "I've never even met you. I don't know whether or not you're telling the truth." My stalker still didn't move. He was so utterly still, I would never have seen him if it hadn't been for that one slight, startled jerk of his head. He stayed motionless as my fingers walked along the line of my books, motionless as I drew one out. . . .

And then he did move, because my hardcover copy of *Breaking Dawn* whacked him full in the face, with all my vampiric strength propelling it.

"HA!" I dived out the window myself as he plummeted. The guy blurred weirdly as he fell, stretching out in a smear of silver—but I had to concentrate on my own landing. I hit the ground hard, rolling to absorb the impact. As I came upright again, I caught a glimpse of something disappearing under the hedge.

Teleport! I thought frantically as I hurled myself at the wall of leaves.

Twigs slapped my face; there was a weird dissolving sensation, and my vision went gray for a second. I blinked, and found myself *mostly* on the other side of the hedge. Tearing my arm loose, I burst clear in a shower of twigs and leaves—and stopped.

The path behind our house was a narrow strip of beaten earth, bordering a farmer's field. The short, flat grass stretched out in all directions, barren and empty under the moon. There was no place for so much as a mouse to hide. And there was no sign of anyone.

With no heartbeat or breath to distract me, I could hear every tiny sound. A car grumbling on the distant main road. The soft swish of the breeze through the grass. And, very close, the rasp of one dry leaf against another as something slunk through the hedgerow.

I whirled, crouching—and found myself nearly nose to nose with a startled cat. It was a funny-looking beast, somewhat like a Siamese in shape, but with sandy, spotted fur. It blinked at me with innocent blue eyes.

Uh-huh. Someone seemed to be under the mistaken impression that I was *stupid*.

"Got you!" Fast as a snake, I grabbed the cat by the scruff of its neck. It squalled as I hoisted it into the air. "Stop that! I know what you are—*werecat!*"

The cat stopped struggling long enough to shoot me a look of pure disbelief.

"Don't give me that. I read books, I know a shapeshifter when I see one. And don't even think that I'm going to fall in love with you." I shook the cat for emphasis. "Now turn yourself back—"

Running footsteps interrupted me. I jumped, my grip slipping on the cat's slick fur; it twisted free and streaked down the path, heading for the street.

"Crap!" I dashed after it, but my foot slipped in the mud as I tried to turn the corner. Going too fast to control the fall, I sprawled belly-first onto the rough tarmac—straight into a dazzling beam of light.

"Ack!" Blinking watering eyes, I looked up. The light wasn't from an oncoming car as I'd feared, but from an ordinary flashlight. The guy behind it gaped at me.

"Uh." I pushed myself to my knees, brushing gravel off my palms. I hoped he didn't notice my teeth. "Hi."

He didn't respond, still staring at me as if I'd hypnotized him. I could hear the harsh catch of his breath, as if he'd been running hard. He couldn't have been much older than me, although he topped me by nearly a foot. He was wearing jeans and a long leather trench coat, but his short-cropped red hair and combat boots gave him a vaguely military look.

Also, he was very, *very* ripped.

I was suddenly and painfully aware that my hair was a twig-tangled mess, my eyeliner was smeared, and I had cat hair all over my black clothes.

"Um," I said, fighting down a blush. At least he couldn't have recognized me from when I'd been alive. I was certain I'd never seen him before—his shoulders weren't the sort a girl would forget. "Look, this is going to sound weird, but did you just see a cat go past here?"

He stared at me for a second longer, then his hand darted into an inside pocket and he flung something at me. Caught off guard, my reflexive recoil was too late—but the impact was so light I could barely feel it.

Paper clips. Just paper clips, bouncing off my skin to chime against the ground.

"Hey!" Without even thinking about it, I reached down to gather them up. "What the—"

But he was already running. The beam of his flashlight bounced as he fled back down the road. Though he was fast for a human, I could have caught up with him without even trying. I *could* have, if I'd tried. But the glimmer of the paper clips against the tarmac was irresistible, catching like fishhooks in my brain. I couldn't leave them there.

By the time I'd picked up the last one, he was long gone.

Chapter 8

"A cute boy threw paper clips at you and ran away?" Zack said that evening, sitting on the edge of the kitchen counter.

"Yeah."

He contemplated this, legs swinging. "Maybe he likes you."

"First, his motivation is not the issue here." I poured gravy over my cereal bowl of raw ground beef in an attempt to make it feel more like breakfast. "Second, I don't care whether or not he likes me. Third, at the time I looked like I'd flung myself through a hedge, mainly because I just had. The point is, he threw paper clips at me, and I couldn't help picking them all up. I'm a vampire *obsessive-compulsive!*"

Zack opened his mouth.

I pointed my spoon at him. "My sire definitely said 'vampire,' so you can forget any word that starts with *z*."

Zack made a face at me and slid off the counter. He wandered over to peer into the fish tank. "Hey, Brains isn't looking too good."

I joined him. The fish looked about as un-good as it was possible for a fish to look without actually being a skeleton. Either vampire blood really was deadly, or Mum had forgotten to dechlorinate the water. I poked at the limp body with the handle of my spoon, and it floated to bob belly-up on the surface of the water. Zack looked as if he might cry. "We could bury it in a nice spot in the garden," I said, trying to console him.

"But how will it rise from the dead?" he said anxiously. "It can't *flop* out of the grave."

In the end we settled for burying the fish at the bottom of the tank, under a mound of neon pink and blue gravel. I went back to my congealing breakfast, trying hard not to think about the fact that there was now either a decaying fish or an undead fish in the kitchen. I wasn't sure which would be worse.

"Hey, Janie . . ." Zack had the speculative tone

that guaranteed I wouldn't like whatever he said next. "Will you take me with you when you run away to join forces with Lily against the evil, bloodsucking vampire Vikings?"

I groaned, sliding down in my chair. "There are so many things wrong with that, I don't even know where to start. Zack, I'm not running off anywhere, at least not yet." Mum and Dad had completely flipped out when I'd wanted to go to a Fang-Girl convention last year. If I snuck out to meet a mysterious, undead woman, I wouldn't be allowed out of my room until the next millennium.

"Oh, come on, it would be so awesome!" he wheedled. "I've already got the perfect outfit!"

"Not only no, but *hell* no."

He folded his arms, glaring at me with all the threat a skinny twelve-year-old in a vintage gentleman's dressing gown could muster. "If you don't let me be your sidekick, I'll tell Mum and Dad that you ran out after cute vampire hunters."

I showed him my fangs. "Or you could shut up and get to keep your blood in your veins."

"Don't bite your little brother, Xanthe," Dad said, coming into the kitchen. His hair was damp from the shower, and he wore paint-splattered jeans and a T-shirt. "One vampiric child is quite enough, thanks." He kissed the top of my head in greeting, then, to my surprise, went to the cupboards and started making himself a bowl of cereal.

"What's up with that?" I asked, nodding toward his bowl.

"Your mother and I agreed that it would be a good idea for me to time-shift to match your schedule," he said, getting the milk out of the fridge. "She has her teaching commitments, after all, but my publishers don't care when I paint, as long as I hit the deadlines."

"Oh." Touched as I was by the gesture, this was going to be massively inconvenient. "That's nice of you, but not really necessary."

"Yes, it is," he said firmly. "Undead or not, you're still my daughter. And you're still a minor. Legally, you have to have a responsible, adult guar—uh." He stared down into the cutlery drawer. "What happened to the spoons?"

"They're over there now," I said, pointing. "I rear-ranged all the drawers so that the biggest items are near the door, and then they go in descending order clock-wise around the room."

Dad looked at me. "Baby Jane," he said, shutting the cutlery drawer carefully. "Are you feeling all right?"

"No!" I scowled down into my empty bowl. "Everything in this house is *out of order!*" Even now, the fact that the saucepans were incestuously piled together under the counters was setting my teeth on edge.

"Hey, Dad," Zack said, shooting me a triumphant glare. "Want to see something funny?" Without waiting for a response, he grabbed a handful of cornflakes out of the cereal box and cast them onto the floor.

"Zack!" Even as I yelled, I was already sliding helplessly off my chair to start gathering them up. "I'm going to kill you!" He wisely fled the room, scattering cereal in his wake.

Dad offered me the dustpan. "Here," he said, his tone gentle.

I avoided his eyes, furious and on the edge of tears. "I have to pick them up one at a time." Despite my best efforts, my voice wobbled. "I can't help it. And I need everything to be arranged properly, or I feel uncomfortable."

Dad was quiet for a moment. Then, "Okay," he said, joining me on the floor. He started picking up flakes of cereal alongside me, putting them in the dustpan.

"You know," he said after a couple of minutes, "this is completely normal."

I sniffed. "No, it's not."

He smiled, crooking a finger at me. I followed him into the living room and watched him hunt around in the stacks of books. "Look," he said, handing me an academic-looking one. "Right there."

I squinted at the paragraph next to his pointing finger. The scholarly language was nearly impossible to decipher, but it seemed to be a chapter on Romanian folklore. Apparently, some legends said that you could get away from a vampire by . . . "Scattering poppy seeds?" I read out loud.

"Yep. Because the vampire will have to stop and count them all." Dad grinned. "Sound familiar?"

"Not really," I said doubtfully. "Is this the book with the tortoise thing? Because that was seriously on crack."

"This particular belief was quite widespread, even if it doesn't turn up in movies now. Maybe the real vampires suppressed the knowledge." He shrugged. "Or maybe it's simply not that scary. Nobody's going to want to watch a movie where Professor Van Helsing overcomes Dracula with the astonishing power of baking ingredients."

I stared down at the page. Dad was right; I couldn't think of any popular vampire story that had *that* in it.

But the guy last night had known it.

"So," Dad said in the fake-casual voice that he used when prying into my personal life, "you didn't wake us up before dawn. Didn't your sire call?"

"Uh . . ." Hmm. How to break the news. *Hey, Dad! I'm a superspecial ubervamp and my sire wants me to run away to be her bodyguard against a thousand-year-old evil vampire with his own personal army!* Yeah, that would go down wonderfully. Was there any way of putting this that wouldn't end up with my parents welding me into a closet for my own safety? "Well . . ."

I was saved by the sound of a muffled yell from the back garden, as if someone had discovered that the tree branch he'd grabbed was unexpectedly spiky, followed by a somewhat louder scream, as of someone subsequently losing his grip on said branch, and a very solid-sounding thud, as of aforementioned person hitting the ground.

I really didn't like people spying on me. I couldn't do much about Hakon and Lily, but normal eavesdroppers were another matter. And so, first thing in the evening, I'd spent some quality time in the back garden with the oak tree and a large reel of rusty barbed wire.

"Explain later!" I yelled to Dad, and zoomed out the back door. Sure enough, a guy had just fallen out of the oak tree. The busted crossbow lying on the ground nearby suggested that he'd had more on his mind than creepy staring. At the sound of the back door, he rolled to his feet, his long leather coat flaring around his broad form.

"You!" God, did *everyone* want to stalk me? Were they taking it in shifts? "Okay, hold it right—"

A shower of paper clips hit me right in the face.

"You are really starting to piss me off!" I yelled at his retreating back. He never broke stride, disappearing round the side of the house at a dead run. But it was only normal human speed—I could moonwalk faster than that. My hands blurred as I grabbed paper clips as fast as I could. "You aren't getting away that easily!"

"Xanthe?" Mum's head appeared in her bedroom window. "What's—?"

"Stay inside!" My anger and frustration felt like a storm cloud pressing against the inside of my skull. Shoving the last few paper clips into my pocket, I sprinted round the house and down the driveway like a dog after a rabbit. I burst out onto the road—just in time to hear the roar of an engine and see an enormous white van barreling toward me. Only vampiric reflexes saved me; without thinking, I leaped straight upward. I caught a brief glimpse of my nemesis's startled face through the glass, before the arc of my leap took me up onto the roof of the van itself.

I promptly discovered that keeping your balance on top of a moving vehicle was a lot more difficult than the movies made it out to be, and fell off. The van fishtailed around the corner with a smell of burning rubber.

"Oh, no you don't." I put my head down, and *ran*. Fire flooded through my veins, spiraling out from my heart until every fiber of my flesh felt incandescent with strength. My shoes were smoking, but I didn't care if my feet wore down to the ankles. We were still in the quiet Lancing backstreets with speed bumps stopping him from accelerating too fast. And there was no one to see me—

Someone darted into my path, far too late for me to do anything about it. I went sprawling, rolling head over heels a good ten feet along the road before I managed to stop myself. I staggered back to my feet to see the van's mocking red taillights disappear into the distance, joining the main road.

"*Damn* it!" My scrapes and bruises were already fading back into my skin, but my head still felt like someone was pulling at my brain. Furious, I spun round to see who had tripped me up.

"Don't move," growled the very large man carrying a gun and a stake.

"Uh . . ." The weird tension in my head had intensified to a distracting white-noise buzz, and the skin between my shoulder blades crawled. I risked a quick glance back, and found that another man had stepped out from behind a Range Rover to block my escape route. From the enormous pistol in his fist, I didn't think he was out for a nice evening stroll. I was guessing I'd run straight into a trap.

I promptly put my hands in the air. "I surrender."

"We don't want you to surrender," said the first guy in a deep, vicious snarl. His eyes were narrowed with hatred above the black scarf hiding most of his face. "We want you to die."

"No, really, let's talk about this!" I gabbled, trying to circle around to get both of them in view at once. They flanked me like wolves, the guns never wavering. "I, um, I know Lily's secret plan! Take me to Hakon, and I'll tell him everything!" My shoulders hit a brick wall; they'd backed me up against the side of someone's garage.

The two men exchanged a glance over their scarves. "What secret plan?" said the second one.

"Who's Hakon?" said the first.

I stared at them.

The first guy shrugged. "Who cares?" He leveled his gun at my heart. "Time to die—"

"Cease!"

We all jumped, my attackers whirling round. Someone stood poised on the roof of the parked Range Rover, silhouetted against the starry sky. In a breathtaking arc, he leaped ten feet, landing crouched in the middle of the road. He unfurled back to his full height, his velvet frock coat billowing around him, the moonlight turning his hair to pure silver. His high-cheekboned, elegant face was set in an expression of icy determination. As he faced my stunned attackers, his lips drew back in a contemptuous snarl . . . exposing jagged, sharp-edged teeth.

He was a vampire.

His pale eyes flicked to me. "Run, *ma chérie*," he said. His voice was as light and golden as honey, with a rich French accent that made the simple phrase sound like an invitation to unspeakable immoral delights. He dropped into a combat crouch, empty hands spread. "I shall take care of these—"

And that was as far as he got, because as my attackers had been conveniently distracted by his appearance, I punted them fifteen feet down the road.

I hadn't actually *intended* to do so. I'd only hoped to knock them off balance to give my unexpected rescuer an opening—after all, a dramatic pose was no match for two guns. So I'd shoved them, with all the strength I could muster.

Which, as it turned out, was quite a lot of strength.

"Quick!" I yelled as they skidded away, trailing shocked swear words. I dashed past the suddenly slack-jawed vampire. "Get them before they escape!" One of my attackers was already rolling to his feet—without thought, my blood roaring in my veins, I leaped for him. We crashed back to the ground, him flailing, me desperately trying to work out some way to subdue him. I grabbed for his hair, yanking upward with the vague thought of slamming his skull back down against the road—

I'd forgotten my vampiric strength again.

"AIEEEEEEEEEE!" I shrieked, reaching a high enough pitch to stun bats. I flung the severed head away with all

my strength. *"AIEEEEEEEEE!"* I hopped from foot to foot, overcome with utter squick.

"Shh, hush, it's all right!" The other vampire's hands captured my flailing wrists. "Xanthe!" Lights were coming on in the nearest house; with a quick look around, he grabbed the corpse by the back of its collar. "Quick, back here." He dragged us both into the shadow of the garage. After a few moments, the lights clicked off again, leaving us in darkness. I felt the tension in the vampire's muscles ease. "Well, that went . . . differently."

I managed to get enough of a grip on myself to speak, though my voice came out in a Mickey Mouse squeak. "Is he dead? Is he dead?"

The vampire looked down at the headless corpse. "Yes," he said. "He is very, *very* dead." He cleared his throat. "You must be wondering who I am."

My legs didn't want to support me anymore. I sat down hard. "What . . . what happened to the other guy?"

"I believe that he has fled, rather understandably. Now, my name—"

"Oh God, he escaped?" Even though I didn't need to breathe, I was starting to hyperventilate. "Is he coming back?"

"No," the vampire said firmly, catching my hands between his own. "Because I will not let him. I'm here to protect you."

I looked at him. I looked down at the corpse. I looked at him.

"Ah . . ." He appeared mildly embarrassed. "I can also help you dispose of bodies?"

"Okay," I said, still feeling a bit shell-shocked. "You sound very useful. Um. Who are you, exactly?"

He let go of my hand and stood, clearing his throat again. "In life, I was the Comte Ebène Bellefleur. Now, I am simply Ebène de Sanguine." He bowed deeply, sweeping back his long, black frock coat with perfect grace, as though this was his customary attire. "I would be pleased if you would call me Ebon. I have come to bring you home."

The best I could muster was a heartfelt "huh?" I was lagging about two minutes behind the conversation. I kept thinking of that horrible *crunch* through my hands.

"I must deeply apologize from the bottom of my soul that it has taken so long for us to send one of the Blood to welcome you," Ebon said, somehow managing to enunciate the capitalization. "I must confess that we were unprepared for your Transfiguration"—once

again I could hear the capitals clanging into place—
"but I can assure you that you will be a treasured jewel
among us. Now, *ma chérie*, we must make haste." His face
turned serious, and he held out a long, white-fingered
hand. "This place is not safe. As you have discovered,
the hunters are closing in. I will protect you with my
very life, but I cannot hold this place secure for long.
You must come."

I struggled to get my brain to concentrate. "Come . . .
with you? Where?"

"To your true home," he said—and suddenly his face
was only inches from mine. I froze, transfixed by the
pale blue of his eyes, as clear and cool as the light at
the heart of a glacier. "Come, Xanthe," he murmured,
shaping the hated sound of my name into something
beautiful and wild. "I long to teach you. To show you
who you are, and the power you will become. It is time
for you to learn everything."

I stared at him, and he didn't become any less real.
There was an actual gorgeous vampire aristocrat in
front of me, vowing to lay down his life in my defense.
All I had to do was take his hand.

"Okay," I whispered, my throat dry. "First let's hide
this body somewhere, and then . . ."

"And then?" he whispered back, his breath cool on my lips. His pale eyes gazed into mine, wordlessly promising to whisk me away from all my troubles.

Or, to put it another way, a very strange man with predator's teeth wanted to get me alone.

"And then," I said firmly, taking his hand, "you're coming home to meet my parents."

Chapter 9

I had to admit, Ebon was somewhat less cool in our living room than he had appeared when dramatically posed on top of a car. What had been an elegant, model-slender physique in the starlight was now the slightly stretched look of a teenage boy who'd hit his full height too quickly, leaving him with gangly limbs and gawky wrists. Sure, his pale blue eyes and razor-sharp cheekbones could have launched a thousand boy bands, but put him in jeans and a T-shirt, and he'd easily have passed as a student at any high school. As it was, the wildly spiked hair, leather trousers, and velvet coat gave the vague impression of a teenager dressing for Halloween as the bastard love child of Edward Cullen and Dracula.

With Ebon seated on the sofa and the three of us arranged opposite him on dining chairs, the whole scene had the air of a job interview. Ebon perched gingerly on the very edge of the cushions, spine perfectly straight, as though afraid the sofa might eat him if he leaned back. His eyes flicked from me to Dad to Zack and back again.

"So," Dad said in a horrible fake-hearty voice that made me cringe in my chair, "you're a vampire, are you?"

Ebon inclined his head stiffly.

"See?" I hissed to Zack, who was staring at Ebon with unreserved interest. "I *told* you so."

"I still think he could be a zombie," he whispered back, loudly enough that Ebon would probably have been able to hear it from the next room. "He looks awfully rigid."

Zack had a point. Ebon's bony hands were clenched on his knees. Rigor mortis seemed to have set in.

Mum came in, carefully balancing a tray. Despite the fact that it was one in the morning and she was wearing fuzzy, leopard-print slippers, her hardwired sense of What We Do When Unexpected Company Appears had kicked in. "I made tea," she said, putting the tray down on the coffee table. "Milk? Sugar?"

"*Mum*," I said, just as Ebon said, "Yes, thank you, ma'am." I'd never seen anyone accept a cup of tea so gratefully. As we all watched in fascination, he gulped down a mouthful as though doing a shot of vodka. Catching our eyes over the rim of the mug, he flushed, lowered the cup, and stared down into the tea as if divining the future.

"So . . . Ebon." Mum sounded as if she was grilling a particularly hapless PhD student on his dissertation. She even had a pad of paper balanced on her knee, a mechanical pencil poised to take notes. "Tell us about yourself. How old are you?"

"The years of my life numbered one-and-twenty, madame." He had both hands wrapped round his teacup, like a boy clutching a teddy bear, but his voice was velvet-smooth again. "But the years of my unlife span considerably longer. I was born in Paris in 1770."

The point of my mother's pencil snapped. The silence was so thick I could hear my parents' hearts beating.

"Oh," Zack said, sounding disappointed. "I hoped you were a Victorian."

We all stared at him, nonplussed.

"What?" he said, looking around at us. "Then he could have helped me make some period trousers. All the steampunks would have thought that was awesome."

"Steam . . . punks?" Ebon said.

"Don't ask," I advised him. "Really."

"Ebon?" Dad said. "How long do vampires live?"

Ebon turned one hand palm up, spreading his fingers. "Until we are killed." He leaned forward, his pale blue eyes intent. "Which is why I have come. There are those in the world who hate and fear our kind, and seek out any newly emerged member of our race. They attempt to slay us in our infancy, before we know how to protect ourselves. And as you have found, Xanthe, they are already here."

Mum stiffened. "As you have found?" she repeated, shooting me a narrow-eyed glance of suspicion.

I avoided her gaze. I hadn't felt the need to share the full details of the night's events with my parents. "I, uh, kind of ran across a few of them. Only briefly. I was perfectly fine! No danger at all, really!"

"Terrible danger," Ebon corrected, supremely unhelpful. "The hunters are a hereditary secret brotherhood, intent on eradicating the Blood from the earth. Throughout the centuries their fanatics have hunted down and slain many of us."

"Well, to be fair," Zack said reasonably, "you are

bloodsucking, undead monsters."

"Hey!" I slapped him on the back of his head as Mum said, "*Manners*, James!"

"I cannot condemn you for holding that opinion, young master." Ebon shook his head, one corner of his mouth twisting. "The hunters have carefully cultivated lies about my kind for uncounted centuries, and the fruit of that harvest is fear and hatred." He gestured in my direction. "As you have discovered, in truth we wish only to live in peace, taking nothing that is not freely given by those who love us. But the hunters care not that we do no harm. They see us as animals, to be hunted for sport."

"Huh," I said, frowning. "Great. As if I need another group of people out there wanting to kill me."

"*Xanthe Jane Greene.*" Dad's parental sixth sense had obviously just pinged into the red. "What do you mean, *another* group?"

That's right—with all the excitement, I still hadn't gotten round to filling my parents in on last night's conversation. "I got that call from my sire," I told them. "Lily. But she wasn't worried about hunters. She said that the real danger is this evil, ancient vampire named Hakon."

"Ah," said Ebon, clearing his throat. "If I may?"

From my mum's and dad's faces, we were two seconds away from complete parental explosion. I charged on in an attempt to defuse the bomb. "Because, you see, they've got this sort of massive feud going on, because he's like the vampire Godfather or something, but Lily managed to escape from his evil organization—"

"Um." Ebon half raised his hand. "I really—"

"And she vamped me in the hospital because she felt sorry for me, but Hakon doesn't like that, so she thinks they might want to get me too. But it's okay!" I said hastily as both my parents drew sharp intakes of breath. I waved my hands at Ebon. "See, she sent Ebon to protect me!"

"*Actually*"—Ebon finally managed to jam a word in edgewise—"Hakon sent me."

Silence fell. We all stared at him.

"Um," he said. His ears were turning pink. "The situation is not quite as you think." He sighed, running one hand through his spiked hair. "*Ma chérie*, I'm afraid that your sire has not been entirely truthful with you. There are no, ah, evil vampires out to kill you. Only the hunters, who always plague us."

I remembered the way my attackers hadn't recognized Hakon's name, and my stomach lurched in sudden uncertainty. "But . . . Lily said . . ."

"Your sire," Ebon said, "is a liar. And very dangerous. Madame, monsieur." He turned to my parents,
his face grave. "I think you will agree that a virtuous
individual would not bring a young girl into this life
without her parents' consent, let alone encourage her to
then run away from her own family."

Mum was nodding. Dad said nothing, his expression
neutral, but his artist eyes were scrutinizing Ebon as
intently as if preparing to paint him. Zack just looked
utterly thrilled with everything.

I crossed my arms over my chest, scowling. "And I
suppose you're going to say that Hakon is actually the
good guy here." Despite my sarcasm, I was badly shaken.
In retrospect, Lily's voice was starting to sound a little
too smug, a little too unnecessarily mysterious. And it
was hard to doubt the sincerity of someone who'd con-
fronted two armed men for me.

Ebon hesitated. "Hakon is . . . Hakon. I cannot claim
that he is the gentlest of souls. He was born a Viking,
which gives him a perspective sometimes at odds with
current mores. But his greatest desire is simply for order
and peace. It is he who keeps us hidden and safe from
mortals—and who keeps mortals safe from those Blood
who would otherwise prey indiscriminately upon them.

Which is why your sire is adamantly opposed to him."

"Hmm." Dad's tone was noncommittal. "And you work for this Hakon? Is he your sire?"

"Alas, no. My own sire is . . . currently in retreat, forcing me to find an alternative patron." Ebon spread his hands, palms up. "It may perhaps stand as a testament to Hakon's character that it is he that I chose to swear myself to, and although I am not of his Bloodline, he accepted my oath."

"So . . . that kind of makes you my adoptive cousin or something?" I had a sinking feeling that vampiric social relations were going to prove even more complicated than school cliques.

He cocked his head at me. "No. Why?"

"Lily said Hakon was her sire's sire."

"I see." Ebon rested his elbows on his knees, his face pensive. "So she does indeed seek to conceal her true name and nature from you. She is not Hakon's descendant, *ma chérie*. She is more ancient than that. She is more ancient than my own sire's sire, who once fought in the great Colosseum at Rome. She is, in fact, the very oldest among us. She is a Bloodline unto herself. She has always walked alone, seeding war in her wake but creating no descendants . . . until you."

"Why?" Mum said, her voice sharp with anxiety. "Why Xanthe?"

Ebon shook his head slowly. "We do not know. But it can mean nothing good. When Hakon learned of this, he dispatched as many men as he could muster to hound your sire, to keep her from returning to complete whatever plan she has."

I swallowed. "You keep saying 'your sire.' What's her real name?"

Ebon hesitated again. "Perhaps it would be best if you continued to think of her as Lily."

"Mr. de Sanguine." *I* wouldn't argue when my mum used that tone. "Tell us."

Ebon struggled for a moment, looking conflicted, then let out a long sigh. "Her real name," he said, "is Lilith."

Chapter 10

Mesopotamian mythology." As usual, Mum barged into my room without knocking. Going straight to my desk, she started unloading books one by one from her massive shopping bag. "Talmud commentaries. Kabbalah traditions. Chronicles of the Vikings. Scandinavian cultures from the seventh to tenth centuries. The French Revolution." She dropped the last book onto the teetering pile. "The librarians must think I'm writing an incredibly odd research paper."

"Good evening, Xanthe," I muttered to my own reflection in the mirror. "How are you? Why yes, Mum, I'm recovering nicely from last night's traumatic events, thank you for asking." I screwed the top back on my lip gloss and turned around with a deep sigh. "Mum, what's all this?"

"Research." She pointed at each group of books in turn. "Ebon. Hakon. Lilith. Though that last one is a little speculative. French aristocrats and Viking warriors have solid historical evidence, but I'm dubious about the existence of a ten-thousand-year-old demon."

"What, and vampires are perfectly logical? Anyway, of course there has to be a Lilith. There's always a Lilith. In vampire books," I explained, at Mum's blank look. I waved a hand at my own bookshelves. "She's always the vampire queen or ultimate sire or some such. And she's usually an utter skank. Um, no offense," I added to the air in case Lily was listening in. "Anyway, Lilith turns up in loads of religions and myths as the mother of demons or whatever, so it makes sense that she'd be real, right?"

"Hmm." Mum did not sound convinced. "And what does she say about all this?"

"Nothing. I can't get a signal, not even at the bottom of the garden." I hadn't dared go farther than that, for fear that the vampire hunters would jump me again. "But Zack's phone isn't working either. Maybe the station is down or something." I picked up one of the

books from the Lilith pile. The front cover had a painting of a fair-haired woman who seemed very happy to
see the anaconda encircling her naked body. I had to
admit, she did look like Lily sounded. "Mum . . . I *am*
really fast and really strong. I think that means that my
sire has to be pretty old. So that part of Ebon's story
checks out. And the werecat and paper-clip guy make
a lot more sense if they're hunters rather than spies for
some ancient vampire Elder. But . . . I don't know about
the rest."

"That's what these are for." Mum patted the stack of
history books. "Here, I've prepared a list for you."

I took the clipboard she handed me and leafed
through the papers dubiously. "What is this, an under-
grad French history exam?"

"Exactly," Mum said in triumph. "So we can find
out if this Ebon really is who he claims to be. You can
subtly work questions into normal conversation."

Yes, I could just see myself ever so casually asking
Ebon to explain the composition of the États-Généraux
in under two thousand words. He'd never suspect a
thing. "Why don't you do this?"

"I tried while you were getting dressed. He's able
to turn any inquiry into vague small talk about the

weather." Mum glared at the books, as though they had somehow failed her. "I think he might be under orders to only talk to you."

"I'll . . . be there in a minute." I turned back to my pale and slightly worried-looking reflection. "I just need to redo my hair."

"Xanthe." Mum took the hairbrush out of my hand. "You look very nice already. Stop fussing." She paused, studying me in the mirror. "Is that why you've been hiding up here? Worrying about how you appear to him?" Her voice fell into familiar lecturing tones. "Now, Xanthe, you know that's a culturally indoctrinated neurosis imposed by patriarchal—"

"God, Mum! Sorry if I want to make a good impression on the only boy of my own species I know!"

"I'm sure he likes you very much," Mum said soothingly—then her tone sharpened. "He hasn't *said* that he likes you very much, has he?"

"*Muuuum*! No!"

"Good," she said, relieved. "So there's no need for anyone to be anxious, is there? All you have to do is talk to him. Find out who he is."

I fidgeted with my lip gloss, looking down. There was no way that I could tell Mum that I already knew *exactly* who Ebon was. It was obvious.

Three words:

My.

Soul.

Mate.

All the signs pointed to it. He was the first vampire I'd ever met. He'd saved me from certain death, kind of. He had unlikely hair, an exotic history, an unbelievably sexy accent, and, for God's sake, *leather trousers*. It was inevitable. I was going to go down there and fall madly in love.

This *sucked*.

I had enough trouble with the mysterious sire who might or might not be an ancient demon, the Viking vampire who might or might not run an evil empire, the zealots who might or might not be out to kill me, and the family who absolutely, definitely, *would* weird out and do something totally embarrassing in front of my fellow vampires at some point. Not to mention the werecat and his van-driving friend, probably lurking behind the hedges even now. I totally did *not* need to add eternal love to my towering stack of problems. Sure, it was likely to all come out okay in the end, but there were bound to be misunderstandings and fights and long brooding fits punctuated by fiery glances. And I'd probably find myself gazing longingly at him when I should be scanning the treetops for paper-clip-wielding maniacs.

"Xanthe?" Mum touched my elbow. "What are you worried about?"

"Nothing." Ebon probably wouldn't even like me until something suitably dramatic happened to make him realize his true feelings. I squared my shoulders. "Guess there's no point delaying it."

"It's a conversation, not an execution, Xanthe." My mum studied my face, and her own softened. "You really are nervous, aren't you? Xanthe, let's talk about this. I've been a teenage girl"—this, I felt, was *extremely* unlikely—"and I remember what it was like. You can share your concerns with me. I've gone through the exact same thing."

"What, having to subtly interrogate an ancient, undead French aristocrat who may or may not be telling the truth?"

"I've had to talk to boys at parties. Now"—taking hold of my shoulders, she steered me to my chair, and sat down opposite me on the bed—"tell me all about it. Don't worry about the vampire for a moment. Your father and brother are keeping him occupied—"

"WHAT?" I went from seated to fully vertical in under a nanosecond. "You're letting *Zack* talk to Ebon?"

She blinked up at me. "Ye—"

I was out the door and halfway down the stairs before she'd finished the word. This was an utter disaster! I'd had to publicly disown Zack in eight different schools, and half the time he'd still managed to get me thrown out of the cool cliques. Even now, his weirdness could have driven Ebon out of the nearest window. Zack could be showing Ebon his collection of goggles. He could be expounding on his latest comic book obsession. He could be—oh my God—*talking about me.*

I burst through the door to the living room, smashing it off its hinges in my haste. Ebon leaped from his seat at the noise. In one fluid motion, he whirled to face me, dropping into a combat crouch with fangs bared and weapon raised, ready to strike.

It would have been a lot more impressive if he hadn't been threatening me with a wireless gamepad.

"Hey, Janie," Zack said, taking advantage of Ebon's distraction to pummel the vampire's in-game avatar. CRITICAL HIT!!!! flashed across the TV screen in excited red letters. "You want to play next?"

"Good evening, Xanthe." Dad was standing behind Ebon's now empty chair. "Do door handles offend your vampiric sensibilities now?"

"Sorry," I muttered. "Uh, Dad? What are you doing with that paintbrush?"

"What? Oh." Dad looked down as if only just noticing he was carrying a two-foot-long camel-hair brush. "I was, uh—"

"Never mind." I'd just spotted the way that he'd carved one end of the wood into a point. I hoped Ebon hadn't realized my dad was threatening him with art supplies. "Er, hi, Ebon." I narrowed my eyes at my brother. "Zack hasn't been boring you, has he?"

Ebon dropped the controller as if it were a live spider. His ears were bright red, but he swept an elegant bow in my direction. "Your brother is most charming," he said, thus convincing me that he could lie *really well* when it suited him. "He has been kind enough to entertain me while we awaited the gift of your presence."

"He's really good, Janie. He didn't know this game, but he picked up all the special moves right away." Zack paused the game and swiveled round in his chair. "Hey, Ebon, is that a vampire thing? To go with the super-speed and stuff?"

"Ah, not precisely." Ebon hesitated, glancing sideways at me. "But I am over two hundred years old, after all." There was a glint of wicked secrets in his ice-blue eyes. "I have acquired a great variety of skills over the centuries."

The way his French accent caressed the rolling *r*'s made it clear that most of those skills did not involve pressing buttons. At least, not on controllers. Oh God, I did not just think that. I tore my eyes away from him, embarrassment sweeping over me from head to toe.

"I guess you must have played everything since . . ." Zack was evidently searching his mind for something suitably prehistoric. "*Doom*. D'you remember, like, floppy disks?"

Ebon's white-blond eyebrows rose. "My young friend," he said, sounding genuinely amused, "the first computer I ever saw was made out of clockwork. I was utterly astounded when Mr. Babbage made it multiply two numbers together."

"Oh, great," I groaned as Zack's eyes went as round as steampunk goggles. "Ebon, you are really going to regret letting him know that you met actual Victorians." Zack was already out of his chair, drawn irresistibly toward Ebon like a small and badly dressed history-seeking missile. I grabbed him, lifting him into the air. "Oh, no you don't. We've got to discuss vamp stuff, not gaslight fashions. Out!"

"But . . ." Zack's feet pedaled at the air as I swept him away. "Babbage . . . difference engine . . . gears . . ."

"I said 'out'!" I kicked him out the door, glaring until he reluctantly set off for his room. "And no eaves-dropping!" I shouted after him, then turned back to Ebon and Dad. "We *do* have vampire stuff to talk about, right?"

"Indeed." Ebon hesitated, looking at Dad. "Ah, mon-sieur, I do not wish to appear ungracious after you have so kindly invited me into your own home, but there are private matters of the Blood I must discuss with Xanthe."

"Well . . ." Dad looked reluctant, as I made "go away" motions at him from behind Ebon's back. "All right. I'll be in my studio, sharpening some brushes—I mean pencils. Shout if you need me."

That left me alone in the living room with a blond, sharp-cheekboned, spiky-haired vampire wearing leather and velvet. Every word I'd ever learned drained out of my brain. "Uh," I said. "So."

"So," he said, his voice smoldering like the heart of a banked fire.

This was immensely unhelpful, in terms of unsticking my tongue from the roof of my mouth. I shifted my weight, staring down at the carpet. My hands felt two sizes too big, flopping on the ends of my arms like dead fish. We were alone. He was a boy vampire. I was a girl. According to my novels, now we would gaze soulfully into each other's eyes and discover an irresistible life-bond connection, possibly accompanied by hot yet chaste psychic sex.

I risked a tentative glance into Ebon's eyes, and discovered that he was gazing at me so soulfully it would have put a basset hound to shame. Oh, wonderful.

"Uh . . . so," I tried again.

"So," he murmured. "Here we are." His head tilted to one side slightly, exposing the long masculine line of his neck, and his voice dropped into a deep, intimate murmur. "*Ma chérie*, there is . . . something about you. Something different from anyone I have ever met. It is . . . strange. As if there is some deep connection between us, even though we come from different Bloodlines. Do you also feel it?"

Unless the mystic bond he was referring to felt identical to total, utter, stomach-clenching embarrassment, no. "Uh, let's talk about, um, vampire hunters!"

I squeaked, backing up and running into the wall. "They're still lurking around, right?"

"They will not attack while I am here," Ebon said with utter confidence. "They have reason to fear my name." A shadow crossed his face, as if he was remembering dark and terrible deeds. "I did not always have the control I do now." He turned away, staring moodily out the window at the front garden. "The beast I must constantly battle, the bloodlust . . ." He trailed off, lost in angst-filled contemplation of his inner pain, or possibly the rhododendrons.

"Okaaaaay." I surreptitiously edged around to put the coffee table between me and the admitted schizoid psycho. "What about Lilith, then?"

Ebon resurfaced from whatever depths he'd been plumbing. "Indeed, she is a greater threat. Many of Hakon's Bloodline are endeavoring to ensure she cannot reach you, but she is as subtle as a snake. She will eventually evade them and return to claim you. Unless . . ." Without warning, Ebon closed the space between us with two long strides, suddenly so close I could have felt his body heat, if he'd had any. "*Ma chérie,* are you brave?"

"No!" My shoulder blades were practically digging

through the wall as I attempted to avoid contact with his chest. If he proposed some sort of psychic bonding, the wall wasn't going to stop me. "And for God's sake, get out of my face! Haven't you ever heard of personal space?"

Ebon took a sharp step back, caught his ankle against the coffee table, and went sprawling. Piles of books cascaded after him.

"Ack!" I dropped to my knees, grabbing for scattered books. I'd restored three to the table before it occurred to me I should probably be more worried about my flattened vampiric bodyguard. "Um, are you okay?"

"Fine!" Brick red and much less Byronic, he scrambled up and started to help me restore order to the table. "My apologies," he muttered, looking utterly mortified. "My intentions—that is, I did not—"

"Uh, Ebon?" I interrupted, distracted by the way he'd moved two books that I'd just put down. "What are you doing?"

He looked down at the stacks on the table, as if only just noticing how he was sorting them. "Oh. As I'm sure you've discovered, we of the Blood can be a touch—ah, obsessive, about items being arranged precisely to our liking."

"Yeah, but look, I already made a pile for small leather-bound books." I pointed at my stack. "See?"

He coughed, sounding embarrassed. "Small leather-bound books with an odd number of letters in the title." He gestured apologetically at the stack he'd started. "Small leather-bound books with an even number of letters in the title."

I stared at him. "You have got to be joking."

"I'm older than you. I'm afraid the tendency strengthens with age." He restored the last book to the table and sat back on his heels, clasping his hands together. "Many of the Elders have such exquisitely refined taste, they can't enter other people's houses. It's not that they can't come in without being invited—it's simply that, if they do, they are overcome by the desire to clean up."

"Huh." I leaned back against the sofa. Ebon was somehow much less intimidating, now that I'd seen him flat on his back under an avalanche of vampire romances. "What was that you were saying about being brave?"

"Uh . . ." Ebon looked as if he was trying to find his place in a script again. "Oh yes." He cleared his throat. "It is dangerous, but there is a way we can hunt down Lilith, if you are willing to learn the powers of the Bloodline. For you—and you alone—have a direct connection to her."

I wrinkled my nose. "Yeah, I know, she can spy on me." I wondered what Lilith was making of all this, if she was listening in. "How does that help?"

"That bond is a two-way path."

I sat bolt upright. "You mean *I* can look through *her* eyes? And sense where she is?"

Ebon hesitated. "You should not attempt to link with her senses yet—not only is it considerably more difficult, it could be highly dangerous. I fear that should you open more fully to her than you already are, she could strengthen her unholy link with you and enslave you to her own twisted desires."

I remembered how reasonable and persuasive Lily had sounded. "Right. Let's not do that. What *can* I do safely?"

"I can teach you to master the other power, of feeling her direction through the pull of the Bloodline. She cannot hide from you, any more than you can conceal yourself from her."

"Holy sh— uh, I mean, wow." Lily hadn't bothered to mention *that*. "Is it hard? How does it work?"

"The Bloodline is like a river, in which we exist as

naturally as fish." Ebon's long, pale hands swam through the air in demonstration. "You will find that there is a current to the Bloodline, which flows from sire to childe. A sire may reach downstream to all of his descendants, though with more distant generations the power of the Bloodline is spread out and weaker—he can still use their senses, but for less time, and he cannot precisely sense their location." Ebon splayed his fingers out like a branching stream, then closed them again. "But with his direct children, the connections are sufficiently strong and focused that he may use it to tell which direction they are from him. Likewise, a vampire can reach upstream, against the current of the Bloodline, to his direct sire— though no higher, as the force of the Bloodline is simply too strong to battle upstream to one's sire's sire." Ebon raised one finger. "As Lilith's only direct descendant, you and you alone possess the power to locate her. I can teach you now, if you are ready."

"Hey, it's not like I had anything else planned. Let's do it. Um, what am I supposed to do?"

"It is like listening to the beat of your heart." His voice lowered, rich and hypnotic. "Except that rather than feeling the tides of ordinary blood, you attune yourself to the gentler call of Blood." I still couldn't work out how he could say the capitalization. "But you must be careful not to allow yourself to be swept away. Center yourself firmly in your own body, then look inward, and feel the beat of Lilith's heart sustaining you, flowing into your veins. Then, simply turn in the direction of the current."

Feeling a bit stupid, and uncomfortably aware of Ebon watching me, I shut my eyes. Without breath or heartbeat, my body felt like an empty cathedral; a vast, silent space, in which even the tiniest sound would echo like thunder. I tried to let my mind expand to fill that expectant void, attuned for the slightest motion.

When we'd lived in a flat, I'd sometimes find myself humming a song under my breath for no apparent reason, only to realize that the music was coming through the wall, from one of our neighbors—too quiet to hear unless you were listening for it, but loud enough for my subconscious to have picked it up. The Bloodline was like that. With my mind turned inward, I could feel something running underneath my own senses. There was the echo of a pulse fluttering in my still chest, the sensation of air expanding my unmoving lungs. Flashes of color sparked behind my closed eyelids, streaking together like an Impressionist painting. And beneath it all, the tide of my blood ran like a river, stretching out beyond the confines of my skin.

One current seemed to be flowing inward, into my veins, just as Ebon had said. But there was also something else. . . .

"What do you feel?" A strange hint of excitement edged Ebon's whisper. I peeked at him from under lowered eyelids. His body was taut, poised to catch my next words.

What was it Lily had said? *Your Bloodline isn't normal. . . . And if Hakon knew, you'd already be dead.*

"I dunno," I said, picking my words carefully. My voice sounded weirdly muffled in my own ears, distorted around the edges by other half-heard sounds. "You said I should only be able to feel one current, my connection to Lilith, right?"

"Indeed." Ebon sounded as calm as a hypnotherapist, but his clasped hands tightened. "Remember to keep steady in your own body. Tell me exactly what you feel."

I really wasn't sure that was a great idea, not until I had at least some clue as to what was going on. Without moving, I tried to picture the Bloodline in my head. One current was definitely streaming *out* of my own heart, not into it. And, when I focused on it, it turned its attention on me.

116

The Bloodline roared in my veins, demanding my attention like a hungry toddler. Whatever was on the other end felt close, very close. In the very next room, in fact.

"*Oh* no," I moaned, opening my eyes. "No, no, no!"

"Uh . . ." Ebon trailed behind me as I rushed to the kitchen. "Xanthe, are—?"

"This totally wasn't my idea," I interrupted. "I swear, I had nothing to do with it!"

Ebon followed the line of my pointing finger, staring bemusedly into the empty waters of the fish tank. "What—?"

The mound of pink and blue gravel heaved, revealing a silver-scaled flank.

"*Good Lord in heaven!*" Ebon recoiled so hard he rattled the kitchen cabinets.

Brains-the-fish struggled free of the gravel, thrashing its tail. It hung in the water, pale as the moon, then drifted forward without visible effort until it was nose to nose with me on the other side of the glass. The look it gave me was way too considering for a fish.

"It's a fish," Ebon said, weakly. "Why have you bitten a fish?"

"I didn't!" I said, locked in a death stare with the goldfish. My eyes started to water. "Blame my mum; it was her experiment. Has anyone ever, um, made a vampire animal before?"

"It is considered extremely perverse. I know of only one who has done so, but that was with cats. I can at least understand cats. Cats are nice." Ebon was obviously rattled, oddly drawled vowels breaking through his polished French accent. "How can a *fish* be a vampire? It doesn't even have teeth."

Brains gave him a look that suggested it was perfectly willing to try sucking him to death without them.

"You know," I said slowly, most of my attention still occupied with the Bloodline. "I think this is going to take me a little while to grasp. I could do with a bit of private practice." I groped for something to keep him busy. "Um, you ever play *Rock Band*?"

His eyes lit up. "You have *Rock Band*?" he gasped as if he'd opened a closet and found Narnia. "Er, I mean." His expression snapped back to his customary polite-yet-brooding look. "Only if you are sure you don't require my assistance."

"No, really, I'm good for the moment. Get Zack to show you."

He hesitated a second longer, practically vibrating with indecision—but duty was helpless before the power of rock. "Simply practice feeling for direction—don't try to make contact," he reminded me and took off. I listened to his eager footsteps go up the stairs and to Zack's room. A few minutes later, two sets of feet thumped back down again, heading for the living room. I waited until I heard the crash of guitar chords.

"So, Brains," I muttered, under the unlikely sound of an eighteenth-century, aristocratic French vampire enthusiastically murdering Iron Maiden. "What do you think he's expecting me to find? And why is he so keen for me not to actually look down these Bloodline things?"

Brains rippled its fins in a piscine shrug, looking up at me.

I knew exactly where it was looking, because I was getting a fish-eyed view of my own face.

Looking down the Bloodline was easy. The connection was a bright, straight road between us. And now that I was able to sort Brains out from the background flow, the rest of the Bloodline was starting to come into focus too.

One current going outward, to Brains. One current coming inward, presumably from Lilith.

So what was the *other* connection I could feel? The one that went in *both* directions?

Chapter 11

It was a good thing Ebon was easily entertained by video games, because I was fully occupied staring at the wall for the rest of the night. It was also a good thing that I was used to tuning out my little brother in order to study, as Ebon's singing was even worse than Zack's favorite Finnish metal bands.

I could easily dip into Brains's senses, but that didn't tell me much except that the life of a goldfish was unbelievably boring. All I could do was ride along as it circled its tank—the psychic connection between us stopped at that. I couldn't take control of its body, and trying to order Brains around verbally just got me a flat-eyed stare. Obviously, the goldfish was not impressed with me as a sire.

I wished I felt as unbothered by Lily. I could feel the tie to her as easily as my link to Brains. After several hours of practice with the fish, I finally psyched myself up enough to try snatching a glimpse through her eyes as well, but it turned out to be almost as uninformative. All I got was a view of motorway rolling past, and the rumble of a car engine. I dipped in and out a couple of times over the night, but I didn't dare stick around too long, in case Ebon's warnings about hijacking Lily's senses being dangerous were actually true. Each time was the same—steering wheel, engine noise, roads. The only useful thing I caught was the name WORTHING on one of the signs, so she couldn't be too far off. I still hadn't decided whether or not that was a good thing.

That left the third connection. Which was . . . weird.

Unlike my other two Bloodline links, this one seemed to flow in both directions, as though whoever was on the other end was both my sire *and* my descendant. I couldn't figure out how that could be possible. Given Lily's earlier statement about not letting Hakon know about my "unique" Bloodline, combined with Ebon's slightly-too-interested line of questioning earlier, I wasn't inclined to ask him about it just yet. All I could do was experiment, comparing it to my links with Lily and Brains.

I could always sense the strange link's direction—nearly due west—but my ability to do anything else with it was oddly intermittent. The first time I gingerly turned my attention that way, it was as if I'd stepped on a greased trapdoor; one second I was behind my own eyes, then *BAM!* my fingers were dancing over a laptop keyboard propped up on my blanket-swathed legs. I wasn't simply watching; it felt like I was *there*, as if it was *my* body lying on that bed. It had freaked me out so much I'd snapped back to my own senses like a rubber band and had had to go and join Ebon on the Xbox for an hour to calm myself down.

But when I'd finally stopped panicking enough to test the Bloodline again . . . nothing. Literally nothing; the Bloodline sucked me down, and my senses went utterly blank. No sight, no sound . . . nothing.

Lily had said that there was no way to block the Bloodline, but apparently this vampire could. Which meant that, whoever it was, he or she was more powerful than a ten-thousand-year-old demon goddess. And was connected to me more strongly than even my own childe and sire.

That thought was enough to keep me fully preoccupied, all the way through to dawn.

Unfortunately, I wasn't the only one who'd been thinking.

"So, Xanthe," Mum announced without warning the next evening, over her dinner and our breakfast, "I've come to the conclusion that you should turn me into a vampire."

Ebon dropped his fork. I stared at her in perfect horror.

"Both of us," Dad added. I swiveled to stare horror-struck at him too. Ebon's knife clattered against the floor.

"And me!" Zack chimed in. I was all out of horror. There was not enough horror in the world.

"No, James," Mum told him, steel in her voice. "Not you."

Ebon had retreated under the table, possibly to retrieve his cutlery, but more likely to hide from the utter insanity of my family. *"Are you all deranged?"* I inquired as politely as possible.

"Really, it's the only sensible solution," Mum said calmly. She speared a sprout and consumed it without haste before continuing, "We can't leave you all on your own."

"If you all go off and become vampires, I'll be on my own," Zack grumbled into his plate. "How come it's okay for me to be alone but not Janie?"

"Do you want to be twelve forever?" Dad said to him.

Zack considered this. "Can I be a vampire when I'm fifteen, then?"

"Twenty-six," Mum said. "That's a good age for a man. Get a degree and start a career, and then we'll see about biting you."

"But Janie—"

I banged my fork down. "No one's making anyone a vampire! *God!*" I shot a mute appeal at Ebon, who had just emerged, red-faced, from under the table. "There are rules about this sort of thing, surely?"

"We shall appeal." Dad nodded his head decisively, looking determined. "We'll make this Hakon see the need for a special dispensation. I'm sure he's a reasonable man."

Ebon broke into a coughing fit.

Dad waited patiently until he'd finished. "Well?"

Ebon looked round at the massed expectant stares. "Oh dear," he said, and dropped his fork again. "Excuse me."

"I'm not making you into vampires," I said, crossing my arms over my chest and glaring at them all. "It would be too weird to be my parents' parent."

"That's easily addressed," said Mum. "Ebon can do it to us."

There was a muffled thump as Ebon hit his head on the underside of the table.

"He isn't going to do it to you!" I yelled, wishing that the ground would open up and swallow me—or better yet, my parents. "Nobody's doing anything to anyone, ever!"

"Do you want to have to watch us all die?" Mum asked, point-blank.

That silenced me. Sure, I knew intellectually that my parents would one day get old and not be around anymore—but that sort of thing wasn't supposed to happen until I was old myself. Not while I was still *fifteen*.

Thing is, I was going to be fifteen forever.

Dad was watching my face. "You see the problem, Xanthe," he said more gently. "How are you going to support yourself—not only now, but in a year, a decade, a century? You'll still look like a teenager. How would you get a job? Where would you live?"

On the other hand, the alternative to no parents seemed to be immortal parents. Talk about a rock and a hard place. The thought of living with my family *forever* was horrifying. "I—look, this is nuts. You can't all become vampires." I waved at Ebon, who'd just put his head cautiously over the edge of the table to see if it was safe to come out yet. "Ebon, *you* explain it to them."

"I, um, I . . ." Ebon quailed as all eyes turned on him again. "I . . . have urgent business to attend to!"

"*Ebon!*" He'd bolted straight out of the room, and indeed from the house. I caught up with him on the driveway. "Where are you going?" I demanded, grabbing his sleeve and hauling him to a halt. "You're supposed to be my bodyguard, remember?"

"Yes, but—!" Ebon was rather wild-eyed. He raked one hand through his hair, causing havoc to the carefully gelled spikes. "Your family is very, um, that is, surprisingly, er—"

"Insane?" I supplied.

"I was going to say devoted." Ebon shook himself, seeming to calm down a little. "But I truly do have urgent business, I'm afraid."

"Really? What?"

"I would prefer not to say."

I gave him a long, level stare.

"Ah—" Ebon had the expression of a girl forced to ask for a tampon. "Actually," he muttered, "I'm hungry."

"You're—oh." I'd *thought* he'd been pushing his ground beef around unenthusiastically. "Okay. Let's find you someone to eat then." I scanned the deserted front garden. "Crap. Where's a lurking vampire hunter when you need one?"

Ebon looked at me a bit oddly. "You . . . are comfortable with this?"

"Ebon, you're a vampire. I'm kind of familiar with the basic concept." I shrugged. "Besides, I'm going to get hungry eventually, so it's not like I can afford to be squeamish." Ebon's look had turned into a flat-out stare. "What?"

"You truly aren't hungry," he murmured. "I didn't believe—well." He shook his head. "In any event, I must ask you to wait while I . . . relieve myself."

An idea burst into my head. I'd never thought anything I'd learned in math class would actually prove useful, but a bit of elementary geometry—two straight lines converge to a point—might answer some questions. "No way. I'm coming with you."

"No, you must not." Ebon's expression turned darkly brooding. "I do not wish you to have to witness my beast—"

"Hello! Fellow vampire here!" I waved my hands in the air. "I've got to learn how to do this stuff too, you know. I'll, like, shadow you."

"No, I—" He stopped abruptly, as if an idea had just

127

struck him too. "I suppose you have a point," he conceded. "Very well. First we must find a suitable donor." He threw back his shoulders, a hunter preparing to stalk his prey across the night . . . and pulled an iPhone out of his pocket.

"You are *kidding* me." I watched as he tapped through screens with practiced swipes. "There's an app for *that*?"

"Hakon keeps a regional list, to help his Bloodline keep to previously bitten humans. This is a convenient way to distribute the information." His mouth quirked. "There's a corresponding wiki for reviews as well, but that's strictly unofficial." He scrolled down the screen. "Here we are. The closest donor is . . . yes, one Lorraine Mitchell. I believe you've met?"

"Lorraine? You want to eat Lorraine? Hang on." I frowned. "How did you know about that?"

Ebon raised one eyebrow and cast me a dark, mysterious smile that insinuated possession of strange psychic powers.

I waited.

When it became obvious that I wasn't buying it, Ebon's mystic expression slid into slight embarrassment. "I must admit I was following you," he said. He shrugged one shoulder. "I have been stalking Lilith for

128

some years now, on Hakon's orders. Fortunately for us all, I came across her as she was unearthing you from your grave."

I remembered the gunshots I'd heard, when I'd first woken up in my coffin. "That was you? You chased her away?"

"I am, in fact, more dangerous than I appear," he said a touch testily. "In any event, after driving Lilith off, I shadowed you. I have been watching over you for a few nights now."

"Huh. Would have been useful if you'd introduced yourself a bit earlier," I said, thinking of Mr. Paper Clip and his werecat spy. "I could have used the help."

"My apologies, but I had to determine whether you were truly an innocent, or Lilith's willing minion."

"It's okay." I caught a flash of movement at the front window; my dad, quietly keeping an eye on us from behind the curtain. I didn't think he'd be wild about the idea of me heading out for a spot of bloodletting. I nudged Ebon, tilting my head meaningfully. "If we want to avoid a long argument, we'd better get moving."

"Easier to ask for forgiveness than permission?" he murmured, following my gaze. "I quite agree." He offered me his hand. "If you would do me the honor?"

I fell into step with him. His hand clasped my own as if we were dancing together, and our feet skimmed the ground as easily as seagulls across the sky. Streetlamps flashed past in a blur of strobe light. Rather than stick to the roads, Ebon took us out into open farmland. We leaped through the fields, hurdling the occasional hedgerow like steeplechasers.

I waited about ten minutes before asking, "Is there some reason why we're going so slowly?"

Ebon missed a step. "You . . . call this slow?"

We couldn't be doing more than about thirty miles per hour. I'd done at least double that trying to catch the van driver. "Well, yeah. You don't have to hold back for me, Ebon. I can keep up."

"Perhaps you would care to set the pace—*aaaaugh!*"

"Sorry," I said, jogging back to his doubled-over form. "Are you okay?"

"I believe I have a dislocated shoulder. I was . . . not expecting you to accelerate quite so rapidly." He straightened, giving me a pained smile. "No matter. It will heal in two minutes or so."

"Wow, you heal slowly too? Are you weak from lack of blood or something?" Ebon was staring at me again. "What?"

"Nothing," he said, taking my hand again—with his other hand, this time. "But I am becoming extremely interested in talking with your sire."

We set off again, with me carefully shortening my strides to match his. Lancing dwindled to a small scattering of lights behind us. Cars rumbled distantly off to our left, marking the main road, while the rolling hills of the South Downs rose to our right. "So," I said. Neither of us needed breath to run, so we might as well talk. "Why Lorraine?"

"Because the Elders require us to minimize the number of people we bite. Every time we feed, we run the risk of passing on the gift of the Blood." I opened my mouth, but he'd already anticipated my next question. "No, it does not matter if we use knives or needles or our own sharp teeth. It is simply the act of taking their blood within us, transmuting it to Blood, that may form the connection."

It was my turn to miss a step. "Are you saying that I may already have made *Lorraine* into a vampire?"

"Perhaps." He shrugged. "If you had fed her your own blood, she would definitely become one of us, but merely feeding from her may have given her the gift."

I could not be Lorraine's sire. The possibility was

too horrible to contemplate. Lorraine, able to borrow my senses whenever she wanted? *Lorraine*, in my blood?

I looked again at that third Bloodline, though I didn't try going down it. "Ebon? Let's say, hypothetically speaking, that I *have* turned Lorraine. Would I feel, um, some sort of connection to her?"

"Yes," Ebon said with a raised eyebrow at my look of horror. He continued, "But you might regardless, whether she has been infected or not. Depending on how much blood we consume, we can form weak, temporary mental links with anyone we feed from. It's not comparable to a full Bloodline connection, and they fade very rapidly, but with practice we can use them to perform minor acts of influence. Another reason to return to your earlier victim—I can demonstrate how to glamour her into forgetfulness."

"Huh." My strange third link was *stronger* than the others, not weaker. And I couldn't think of any reason why Lilith would want to protect Lorraine from Hakon, especially considering that he obviously knew about her anyway.

Well, at least going to Lorraine's house would determine whether it *was* her. I realized that Ebon had changed our course, angling us farther inland. "Hey, you're going too far north. Lorraine lives in Angmering."

"I know." He pointed ahead, to where a tall hilltop rose against the starry sky. "I thought we might make a small diversion, to Cissbury Ring. I . . . want to show you something."

"Well . . ." Ebon turned an earnestly angst-filled expression on me, like a very Goth puppy. I mentally shrugged. "Okay, if you want." Heck, if he got too weird, at least I knew I was stronger and faster than him. And the height would give me a better view of the surroundings . . . ideal for the Bloodline experiment I had in mind.

We scrambled up the rising ground, plowed earth giving way to tussocks of grass and gorse as we ascended. Cissbury Ring was actually an Iron Age fort, though it didn't look like much. Just a tall hill topped with a mile-long ring of grassy embankments, which had once enclosed a wooden fort. Now there was nothing more than long grasses and low, scrubby trees, growing where once Iron Age people had . . . done Iron Age things, I suppose. Presumably involving iron.

"I have always enjoyed it up here," Ebon said, gazing down at the farmland spreading out below us. On the horizon, the lights of Worthing cast a dull red stain into the sky, but up here the night air was cool and clear. A car engine rumbled on the other side of the hill, then stopped, leaving nothing but the sound of wind in the grass. "It makes me feel . . . young."

"Hm? Um, yeah." I had other things than the view in mind. As we started to stroll along the embankment, I reached inward, feeling the directions of my three links. By comparing the lines to what I'd felt from my house, I could triangulate on the other vampires. It would have been easier with a compass, but I could get a rough feel for their locations. . . .

"Is not the moon beautiful tonight?" Ebon said, breaking my train of thought.

"Uh, sure." It was the moon. I'd seen it before. Now, from the feel of it Lilith was somewhere to the north, maybe ten miles or so up the A24—

"It comforts me that there are some things that never change," Ebon interrupted yet again. I resisted the urge to smack him. "The moon at least remains constant, as eternal as we are . . . *ma chérie.*" His pace slowed a bit. "May I share something with you? Something . . . personal?"

"If you want." As long as he didn't expect much response. It was an effort to hang on to my mental map, but I was pretty sure the source of that mysterious third link had to be somewhere in Worthing. . . .

"It's only . . . do you remember when I said that I felt there was a connection between us?" Damn it, I was trying to concentrate!

Ebon continued. "I think it's because we share similar origins, you and I." He was gazing so earnestly into my eyes that I felt like a teleprompter. "Like you, I too am an orphan."

"Oh my God!"

Ebon bowed his head solemnly. "Yes. I too am estranged from my Bloodline, alone in this world. You and I . . . we are not like the others. We are the progeny of beasts. The offspring of monsters. And . . . you will find that there are those who scorn us for it."

I didn't tell Ebon that my exclamation had nothing to do with his history. I'd just tried reaching down that third Bloodline again . . . and now it wasn't black.

Whoever was on the other end had stopped blocking me. Once again I could see through the other vampire's eyes . . . which were looking at a website on a laptop screen. A very, *very* familiar website.

Fang-Girls.net.

Ebon was rambling on, something about darkness and blazing eyes and nightmares made flesh. I barely heard him. His earnest voice was like a safety cord running back to my own body, keeping me a little bit back from the unknown vampire. I didn't know if they could sense me, but someone more powerful than Lilith was not someone to risk pissing off. I stayed very still and small, watching as the vampire scanned the recent activity on the site, then clicked the log-in button. The screen updated itself, and what I saw in the top corner shocked me all the way back into my own body.

SIGNED IN: SUPERLUMINAL

"Xanthe?"

"Huh?" I was jerked back to my own senses. Ebon was gazing down at me as if his entire future happiness rested on whatever I said next. I desperately tried to remember what he'd been talking about. Something about being attacked by a beast and subsequently shunned by vampires? Still reeling from the Superluminal bombshell, all I could do was take a wild stab at an appropriate response. "Uh . . . that sucks, I guess?"

I was talking to thin air. Ebon had stopped abruptly, letting go of my arm. I turned back in confusion and was horrified to discover that he had both hands over his face. Was he *crying*? "Ebon? I'm sorry, I was thinking about something else—"

"Xanthe." He raked both hands back through his hair. He wasn't crying, to my relief, though he looked like he might be about to. That, or burst into hysterical laughter. "Am I doing something wrong?"

I blinked at him. "What?"

He flung his hands into the air. "I tell you my dark, secret past, and all you have to say is *that sucks*?" Words suddenly spilled out of him in a torrent, as if his angst had finally burst the dam of his control. "I tried wearing the right clothes, I tried the right accent, I tried saving your life, I even tried telling you my tragic history, but none of it has *worked!*" His shoulders slumped. "You still aren't . . . impressed."

I snickered.

I couldn't help it. It was just too funny. My snicker grew into full, helpless, doubled-over laughter, as Ebon's face slid from self-pity through confusion and then toward icily offended dignity.

"I'm sorry, I'm sorry!" I gasped, catching his sleeve before he could sweep away in outrage. "I'm sorry, I was distracted when you were talking before, I didn't mean to insult you. But, Ebon . . . are you saying that all this angstastic drama-queen crap you've been pulling is an *act*?" I dissolved into giggles again. "Oh my God, you utter dork. Why the heck would you do something like that?"

Ebon's expression was veering toward confusion again. "But I . . . thought that was what you liked? With your website and, er, stories—"

"You read my fanfic?"

He went bright red. "Er, ah, I . . . I only wanted to learn what you liked." He looked mortified, as if he'd been caught watching porn. Then again, if he'd been reading some of the spicier fanfic forums . . . "So I could make a good impression."

"And you stumbled onto Fang-Girls?" Dear God, how many vampires *were* there in fandom? Though I bet Ebon hadn't realized what he was getting into. Unlike Superluminal, who I *knew* was a long-term fan . . . I put that thought aside for now. I needed to get back to an internet connection to do some checking, but first I had to prevent Ebon from going into full-on meltdown. "Wow. I'm so sorry. I hope you weren't too scarred by the slash section."

Ebon had the slightly stunned expression of a man who was replaying the last five minutes in his head, trying to work out where it had all gone horribly wrong. Still chortling, I took his hand, tugging him along the path again. "So you aren't usually quite so . . . intense? I have to say, I'm kinda relieved. The hints of undying obsession were starting to get a bit freaky."

"But I thought you liked undying obsession," he said rather plaintively. "All of your books and TV shows are full of it. I thought you wanted a . . . a dark and tormented protector."

"Ebon, that's fiction. Everyone likes Mr. Tall, Dark, and Dead in fiction." I shrugged. "But, y'know, brooding angstmuffins are like Majorca. Awesome fun for a holiday, but heck, you wouldn't want to live there."

We walked in silence for a few steps more, before Ebon burst out, "Xanthe—"

"Before you ask, yes." I squeezed his hand. I wasn't sure I *trusted* him, but I did know one thing. "I do actually like you. Though more when you're geeking out over *Rock Band* than when you're getting your Goth on."

For the first time, I saw Ebon's real smile. It was nice, shy and sweet and kinda awkward. And also very brief, because at that moment someone jumped out of the bushes and cut his head off.

Chapter 12

*E**bon!"* I screamed as his body toppled. Metal flashed in the corner of my eye; I jumped back just in time to avoid losing my own head to the return swing of the ax. The guy on the other end of it let out a short hiss of frustration. He was redheaded and broad-shouldered, wearing a long, black leather trench coat and a determined expression. His green eyes met my own, and narrowed.

It was the vampire hunter. The really hot one with the paper-clip obsession. Guess he'd upgraded his weaponry.

There was nothing I could do for Ebon; I'd seen his head go flying into the bushes. I whipped around—but before I had fled more than three steps, a soft hail of paper clips fell around me, glittering. Although I knew I had to run, that this was *insane*, I slid to a helpless stop, dragged back as though connected to the paper clips by invisible steel cords. As I ducked to snatch at them, I felt the ax slice through the air where my head had just been.

I dodged backward, avoiding a second powerful blow. The paper clips winked at me. I wasn't abandoning them, I told the crazy part of myself as I flung myself to one side, snatching up a paper clip as the blade whistled past again. I was going to pick them up *gradually*. When I could. Without being bisected. In fact, maybe I could come back to get the paper clips later . . . ?

The spark of an imminent migraine stopped me from any further attempt to ignore this stupid compulsion. Still, this wasn't too bad. The hunter might be fast for a human, but I was still faster. And I could run all night, whereas he was already panting. All I had to do was evade him until I'd picked up all the paper clips, and then I could escape. Or, even better, avenge Ebon. White-hot rage filled my chest. Leaping over the vampire hunter's head, I managed to scoop up an entire handful before he'd had time to turn. Oh, he was going *down*.

The vampire hunter backed off for a moment, chest heaving, his ax held defensively across his body. I smiled sweetly at him, showing my fangs. "Bring it, Van Helsing," I told him. "I can keep this up all night."

He scowled at me. Flipping his ax to one hand, he plunged the other into his pocket. The scowl morphed into an evil grin, and another hundred or so paper clips hit the ground.

"Okay," I said, dropping into a crouch. "Now you are really getting on my nerves. I am *so* taking you out."

"Die, foul fiend," he snarled, charging once more.

"Foul fiend?" I said, nearly getting clipped by the blade due to disbelief. I rolled to pick up a few more paper clips. "Did you *actually* just say that, like, non-ironically?"

His mouth shut with a snap, and his next few blows seemed to have rather more feeling behind them. On second thought, maybe it wasn't such a good idea to wind up the huge, ripped guy holding the ax. "Look," I said, deciding to try reason. "You don't really want to do this. I'm a good vampire—I mean, like, a vampire with a soul, not that I'm really good at, you know, vamp-stuff. I'm not some monster. Heck, I've only been a vampire for less than a week! I've never even sucked anyone's blood!" I ducked under the blade and back-flipped away. "Really! You can ask my parents! My mum's a university professor, she's a very trustworthy character reference!"

The hunter paused for breath, resting the tip of his ax on the ground but never taking his eyes off me. Sweat stuck his T-shirt to his broad chest. "Please be quiet and die," he wheezed, sounding somewhat plaintive.

"No way, you Blade wannabe—*AIIIIEEEE!*"

My scream scared the hunter so badly he fumbled the ax, but I couldn't take advantage of the opening to attack. I was too busy trying to flail away from whatever had just grabbed me. *Oh God, there's the werecat and now I'm dead* was the rather ignoble last thought that ran through my head—but whoever it was released my arms. I leaped aside, and it blundered past me, hands outstretched blindly.

It was Ebon's headless corpse. Upright. Walking.

I stared at it, rooted to the spot for an instant of sheer disbelief—and nearly lost my own head. I felt the blade score a thin line across my shoulder as I flung myself out of the way.

"You'll have to do better than that," I said, circling. Ebon's—corpse? Zombie? Unholy freak of nature?—had disappeared into the bushes, though I could hear it crashing about. The wound in my shoulder had already closed.

Was it possible that Ebon could heal his decapitation in the same way?

"Pretty soon it's going to be two on one," I said to the hunter, hoping it was true. "So if you've got any more moves, now's the time."

The vampire hunter's eyes gleamed above the curve of his ax. Keeping his gaze fixed on me, he lifted the blood-edged blade—and licked it.

"EWW!" I recoiled. "What kind of a pervert are you?"

"This kind," he said with a twist to his lip. And then he shut his eyes.

This was weird enough that I wasted a whole two seconds gaping at him before I realized I should probably be taking advantage of his stupidity. With a mental shrug, I launched a punch at him that would have caved in his rib cage, if it had connected.

Except it didn't. He waited so late to dodge that I swear my knuckles skimmed the front of his T-shirt, but somehow he still managed to get out of the way. In a blur of superspeed, I struck at him again—but again, at the last nanosecond, he wasn't *there*. Now I was the one who was flailing, spinning as I tried to follow him, while he barely seemed to move. No matter how fast I was, how hard I pushed myself . . . he seemed to respond even before I'd started to swing, despite the fact that his eyes were still shut tight.

Panicking, I swung too hard at his head. My fist whistled through empty air, carrying me off balance. I stumbled—and the hunter was suddenly inside my guard. I grabbed at the ax, catching the shaft more by luck than judgment and managing to rip it out of his hands. Even as it clattered away into the darkness, he was still attacking, driving his shoulder into my chest. We both went down.

He landed on top, jamming his forearm across my mouth. Immediately, I bit down, only to have a horrible grating sensation reverberate through my jaw as my teeth skidded across a metal bracer hidden under his sleeve. I raked at his eyes with my nails, arching my spine—but he reared back, keeping his face out of reach while still keeping my head and shoulders pinned against the ground. His face had gone calm and still, looking oddly preoccupied as though trying to solve an algebra problem in his head. The world spun as he flipped us over somehow, in a movement too fast and complicated for me to follow. Before I could even think of using the momentary opening to break free, he was straddling me, his arm still jammed agonizingly into my mouth while his knees pinned my own arms down.

That left him with one free hand. A hand that was suddenly holding a wooden stake, pointed directly at my chest. The last thing I saw before my world narrowed to that sharp, wicked point were his calm green eyes: relentless, remorseless.

He drove the stake through my heart.

Chapter 13

We both looked down at the stake through my heart.

Funny. I would have thought that should hurt more.

From the look on the vampire hunter's face, he thought it should hurt more too.

I shoved him off me, this time easily flinging him aside. "You staked me," I said stupidly. I prodded at the protruding end. I could feel the wood wobbling around, deep inside. It was like when I was a kid and had a loose baby tooth that I could wiggle right around with my tongue: not painful, but awesomely disgusting. "I can't believe you actually staked me." Anger started to swell within me, displacing bafflement. I grabbed the lapels of his coat, hauling his stunned face close to mine. "I was lying there helpless, and you staked me, you—you—you total *dick!*"

A terrified squeak escaped from his throat. He fumbled inside his pocket, then shoved me hard enough that I lost my grip. As I staggered back, I felt liquid splash over my clothes and face. My eyes and nose stung at the acrid, bitter scent. I gagged, trying to scrub my eyes clear. "What the—"

I heard the soft *click* of a lighter.

"*Oh shi*—" I dived, but it was too late. Heat roared up around me, hiding everything in a curtain of fire. I flailed frantically at my clothes, but the flames shot through the oil soaking me. I could feel it like near-scalding water pouring over my skin, matched by an equally urgent heat shooting through my veins.

Like the stake, it was surprisingly painless. I squinted through the smoke and light, trying to look at myself. As fast as the flames gnawed at me, my body was healing itself; patches of skin shimmered as they blistered and nearly instantly reformed.

Okay. So now I was pissed off *and* on fire.

"YOU ARE IN FOR A WORLD OF PAIN," I roared, shaking off my disintegrating top. The flames around me started to die down, running out of fuel. "I am going to rip your heart out, do you hear me?" I slapped out a last tongue of flame from my shoulder, then curled my hands into fists. "I'm going to rip your heart out, and then I'm going to eat it raw in a bun with *ketchup!*"

I had to admit, the hunter had guts. Even faced with a homicidal, half-naked, smoking vampire, he still attempted to raise his ax. It shook so badly that he nearly took his own head off, but it was pretty impressive, under the circumstances.

Something blurred between us; a loud *smack* rang out, and the vampire hunter spun in two complete circles before collapsing into a heap. Ebon skidded to a halt, his eyes wild and his hair standing on end and his head very firmly attached to his neck. "Xanthe!"

"Ebon!" I gaped at him.

He ignored this, grabbing me by the shoulders. His frantic gaze searched my face. "Be thee hart?"

I blinked. "Huh?"

"Me haid warn't anigh, I couldn't find 'ee in time. . . ." he moaned mystifyingly. His French accent was totally gone, replaced by the broad, drawling tones of . . . Somerset? He sounded more like a farmhand than a vampire. "Be thee hart? Thee peer—" He looked down at my chest and stopped dead.

I looked down too. My flesh had closed up around the stake, leaving a four-inch stub of wood sticking up from my skin.

My totally naked skin.

I yelped, crossing my arms over my chest. I hobbled over to the unconscious vampire hunter and tipped him out of his coat as fast as I could manage. It felt like an age before I could finally swirl its heavy weight over my shoulders. The coat was still warm from the vampire hunter's body, and it smelled of sweat. With it covering me from neck to ankle, I was able to summon the courage to look round at Ebon again.

He was still frozen in place, staring at me. My face went instantly scarlet.

"Uh . . ." I dug my hands into the pockets of the coat, encountering numerous mysterious objects. Something sharp strapped into the lining dug into the small of my back. "Hi. So . . . neat trick with the head. Can I do that?"

Ebon swallowed. "Stake," he croaked, pointing at my now safely covered chest.

"Oh. Right. Yeah, he got me too." I loosened the coat

enough to peer down at the stub. "I guess it's gotta come out. Can you give me a hand?"

"Stake?" he repeated, his voice going high and wobbly.

I gave him a level look. "Don't tell me you're squeamish about blood."

The whites showed all around Ebon's eyes.

Obviously, there was no help from that corner. Bracing myself, I wrapped my hand around the stub, and yanked. It took quite a bit of force to part it from my body, but at last the wood slid out with a horrible *slurp*. Almost immediately, I could feel the bones spring back outward, new flesh welling up to fill the gaping hole.

Glancing up at Ebon, I summoned a weak smile. "Good thing that myth isn't real, right?" I said, tossing the bloodstained stake to clatter near his feet.

Ebon's eyes rolled up in his head. Perfectly rigid, he toppled over in a dead faint.

I stared from the prone vampire hunter to Ebon's unmoving form, and back again. With a sigh, I pulled my slightly scorched mobile out of the ruins of my jeans, and stalked off in search of a signal. I had to go nearly to the other side of the Ring, but at last I found one. I dialed.

"Hi, Dad," I said. "Um . . . can you come pick us up?"

Chapter 14

The next evening found me having breakfast with a ridiculously hot guy. It was typical of my life that this would only happen when said guy was tied up.

I stirred my tea, contemplating the vampire hunter across the kitchen table. "Not only do you try to kill me, you have to go and get me grounded for the rest of my existence," I said resentfully. Thanks to the hunter's little trick with the oil and the lighter, my dad had turned up to find me dressed only in a borrowed trench coat, with two unconscious men. There's really no way to put a good spin on that sort of situation. "I hope you're happy."

The vampire hunter did not look happy. This

probably had something to do with the fact that he was duct-taped to his chair. He should count himself lucky. Mum and Dad were still out in the garage, hunting among the unpacked boxes from the move and arguing about where the handcuffs and spreader bar had been stored. I really, *really* didn't want to know.

"So, Brains," I muttered to the fish, who was eyeing the hunter with distinct interest from its tank on the work surface. "Got any ideas about what we do now?"

The silver goldfish sucked in water, somehow contriving to make its perfectly round, toothless mouth look positively horrifyingly.

"I'll bear that in mind." I drained the last of my tea, and rose to loom with what I hoped was ominous menace at the hunter. "Okay," I said, showing him my fangs. I felt awfully dumb. "Are you going to talk, or am I going to feed you to my childe here?"

The vampire hunter glowered at me, radiating unyielding determination. Oh, joy. I wished Ebon were awake to deal with this, but he got up a lot later than I did, presumably due to his greater age. In the meantime, it was up to me to interrogate this guy, and I wasn't sure how to begin. In the stories I'd read or seen, only bad guys ever had people tied up and helpless. Should I slap him? Threaten to electrocute him with the toaster? Offer him a cup of tea? I was the heroine—wasn't he supposed to have a change of heart and spontaneously come over to my side, having fallen hopelessly in love with my unique specialness?

I couldn't help casting a speculative eye over the hunter's impressive muscles, wondering if maybe a little vampiric seduction might work in this situation. Unfortunately, for his part, the vampire hunter looked more like he was checking me out for vulnerable spots rather than appreciating my irresistible charms. I sighed, giving up the idea. Probably for the best, given that the only seduction I'd ever attempted had gone downhill after my initial DO U FANCY ME Y/N? text message to the boy in question. I'd been *really* glad to change schools in the wake of that disaster. He and his friends were probably still laughing about it even now.

Well, at least I could find out the vampire hunter's name. His coat was draped over the table in front of me; spreading it out, I started going through the pockets.

This turned out to take some time.

There were a *lot* of pockets. The whole inner surface of the coat was covered with them, each precisely sized for the item inside. They were even labeled, the words

154

embroidered on the same sort of ribbon that parents used to sew name tags into their kids' school uniforms. This guy made my categorizing obsession look *normal*.

Some of the items were about what one might expect to find in a vampire hunter's outfit—a couple of crucifixes (they didn't seem to bother me, which made me wonder why he was carrying them around), a whole load of stakes, a few flasks of oil (one missing)—but there was also a whole row of pockets marked PAPER CLIPS. Also another for SEEDS, and yet another marked FLOUR.

"At least you don't seem to have a pocket labeled 'tortoise, live,'" I said absently, examining the handful of small rubber balls I'd just taken out of a pocket helpfully labeled BALLS, BOUNCY. "I'm not sure I could have coped with that. Shouldn't you be carrying some actual, you know, weapons?"

The hunter didn't say anything. He glared.

"Look, you're going to have to start talking sometime. And believe me, I'm by *far* the sanest person around here. My name's Jane." I finally found the pocket labeled WALLET, and flipped it open. "And you are—" I stopped, reading the name on his bank card. "Oh, come on. Don't you have any imagination?"

"No." His voice was a rough, dry rumble. He glowered at me.

"No kidding. That's gotta be the worst pseudonym ever. Don't you get a lot of comments?"

"Yes," he said in tones of deep resignation. "Because it's my real name."

I stared at him. "You're joking."

His face was a study in stoicism.

I flipped through his driver's license and bank cards. There it was, on every one. "Van Helsing? Your actual name is actually *Van Helsing*?"

From Van's weary expression, this was a question he got a lot. "It's a family tradition."

I shook my head. "Wow, and I thought my parents were evil." According to the date on Van's driver's license, he was seventeen. Somehow he'd looked a lot older when he'd been trying to cut my head off. "Sooooo . . . you're a vampire hunter, right? What's up with that? I mean, what have we ever done to you?"

Van's look suggested that I'd moved into the top spot on his personal list of Most Idiotic People I Have Met. "For a start, kidnapped and ra—" He stumbled on the word, breaking off for an instant. "That is, kidnapped and tortured my mother."

That kind of stopped me dead. "Uh, okay," I said, after a second. "I'm really sorry to hear that. But I didn't do it *personally*, you know."

Van really did have an astonishing variety of glares. This one clearly indicated that he was plotting at least three ways to kill me using nothing but the available kitchen utensils. "You're all evil, bloodsucking monsters who slaughter and eat people."

"I do not!" I protested hotly. My words were punctuated by the door banging open. "Hi, Ebon," I said over my shoulder. "Tell this guy vampires don't kill—"

"Who sent you?" Ebon crossed the room in one long stride, seizing hold of the front of the hunter's T-shirt. He shook him, chair and all. "*Who sent you?! Tell us or I'll eat you myself!*" At least, I think that's what he said. The hill-billy Somerset accent was back, so thick that he sounded fresh off the farm.

"Ebon, relax!" I grabbed his arm, pulling him away from the hunter. I hadn't expected Ebon to throw himself into the role of bad cop quite *this* enthusiastically. "And what's with the voice?"

"You!" He turned his wild-eyed gaze on me, looking utterly freaked out. He must have charged down here as soon as he'd woken up; bits of twigs and grass still stuck up out of his hair. "What in the name of all that's holy are you?"

"Ooookay." I steered him into a chair. I guessed he was entitled to a small meltdown, seeing as how he'd had his head cut off last night. "Let's try to relax for a second. Take deep breaths. Uh, actually, I guess that won't help, but you know what I mean." I patted his shoulder reassuringly. "We're all safe now. We got the vampire hunter nice and secure—"

"But he's not supposed to *be* here!" Ebon wailed. "We weren't expecting a real one!"

Could he have amnesia? "Those other two were pretty real, remember?"

"What other two?" Van said.

"Oh, don't give me that," I snapped over my shoulder. "And I know about your werecat friend. So don't think they'll be able to rescue you!"

The hunter had the most perfect "WTF?" expression I'd ever seen. "What friends? I don't have any friends. The cat's *your* friend." He jerked his chin at Ebon.

"Huh? He's not a cat, he's a—" I swung round. Ebon had gone stark white. He stared up at me, face stricken. GUILTY practically flashed in neon above his head.

" . . . vampire?" I finished, lamely. "Ebon, what's going on?"

"I—I *am* a vampire," he said. His thick country accent clashed badly with his velvet frock coat. "But . . . I . . . I'm not quite who you think."

"Ebenezer Lee," Van supplied. He closed his eyes, evidently reciting by heart. "Born on a farm near Nether Stowey, 1842. Died in a fertilizer factory, Bristol, 1859. Bloodline: Mr. Tibbles, from Sekhmet." He opened his eyes again and shrugged as best he could, bound as he was. "That's as far back as we know."

I stared at him, then at Ebon. *"Mr. Tibbles?"*

Ebon's hands twisted together. "I did say I wasn't part of Hakon's Bloodline." He looked as though he could sink through the floor in mortification. "And that my sire was a beast. I wasn't lying."

Ebon's form shimmered. All of him—including his clothes—came apart into a dense gray mist, which coiled down to re-form into a small and very dejected cat.

"It was you outside my window!" I recognized that spotted, sand-colored fur. I should have known; he was as long-limbed and gawky in this form as in his human one. His eyes were even the same pale shade of blue. "I chased you! Ebon, or Ebenezer, or whoever you are— you'd better start talking right *now.*"

"Mrow," said the cat, ears drooping. Mist swirled,

and Ebon sat there once again, thankfully still fully clothed. "I only wanted to impress you." He dropped his head. "Hakon said I had to seduce you, win you over to our side. He wasn't happy about having to rely on me, but he didn't have anyone more suitable near enough— there aren't that many physically young vampires. It was my huge opportunity to show him I was worthy of a permanent place in his organization. I couldn't risk ruining it. So I . . ." He swallowed, then said very fast, "I persuaded two of Hakon's people to pretend to be vampire hunters so that I could rescue you from them."

"Those guys were *vampires?*"

"I wondered what they were doing around here," Van muttered.

Ebon held up his hands pleadingly. "I had to do something, Xanthe! How could I have presented my true self to you and have a hope of persuading you to accept my protection? You'd never have trusted this voice," he savagely exaggerated his accent, "instead of Lilith's. She's the mistress of seduction! And I'm a Victorian farm boy who isn't even a proper vampire."

"So you lied to make yourself seem more romantic."

He nodded, barely moving.

"You do realize that was really, really stupid, right?"

Every line of his body showed that he did.

I contemplated him in silence for a moment. "Ebenezer, huh?"

He winced. "It *used* to be a perfectly normal name."

"Tell you what." I stuck out my hand in his direction. "I'll call you Ebon if you'll call me Jane."

Ebon looked at my proffered palm, then up at my face. Solemnly, he took my hand in his own. "Thank you."

I tightened my grip for a moment, staring him in the eye. "That *is* the only thing you've been lying about . . . isn't it?"

Ebon put his free hand over his heart, bowing slightly. "On the honor of my Bloodline, I swear."

"Your sire," Van said under his breath, "is a cat."

"Don't make me come over there and bite you," I said to him. "I haven't eaten anyone yet, but if you piss me off enough, I may start."

"Liar." Van's impressive shoulders bunched, straining against the bindings. "You cannot hide your evil deeds from me, monster. You must have killed many innocents, but they will be avenged. I shall destroy you."

"I've hardly killed anyone!" I paused. "Hang on. Ebon, that guy whose head I ripped off . . . ?"

"Sven? He's fine. Just a little, ah, aggrieved. Hakon

called him and his brother back before there could be any further . . . escalation." Ebon sighed. "I'm going to have a lot of apologizing to do."

"There, see?" I turned back to Van, hands on my hips. "I haven't killed anyone."

Van's jaw clenched stubbornly. "I fought you. I saw your speed, your strength. You could only gain such power through gorging on blood."

"You also saw her heal a heart wound," Ebon said flatly. "Explain that."

Van blanched. "I . . . must have missed?" He sounded more as if he desperately wanted it to be true than that he actually believed it.

"What?" I said, looking from one to the other. "Ebon, you stuck your head back on. That's got to be harder than healing a mere staking."

"The vampire digests the blood of the living not with its stomach, but with its heart." Van could only have been reciting from a textbook. His school must have been *really* exciting. "It is the only part of the vampire's body that is vital to its unnatural existence, and the only part that cannot be regenerated. Destroying the heart, by any means, thus returns the vampire to true death." He had a slightly panicked expression, as though he'd just opened his end-of-year exam and discovered that he'd studied the wrong topics. "You are a vampire. You must drink human blood. And you're supposed to *die when I stake you!*" This last was nearly a wail.

I looked at Ebon for confirmation. He nodded mutely. "Well, I don't," I said firmly. "Look, isn't it simple? This must all have something to do with Lilith." And, I didn't say, "Superluminal" . . . whoever the hell that was.

"Who?" Van said blankly.

"My sire," I said to him. "Lilith." I looked over at Ebon. "This whole heart thing could be another effect of that, right?"

"No," Ebon said very firmly. He scrubbed his hands over his face, staring at me over them as if I'd suddenly turned into a werewolf. "You are an impossibility. If all this truly is Lilith's doing, then we are in a dire situation indeed."

"There isn't a Lilith," Van said, frowning. His green eyes flicked from side to side as if reading an invisible index. "Deceit will not protect you. I will find the truth."

"Even your kind haven't discovered all our secrets," Ebon snapped at him. "And you should hope that you never do." Van matched his glare.

"O-*kay*," I said, stepping between them before the entire room filled up with testosterone. I turned to Van. "Look, now that you know I'm not some sort of monster, will you stop trying to kill me? I can't have you lurking everywhere I go, and I really don't want to have to keep you tied up. What do you say?"

He didn't even take a second to consider it. "No."

Before I could inform him how utterly unreasonable he was being, the door banged open. "Hiya!" Zack said brightly, barging in. "How's the torture going?"

"Ever heard of knocking?" I scowled at him.

"Why, are you worried about corrupting my innocent soul with terrible scenes of agony?" He patted me affectionately on the arm. "That's real sweet, Janie. Look, I brought pliers!"

Van leaned back as far as the bonds would let him, evidently far more worried by the enthusiastic twelve-year-old than by any of the vampires in the room. I didn't blame him. Zack had scrounged quite a collection of replica Victorian medical equipment from eBay—"accessories," he called them—and they made an intimidating display in the bandolier around his chest. The goggles and wipe-clean PVC trousers weren't exactly reassuring, either.

"Don't poke my prisoner," I said, intercepting Zack as he brandished a corkscrew-shaped piece of metal at Van's nose. "Unless he continues being difficult, of course." I stared levelly at Van. "You want to tell us how you found us?"

Van appeared to contemplate his options for a moment. He sighed. "I got a phone call from my employer, informing me where you would be."

"You mean you can get *paid* to be a vampire hunter?" Zack sounded as if a whole new career prospect had opened up before him.

"It would be difficult if we didn't."

"I knew it!" said Ebon. I noticed that he'd reverted back to his fake French accent now that Zack was present. "Tell us who sent you!"

Van shook his head. "We're always hired anonymously. She only told me where to go and who to stake." His lips compressed for an instant, then he nodded in the direction of his coat. "You can check the call record, if you want to find the number."

I searched through his coat until I found the pocket labeled PHONE, which more accurately could have been labeled BRICK. "My God, Van, is this a phone or an offensive weapon?" I said, hefting the mobile.

"In an emergency, I could use it to crush a vampire's skull." As far as I could tell, he was perfectly serious. "Everything can be a weapon."

Following Van's instructions, I eventually found the list of recently received calls. Sure enough, there had been a string of them last night. "There's two different numbers here," I said, scrolling through the list. One of the callers seemed to have been trying to contact Van at least once an hour. "Wow, someone really wanted to talk to you. Is that one your employer?"

Van jerked his head up as though a thought had just struck him—then he hesitated, indecision breaking his impassive face. "No," he said eventually. "The other one."

"Uh-huh. And that wasn't suspicious at all." I rolled my eyes. "Let's see who you don't want us to know about, shall we—aw, no." The display showed no signal available. "The station must still be down. Can't make a call."

Ebon's eyes shifted from me to Zack. "Er . . ." He sighed, reaching into his jacket. "No more secrets," he said apologetically, pulling out a small black box.

"What's that?" Zack and I both asked at once.

"Mobile phone jammer," Ebon muttered. He cast me a pleading look. "I really couldn't risk Lilith contacting you."

I held out my hand, and he dropped the jammer into it, a bit reluctantly. "Don't think we're not going to talk about this later," I said to him as I thumbed it off. I hit REDIAL on Van's phone, putting it into speakerphone mode so we could all hear.

It only took half a ring before the call was picked up on the other end, as though someone had been waiting poised by their own phone, ready to snatch it up. "Van! At last!" said a deep male voice, sounding incredibly relieved—then, with the sort of instant shift into anger that I'd heard from my own parents when they'd been worried sick about me: "Come home *now*."

Van winced.

"Hi," I said into the phone.

A momentary, perplexed silence came from the other end. "Van?"

"I don't *need* help, Uncle," Van said, his voice surly but clear. "But just for your information, I'm at—" The sentence degenerated into a muffled mumble as Ebon slapped a hand across the vampire hunter's mouth, gagging him.

"What?" The man's alarm was clear even through the tiny speaker. "Van!"

"Sorry, Van can't come to the phone right now," I said. "He's kind of all tied up. Do you know anything about vampires, by the way?"

Another tiny silence. "Few things," the man said, rather dryly. "Who is this?"

"You can call me Jane. Who're you?"

"You can call *me*," he mimicked my intonation, "Quinns."

Ebon yelped. He leaped for the phone, snatching it out of my hand, and mashed the END CALL button. "Oh, clever," he snarled at Van, who'd been knocked over backward by the force of Ebon's movement. "*Very* clever."

"Right," I said, rubbing my elbow where he'd slammed me into the kitchen cabinets. "So I'm guessing that name meant something bad?"

"Hunter-General Quincey Helsing," Ebon said grimly. He jerked his head in Van's direction. "The leader of the vampire hunters."

"Oh. Ouch." I grimaced as I realized how close we'd come to disaster. "At least it sounded like he didn't yet know where we are. Good reflexes, Ebon." I hauled Van's chair upright again, resisting the urge to kick him while he was down. "You are a real pain, you know that?"

Blood ran down Van's chin from where Ebon had whacked him in the mouth, but there was a satisfied gleam in his narrow green eyes. "Bite me."

"Don't tempt me," Ebon growled. He flexed his hand. "I *still* haven't eaten."

Crap, I'd forgotten that not all of us were superspecial magic princesses. I eyed Van. Well . . . why not? Serve him right. "Ebon, you won't flip out and kill him in a blood-frenzy or anything, right?"

"I only need half a pint or so. He'll survive." Ebon showed his teeth. "I can make it quite unpleasant if you like, though."

"I'm not afraid of any of your foul kind," Van said, lifting his chin defiantly. "Do your worst."

"Have a ball, Ebon," I said, stepping to one side with a flourish. Van suddenly looked extremely worried. "Um, I didn't mean that literally. Zack, out."

"But I want to watch!" he protested as Ebon advanced on Van. The vampire hunter clenched his fists, twisting his forearms, but his bonds stayed firm. In a blur of superspeed, Ebon was on him. Fangs flashed—

Van went flying over backward again as Ebon recoiled from him, retching. "Uh," I said, watching Ebon double over, scrubbing the back of his hand across his mouth. "Doesn't he taste good?"

"Oo! Oo!" Zack stuck his hand in the air, bouncing

like a teacher's pet. "Eat me! I'll wash the taste away!" Ebon waved him back, still gagging.

"What's wrong?" Van's muffled voice came from the floor, sounding slightly surprised but still infuriatingly smug. "Not tender enough for you, fiend?"

"No." Ebon straightened, wiping his sleeve across his mouth. His complexion had gone the faint green of someone who'd swallowed something rotten. "So *that's* what you are."

"What—uh." There was a sudden appalled silence from Van's direction, like someone getting to school only to discover they'd inexplicably left their pants at home.

I dragged Van upright yet again. You'd have thought he'd have been *relieved* that Ebon didn't seem to want to eat him, but he didn't look it. He'd gone as pale as if Ebon had actually drained him. "It's not what you think," the vampire hunter said quickly. "No, I taste bad because of . . . steroids. Yes. Full of drugs. Definitely."

"I think not." Ebon took a polite but firm grip on my elbow. "Jane, we have a somewhat severe complication. A word, please?"

"Watch him for a sec," I said to Zack. I threw a glance at the tank, where Brains was still ogling Van, undaunted by Ebon's reaction. "You too, Brains. Ebon?"

I thought we'd just go into the next room, but Ebon led me all the way upstairs, into the guest bedroom. He shut the door behind us, with a nervous backward glance. "I hope that's far enough," he said. "I don't want the hunter overhearing."

"What's up? Has Van got poisonous blood or something like that?"

"Something, indeed," Ebon said, expression grim. "Suffice it to say that he is quite extraordinarily dangerous." He took his iPhone from his pocket as he spoke, fingers swirling across the screen. "I have to contact Hakon. Now." He put the phone to his ear and, as far as I could tell, started talking backward.

"What—"

He shushed me with an apologetic wave of his hand, listening to someone on the other end. A wince crossed his face. When he spoke next, his voice had dropped into a groveling tone that sounded like a kid who'd just kicked his ball through the neighbor's brand-new window. The exchange went back and forth for a few moments, Ebon growing progressively paler. Though I couldn't understand anything that was said, it was clear that the news wasn't being well received. When he finally hung up, he looked wrung out.

"What language was that?" I asked.

"Swedish," he said absently, rubbing the bridge of his nose. "Or at least, what the Swedes were speaking in 950 AD."

"Wow," I said, digesting this. "Will I have to learn that?"

"If you want to please Hakon. He regards it as the only civilized language." Ebon slipped the phone back into his pocket with a grimace. "Anyway, he's sending some of his people to collect the hunter, right away."

"Van's really that important? Why—" I cut myself off, cocking my head. I'd thought . . . "Ebon, did you hear that? Sort of a thump, from downstairs?"

We stared at each other for an instant. Then, moving as one, we leaped for the door. I got there first, with my superior superspeed; I slammed it open, charging down the stairs. Ebon ran into my shoulder as I stopped dead in the kitchen doorway.

Zack was laid out on the floor like a corpse, surrounded by a glittering sea of paper clips. The back door was open. And torn duct tape hung from the arms of the empty chair.

Chapter 15

'm fine, Mum," Zack protested, squirming under the
ice pack. "Stop fussing."

"Don't move," Mum ordered, shoving him back
down onto the sofa with a firm hand on his chest. "You
might have a concussion."

"I'm going to kill him," I snarled, my hands flexing.
"I'm going to tear him into pieces."

"No you won't." Despite not having fangs, Dad
looked twice as homicidal as I did. "*I* am going to hunt
him down and rip him limb from limb. *You* are never
leaving this house again. Either of you," he added with
a glance at Zack.

"It's not my fault it turned out that he could tear the

arms off the chair and club me with them!" Zack protested indignantly. "Why am I grounded?"

"It's for your own protection," Mum told him. "With this lunatic on the loose, we can't take any chances."

Ebon came back in, having excused himself in order to "commune with the Elder." He raised an eyebrow at me and jerked his head in the direction of the door.

"We're just gonna go and, uh . . ." I couldn't think of an excuse, but my parents were too preoccupied with caring for Zack to notice our departure anyway. We went back into the kitchen, and I closed the door behind us for privacy. "What did Hakon say?" I asked him.

"Many things, all of them unrepeatable. I think I am now officially bereft of his patronage." Ebon dropped into a chair with a sigh. "Well, at least that is certain to be the low point of my night."

"Hey," I said, distracted. "Brains is gone!" The lid of the tank was ajar, and the waters were devoid of undead killer goldfish.

Ebon's entire body froze. "Jane," he said very calmly, "would you please be so kind as to look down your Bloodline and tell me if the fish has been killed?"

I focused inward, searching. "No, Brains is still there," I said in relief. I could feel the thread that bound us, stretching off into the distance. "Maybe it's chasing after Van." I tried looking through the goldfish's eyes, but all I got was blackness and an impression of being jostled. Switching back to my own perspective, I was startled by Ebon's suddenly aghast face. "Ebon, what is it?"

Ebon spat out something that could have been ancient Swedish, or could have been Somerset dialect, but which was definitely a swear word. "The hunter stole it."

I blinked at him. "The vampire hunter stole my goldfish." It didn't make any more sense the second time either. "What?"

Ebon scrubbed his hands over his face. "His blood tasted terrible," he said, muffled.

"Yeah? So?"

He dropped his hands, his features drawn and pale. "He's a dhampir."

"Okaaaaaay." I pulled out a kitchen chair and sat down opposite him. "I think this is going to be a long one. You mean dhampir as in a vampire-human hybrid?" Ebon stared at me. "Don't look so surprised. I read, you know."

"Well then . . . yes. Dhampirs are the result of a vampire breeding with a human. As they're part-undead, we can't digest their blood, hence the taste." Ebon's lip curled, as if the flavor of Van's blood was still lingering on his tongue.

"They're very, very rare—not only because we aren't very, ah, fertile, but also because their creation is banned by every Bloodline. The origins of this one will be of *great* interest to the Elders. Whoever is responsible will shortly find their existence becoming very unpleasant indeed."

"He mentioned something about his mother being raped." I remembered the way that Van had stumbled on the word, correcting himself; he must have been trying to keep his vampire parentage secret. "But what's the big deal? I mean, okay, he was pretty fast and strong, but I was still able to backflip rings around him." Until, I realized, he'd licked my blood off his ax.

"Dhampirs inherit only a shadow of our strengths, true, but they are also only burdened with a pale version of our weaknesses." My mind flashed to the neatly labeled pockets in Van's coat. "They can go out in daylight, although they tend to prefer the twilight and evening, for example." Ebon shook his head. "But their physical nature is not the danger. They can use the Bloodlines."

"Wouldn't they only be linked to their vampire parent, though?"

"They can use the Bloodlines," Ebon repeated, "to *any* vampire. All they require is a taste of a vampire's blood, and they can then track any vampire in the same family. Not just the direct line. Not just one generation. Everyone."

I swallowed. "And if he's got Brains—"

"A dhampir's tracking ability doesn't last long, but with the goldfish, he's got a constant supply. All he has to do is keep drinking a little of its blood every hour, and he'll be able to track you, your sire, her progenitors, and other relatives—all of you." Ebon's knuckles whitened where his hands were clasped together. "With one initial lead, a dhampir can slaughter an entire Bloodline." He squared his shoulders, reaching into his pocket. "And now I get to tell Hakon, who's probably going to slaughter *me*."

"It's only me and Lilith at risk though, isn't it?" I asked, watching him dial. "You said she didn't have any other descendants."

"What? Oh. Yes," he said rather vaguely. "Still." His phone beeped, and he switched into Swedish again. If the last call had sounded like a little boy trying to apologize for a broken window, this one was more on the scale of a guy having to admit to his girlfriend's shotgun-owning father that daddy's little girl was knocked up. Even from across the table, I could hear the blast of archaic Swedish from the tiny speaker. Ebon's face went from white to gray as the call progressed. By the time it finally ended, he was soaked with sweat, and shaking. "I'z ne'er haz to deal wi' Hakon like *that* afore." He took a deep breath, his accent smoothing out again to just a hint of country drawl. "Hakon's going to have the entire county swarming with vampires by the end of the night. We'll need your assistance, Jane. You can find the fish—if we can recover that, half the threat is neutralized. The dhampir must know that, so he'll presumably be aiming to move quickly, strike as fast as he can . . . but we've got a small amount of time on our side. There's no one in your Bloodline near here for him to reach."

I froze. Because there *was* someone near here.

I tested my three connections. Lilith's still stretched north . . . but the other two were precisely aligned. Brains—and therefore Van—was headed straight toward Superluminal.

If Hakon knew . . .

"Ebon," I said, making my decision. "I know where he's going."

Chapter 16

Worthing hospital?" Dad said dubiously, eyeing the long, low building over the top of the steering wheel.

"Evidently." The pull of the Bloodline was unmistakable. "Maybe Superluminal's a doctor. It would be an easy way to get blood." I felt nervous, exposed, despite the fact that I was squashed into the backseat with Ebon and Zack. At this hour, the hospital parking lot was nearly deserted, apart from a line of staff cars. I tapped my dad's shoulder. "Drive down a bit farther." As we crawled past the main building, I concentrated on the Bloodlines, making careful note of their directions. "Well, Brains and Super-luminal are definitely inside." I tried looking through each set of eyes in turn. "They're both still in the dark. Maybe Van hasn't found the right room yet." I hoped so. For all I knew, Superluminal might be capable of bouncing Van off the ceiling with one hand, but Lilith had seemed anxious to keep my weird Bloodline a secret. It couldn't be good to have my worst enemies finding out about it.

"We'd better try to get inside quickly." Dad swung the car into a space marked RESERVED, and killed the engine. "Any ideas?"

"Visiting hours are over," said Mum from the passenger seat. There were hardly any lights on in the bulk of the hospital, though the Accident and Emergency department entrance was still lit up. "Can we break in?"

"I believe that shouldn't be too difficult," Ebon said, looking up from the text message he was sending to let Hakon know where we were. His eyes narrowed as he studied the building. "There," he said, pointing at a ventilation duct. "We may obtain entrance through that shaft."

The duct was barely longer than my forearm, and covered with a slatted metal grill. "Uh, I'm seeing a slight flaw in your plan, Ebon."

He cast me a small smile. "*Ma chérie*, I believe it is time for your next lesson in the ways of the Blood." He shimmered, and I thought that he was going to turn into a cat again—but he just went dim and flickery, as if he were a hologram projected into a smoky room. I couldn't feel his hip against mine anymore.

"That's. So. *Awesome*," breathed Zack.

Ebon coalesced back into solidity again. "The old legends of vampires turning into mist, or flying, or becoming invisible, or even shape-shifting, are not entirely unfounded in reality."

Mum was staring at Ebon as if he was a personal affront to her worldview. "How can you do that?" she spluttered. "It's not physically possible! It's—you're— *breaking the laws of thermodynamics!*" Clearly, she thought this should be punishable by execution, or at least a severe fine.

"Madame, I'm a walking corpse that feeds on blood. I violate several fundamental physical principles."

Dad patted Mum's hand. "Don't worry, honey. It's probably something quantum."

"I prefer to call it 'magic.'" Ebon shrugged. "In any event, our physicality is somewhat a matter of habit. If one is able to overcome one's own self-image, one can achieve a number of interesting effects."

"I actually think I've done the mist thing before,"

I said, thinking back to my experiences with "teleporting." "Hey, Ebon, does this mean I can learn to shape—er, do that thing that you do?"

He turned faintly pink. "I'm . . . somewhat of a special case. I have an, ah, inherited, alternative self-image. Some others *can* alter their appearance, but it seems to require both a certain aptitude and a great deal of practice." He shook his head. "But simply de-cohering is mostly a matter of instinct. The two of us can get in."

"Perhaps," Dad said. "But the rest of us can't."

"I *told* you we should all have become vampires," Zack muttered.

"Ah." Ebon hesitated. "Monsieur, madame, I fear that we're going to have to ask you to perform the duty of rearguard."

"Absolutely not—" Mum started.

"Mum, Dad, we don't have time to argue about this! We can't let the vampire hunters discover Superluminal, whoever it is." I was already opening the car door. "Look, do any of you have your mobiles?" At their head shakes, I passed Mum mine. "Okay. You wait here while Ebon and I scout ahead. Once we're inside, we'll use Ebon's phone to call you, and then we'll leave the line open while we explore. That way if anything goes wrong, you'll hear, and be able to get help."

Mum and Dad looked at each other uncertainly. "Well," Dad said after a moment of silent parental communion. "All right. Be careful, Baby Jane."

I nodded, slipping out of the car. I could feel their worried gazes on my back as Ebon and I slunk through the shadows to the ventilation grate. It really was awfully small. "How exactly am I supposed to do this?" I hissed to Ebon. "Do I concentrate, like on the Bloodlines?"

"Simply move. Your body knows what to do." He put his hand over the grate. "Don't think about it. I'll meet you on the other side and guide you." He dissolved into pale gray mist, streaming through the slits.

"Ebon!" That was it? Feeling stupid, I put my own hand against the grate. It was cold and hard and very, very solid. I pushed experimentally, the metal pressing into my hand. This was dumb. There was no way I could fit through there, no matter how much I needed to be—

On the other side of the grate.

I was so surprised that I started to go solid again, which was really not the right thing to do in a small pipe. My body instinctively fuzzed back into mist again as the walls pressed against my flesh, like the way that your hand jerks back from a stove even before your brain has registered it as hot.

I couldn't see or hear anything. I could sort of feel the sides of the pipe, but only where my mist was directly in contact with it. Cautiously, I roiled forward a little. It was a weird sensation, my entire body churning through itself randomly as I moved. I had no sense of any part of myself being different from any other part; it was all *me*.

Something tickled at my edges, like someone tapping on my shoulder. I flowed forward and found myself engulfing a small, warm, furry form. I swirled around it, trying to make sense of what I was feeling. A sort of horizontal cylinder, with four appendages supporting it . . . a long, twitching thing, and two upward pointing triangles—it clicked into perspective. A cat.

Ebon.

His tail twitched. He slunk off down the pipe, pausing to make sure I was coming with him. I quickly lost track of the twists and turns, or even which way was up. Completely dependent on his eyes and ears, all I could do was keep in contact and trust him to find the way.

Cat-Ebon suddenly fuzzed into nothingness. I sensed trailing wisps of smoke against my own as he poured himself through a thin crack. I went through the same gap and panicked, flailing as I tried to find him again. All I could sense was some strange, tall, complicated shape—which, I realized, *was* him, back in his usual shape. My panic redoubled as I realized that he hadn't told me anything about how to go solid again. I clutched at him, my mist self swirling over his shoulders, trying to remember how I normally felt—

"Oof," Ebon gasped, collapsing under my sudden weight. After an agonizingly long and embarrassing couple of moments untangling my legs from around his neck and my arms from his knees, we were both back on our feet again. Ebon straightened his jacket. "That went remarkably well, all things considered," he said kindly. "But I think it's best if we continue on foot. An indoor fog is somewhat noticeable, and while there are ways of becoming more diffuse, I don't think we should tackle that form of invisibility quite yet. It would not be a good moment for you to lose your head."

Given that he didn't sound like he was speaking metaphorically, I was in wholehearted agreement. "Give me your iPhone." Once I had Dad on the line, I tucked the phone in my pocket and turned on my heels, concentrating on the Bloodline. "This way," I said, pointing off down the corridor.

One of the many advantages of being dead was that

you could move awfully quietly when you set your mind to it. It was no trouble at all to ghost past the occasional cleaner or night nurse, even when solid. Apart from whispering to my parents to let them know that we were still okay, we were noiseless. The hospital's wide, echoing corridors were eerie in the dim night lighting. Combined with our own silence and the coursing tide of the Bloodline, it gave me the impression that I was drifting through a dream, the surreal sort where you know that everything could run like water and change at any moment.

Ebon tapped my shoulder and pointed up at a sign: CHILDREN'S WARD (LONG TERM). The Bloodline was pulling more insistently now, as though if I lifted my feet off the floor I'd be swept away. I followed it down a narrower corridor, and again down an even smaller one lined with identical doors, each with a number like in a hotel.

The surge of the Bloodline nearly made me stagger, sucking me toward a particular door. I jerked on Ebon's sleeve, tilting my head in the direction of it. He nodded and lifted one hand in a "wait" gesture. He laid his ear against the heavy wooden door, listening intently. I followed suit, but all I could hear from inside was the wheeze and beep of some sort of medical equipment, sounding as loud as an alarm clock's ring to my heightened senses. The noise drowned out everything else, making it impossible to listen for a heartbeat or someone breathing.

Ebon seemed to come to the same conclusion as he drew away from the door with a slight grimace. He cocked his head at me: *Now what?*

I gestured at the door: *We go in.*

With infinite patience, he turned the handle, so slowly that there was only the slightest hiss of metal on metal. The door swung inward, revealing a sliver of the room within. All I could see was a white-painted wall, with a couple of vampire movie posters tacked up onto it. Ebon kept pushing the door, rigidly controlling its movement, his knuckles white on the handle. A chair. A metal stand with an unused drip hanging from it. A cart full of mysterious electronic boxes with dim green screens, clicking and beeping to themselves. More posters, some of which I recognized—I had the same ones up in my own room. The foot of a metal-framed hospital bed, with charts clipped to the bottom. White sheets mounded over someone lying on the bed, hiding everything except long dark hair fanned across the pillow.

The Bloodlines to both Brains and Superluminal tugged at me. Ebon and I exchanged a glance, then I ducked under his arm. My mouth was dry as I approached the bed, placing each foot carefully so as to make no sound. The figure didn't stir. The edge of the sheet was covering her face. Reaching out, I twitched it down.

A girl about Zack's age stared up at me, brown eyes wide with fear and a knotted strip of fabric gagging her mouth. A sealed jam jar containing a very angry-looking Brains was tucked into the crook of her arm like a teddy bear. I could feel the heat of her skin; hear the rasp of air in her lungs as she struggled for breath around the gag.

She wasn't a vampire.

There was no warning. One instant Ebon was behind me, the next he was thrown backward as a dark shape exploded out of the shadows behind the door. I bit down on my scream and instead threw myself at the struggling figures. My clawing fingertips brushed leather; a powerful blow snapped my head back, making my ears ring. I fell backward onto the bed, the girl struggling underneath me and ruining my attempts to spring back to my feet. Distantly, I could hear a muffled buzzing from the pocket of my coat, as my dad shouted questions from the other end of the phone line. I rolled off the bed, expecting at any moment to feel a stake between my shoulder blades—but I came to my feet unharmed, my back to a wall.

"If you move, I'll stake him," said a low, harsh voice.

I found myself staring at the pointy end of a crossbow. Van had another in his other hand, trained on Ebon, who was nailed to the floor by a pair of slim, silver spikes through his shoulders. Ebon's jaw clenched with pain, but he stayed motionless, eyes focused on the bolt aimed at his heart.

Slowly, never taking my eyes off Van, I raised my hands into the air. "Van, I can see the stakes in the crossbows you've got pointed at me and Ebon," I said, pitching my voice low but clear. My pocket was silent; I prayed that my parents would have the sense to stay quiet.

"Don't move," Van said, sweat beading his forehead. His fingers were holding the triggers half-squeezed, without even a millimeter of slack. "I may not be able to harm you, but I can turn your boyfriend to dust."

"I'm not going to try anything. But listen. You don't want to do this. You can't get away. The police will be here any minute." *Hang up, Dad,* I urged mentally. I heard the faintest of clicks from my pocket and let out a silent cheer in my head. I hoped that the Worthing police had someone trained in hostage situations, because I had no idea how to talk down a twitchy, teenage vampire hunter who looked ready to explode if someone so much as coughed. I also hoped my parents could come up with a plausible explanation for the situation, because I was pretty certain the police wouldn't have procedures for handling complaints about the undead.

The girl was chewing ferociously at her gag, spit drooling over her chin. Now that the sheets had been pulled off, I could see that Van had bound her hand and foot to the bed. At least he couldn't harm her while still keeping the crossbows trained on us. The Bloodline hummed between us, her anger and fear bouncing back and reinforcing mine, like a sunbeam caught between two mirrors.

"You can't win here, Van." I didn't even blink. The instant his attention flickered I was going to punt him through the window so hard he'd hit the ground in France. "The police are going to come, and after one look at this situation they'll lock you up and throw away the key. We three will be able to just walk away."

"You think you can explain to the police why you don't have a pulse? You can't afford to be taken any more than me." The points of the crossbows stayed rock-steady. "Let's make this quick. Tell me how you created this perverted bond, and remove your evil mark upon her, or I swear by my blood I will hunt down and destroy your entire Bloodline."

The girl redoubled her efforts to escape, obviously having come to the conclusion that everyone in the room was stark-raving nuts.

"Believe me, we're as much in the dark as you." I lowered my hands slightly. "Look, let's all—"

There was the nasty, almost imperceptible *creak* of a crossbow string being put under extreme pressure. I froze again.

"Neither of us has been anywhere near here," said Ebon through teeth gritted in pain. "You're making a mistake."

"Ending your kind is never a mistake." Van gestured with the crossbow tip, motioning me to step away from the bed. "Every last one of you should be hunted down like the animals you are. I protect the innocent with my blood."

I raised my eyebrows. "By . . . gagging her and tying her to the bed?"

Van at least had the decency to look slightly embarrassed.

"I had planned to sit in the corner and watch over her as she slept," he muttered. "But she woke up."

"Listen, Van, there's only one person in this room who might know what's going on." I turned my head to face the girl, who was eyeing everyone else as if trying to work out who I meant. "Hi. I'm Jane—JaneX, you know, from Fang-Girls? You're Superluminal, right?"

The girl paused for a moment, as if working through whether it would be better to confirm or deny her identity to the crazed intruders. She nodded reluctantly.

"And you really aren't a vampire?" The only response I got was the most epic glare I'd ever received, even including Van's. "Sorry, I guess that was kind of obvious. What's your real—wait, no real point in asking you. Van, what's her name?"

Van shrugged in total disinterest, as though this was entirely irrelevant.

"What were you, raised by *wolves*?" Leaning over, I unhooked the medical charts from the end of the bed and glanced at the first page. "Hi," I said to the girl. "So, you're . . . Sarah? Sarah Chana?" I flipped to the next page. "And you're in here because—" I stopped dead, staring down at the paper. Amid the medical jargon and mysterious numbers, two words screamed out:

HEART TRANSPLANT

"Oh my God," I whispered. I could feel the fluttering in her chest as if it was my own heart, because—"You had a heart transplant. *My* heart."

"What?" Ebon and Van spoke simultaneously.

"I was in a coma." I could see the pieces falling into place in my head. "My dad *said* I was in a coma! When they finally had to give up, they must have given permission for my organs to be used, but—when I became a vampire I must have healed, and, and—*Ebon!*" I half shrieked in triumph, nearly scaring Van into turning us both into kebabs. "That's it! It's not Lilith, it's *Sarah's* blood, flowing directly through my heart! That's why I haven't been hungry, and why I've been feeling her through the Bloodline!"

You are a crazy, crazy person, Sarah's eyes plainly stated. Ebon looked as though he might share this opinion, but Van had gone pale. "That's why I couldn't stake you?" he asked, horrified.

"Right! You couldn't destroy my heart, because it's not in my chest, it's over *there!*" I stabbed a finger triumphantly at Sarah. "It all makes sense! Except . . . except for the part where my heart's over there instead of in my chest."

"Abomination," Van spat, leveling the crossbow at me with renewed enthusiasm. "To do your foul experiments on——"

"This wasn't my idea!" I protested. Van twitched, looking ready to snap, and I quickly shoved my hands in the air. "Sarah? I'm guessing you don't have any idea what's going on here either. Well, the guy with the crossbows there is a complete psychopath, as I guess you've gathered. If I let you go, can I trust you not to make any sound?" I shifted my weight to move toward her, slowly so as not to spook Van. "Otherwise, Ebon—that's my friend on the floor there—anyway, if you make any noise, Van will shoot him. That would be bad. Ebon's on your side, he's a cool guy, you can trust him. Do you understand?"

She nodded again. I hoped she meant it.

"Okay then," I said. I was within arm's reach. "Van, don't freak," I warned, and leaned over the bed.

Predictably, he freaked. "I said *stay away*," he snarled, turning his body toward me—which meant that the second crossbow drifted, just for an instant, away from Ebon's heart.

A lot of things happened, all at once:

Ebon ripped himself off the spikes, shivering into mist the second he was clear.

Van squeezed both triggers.

I flung myself to one side with full vampiric speed.

And Sarah convulsed.

I didn't have even an instant to spare to see if she'd been hit by the stray bolt. I hurled myself at Van, knocking his crossbow out of his hand. With the same eerie reflexes he'd demonstrated in our earlier fight, he dropped out of the way of my follow-up blow, whirling to strike at me with the second, now empty crossbow. I ducked, he missed, and that was all the chance he got, as a fully resolidified Ebon dropped onto his head.

"Don't kill him!" I dove onto the struggling pair, pinning Van down with a foot on his neck while hauling back on the collar of Ebon's coat. Ebon's arms hung useless at his sides, but his jagged teeth were bared and there was blood smeared all over his mouth. Van's shirt was torn, a savage bite mark on his collarbone showing where Ebon had missed his neck. The vampire snarled, struggling in my grip; I felt Van twist under my foot, and pressed down heavily, cutting off his air until he went limp.

That was when the door slammed open, and a dazzlingly bright light pinned us all in place.

"FREEZE!"

I automatically put my hands in the air, cringing. This meant that I let go of Ebon, who, demonstrating remarkable persistence, instantly darted his head down to strike at Van again. Fortunately for Van and unfortunately for me, my foot got in the way.

"Ow!" The pain lasted only a second. Hands grabbed at me, hauling me away. Disoriented in the harsh light, I couldn't even tell which way was up; I was manhandled like a rag doll until my arms were twisted up behind my back and my face was pressed against a flat surface. Someone slammed a knee down onto my shoulder blades. Through the ringing in my ears, I heard the *crack* of a fist against a face, and an answering feral snarl.

"Ebon, no!" I managed to yell, before the security man on my back squashed me too flat for speech. I drew my legs up underneath me and heaved, twisting with all the strength I could muster. He was only a normal person; compared to Van's dhampiric strength, he was a clinging toddler. I shook him off easily, surging to my feet. The room seemed full of people, colors swimming together in my blurred sight. Even my Bloodline sense felt confused, fuzzy. *"Ebon!"*

I caught a flash of white-blond hair, and an instant later Ebon's shoulder pressed against mine. "Thee a'right?" he said, the country accent incongruous with the blood streaked over his chin and the desire for murder in his eyes.

"Jesus Christ," someone said, his voice shaking. Squinting against the light, I saw a hospital orderly staring at us in terror, holding a radio. "What *are* you?"

"No!" I grabbed at Ebon's sleeve as he lunged forward. "They're ordinary people; we can't hurt them!"

"Emergency, intruders in room 117, call the police," the orderly gabbled into his radio. Another white-uniformed figure lay sprawled at his feet. A nurse was struggling with Sarah's limp body, trying to untie the bonds holding her to the bed. There was too much going on. The Bloodline filled my head with a roar like the ocean. I was drowning underneath it, the tides of my blood rising to sweep me away.

"Surrender or I will use force!" The security guard I'd knocked off my back was up again, all six feet six of him. His face was contorted with fear, but he still squared into a fighting stance. Next to me, I felt Ebon's muscles tense. "Hands up! Against the wall!"

Running feet echoed down the corridor. I felt a strange surge of recognition, as if whoever was coming was someone familiar, someone connected to me.

A plain, dumpy, middle-aged woman in a pristine white nurse's uniform appeared in the doorway. She took in the whole scene at a glance. Not a trace of surprise showed in her face.

"Oh my," the woman said in a rich, rueful voice that shot fire through my veins. "Now this is certainly going to tax my powers of improvisation."

"M-matron?" stammered the nurse who'd been untying Sarah.

"Well." Lilith smiled, exposing sharp-edged teeth. "Not exactly."

Chapter 17

Lilith cocked an eyebrow at the confused security guard. "I don't suppose I can convince you that these are approved visitors?"

He gaped at her.

Lilith sighed regretfully. "I didn't think so. In that case . . ." She drew back her hand, pointing her fingers— and, still smiling, thrust it straight through the security guard's chest.

The humans never had a chance. Even as the guard started to crumple, Lilith was moving in a blur of superspeed. Two sharp cracks rang out, and then Lilith was back where she had started, still wearing that small, pleased smile. The security guard's body hit the ground, immediately followed by the orderly and the nurse; limp, necks broken.

"We'll have to do this the other way." Lilith licked delicately at the blood covering her fingers. She stepped over the bodies, her gaze sweeping over both Sarah and myself. "Are you quite all right, my darlings?"

Ebon interposed his own body between the woman and myself. His hands were raised defensively, though his movements were stiff, the wounds in his shoulders still only half closed. *"You."*

"Me," Lilith agreed. She shimmered for an instant, mist rippling down her form from head to toe. When it cleared, she stood six inches taller: a straight, elegant figure with a narrow chin and razor-sharp cheekbones, her dark hair in a geometrically precise bob. She exuded an effortless chic so compelling that I wanted to do nothing more than sit at her feet and stare up at her.

Her black, slanted eyes watched Ebon warily. "Xanthe darling." Her voice was like chocolate over caramel; it even made me like the sound of my first name. "You must have a lot of questions."

"Uh—" I was sure that I *had*, but at the moment my mind was completely blank. She was like every head girl, every clique leader and trendsetter and sports team captain that I'd ever wanted to impress, all crammed into one package. And all I could think was that I was short and squat and had a stupid haircut.

Oh God, she was *looking* at me. What had the question been again? "Yes?" I squeaked, panicked.

"As soon as we get out of here, we'll have a lovely, long chat, I promise." My blood sang in my veins as she smiled at me. She liked me! She wanted to talk to me! "But first I need you to help me with a little something."

"Jane!" Ebon shouted. I glared at him. How could he be so rude as to interrupt *her* when she was speaking? "Jane, no, don't—"

"I just need you to help me kill this man," Lilith said, raising one long, elegant hand to wave languidly at Ebon.

This seemed eminently reasonable. After all, he was evasive and weird and had a dumb accent. One of the silver spikes that Van had pounded through him earlier was lying next to my foot; dreamily, I reached down and picked it up. All I had to do was stick it straight through his chest, and all my problems would be over.

"Jane, no." Ebon backed away as I straightened. His eyes flicked from me to Lilith and back again. "Jane, wake up!"

"What's going on?" Sarah's voice sounded wobbly as she struggled back to consciousness. She pushed herself upright with an obvious effort, rubbing at deep red marks ringing her wrists and ankles where her bonds had cut into her flesh. I could feel the blood moving through the veins under her skin, as strong and sweet as if it beat in my own. I felt the jolt that went through her as she saw Lilith. "What's happening?"

"Wait a sec," I said to her reassuringly over my shoulder. Ebon was backed into the corner; he tried to duck past me, but I caught him with a hand round his throat. "I just have to kill this man, and then I'll explain everything."

"Huh?" Her confusion beat through my heart, fogging Lilith's brilliant light. "I thought—isn't that your friend?"

"Fight it, Jane!" The man's hands clawed at my own, but I was easily stronger than him. "You know me, remember?"

"Wait!" Sarah pitched herself off the bed, stumbling forward to grab my sleeve. "You said he was a good guy."

"Hush, Sarah darling," commanded Lilith, impatience biting in her voice. "Xanthe, *now*."

I stared at the man I held pinned against the wall.

Did I know him? I could feel his throat vibrating under my palm—he was humming something, desperately, his eyes locked on mine, willing me to remember.

Iron Maiden. He was humming an Iron Maiden song.

My living room, colored notes flashing up on the TV screen, his long, elegant hands flying over the buttons, his blue eyes alight with glee.

When it came to a choice between the exotic vampire sire I'd seen kill three people, or the dork I'd watched rocking out on a miniature plastic guitar, there was *no contest.*

I flipped the spike around, pressing it into his hand as I released him. "Ebon, *go!*" Lilith blurred, but he was even faster. There was an instant of confused motion, then they were both stationary again, but at opposite ends of the room. There was a tear in the collar of Ebon's coat; Lilith's perfect bob was slightly mussed. They stared at each other, perfectly motionless.

"No, stop!" Sarah's hand clutched at me as I cast around frantically, looking for something to use to help Ebon. "Make them stop it!"

"Lie low!" I pushed her back onto the bed. The place where the second spike had been was covered by Van's massive, prone form; I knelt to try to roll him out of the way. He stirred under my hands, groaning, and his eyes fluttered open.

"Watch out!" I ducked at Sarah's shout, covering Van. Something flew past my head and crashed into the wall: Ebon, springing instantly to his feet. Four long, parallel cuts from Lilith's fingernails gashed his cheek and nose, barely missing his eyes and covering his face in a mask of blood.

"How pathetic," Lilith said. She sounded as languid as ever, but there was blood trickling from the corner of her mouth. An angry light filled her dark eyes. "This is what I've been running from all these years? If I'd known you were this slow, I'd have turned and squashed you long ago."

Ebon shook his head, bright drops of his blood scattering over the white bed linens. His lips drew back in a snarl.

"What are you holding back for?" Lilith spread her arms in invitation, though her eyes never left Ebon's. Down the Bloodline, I felt her muscles tense in anticipation. "Here, kitty, kitty."

Help us, I mouthed at Van as I grabbed the silver spike from underneath him. *In three. One—two—*

Van's eyes widened as he looked past me to Lilith. "No, wai—" he started, but I was already hurling myself forward. I caught Lilith completely off guard; before she could get out of the way, I'd crashed into her knees, knocking us both to the floor. I felt her leg start to dissolve under my hand, as if she was trying to turn into mist to get away. I slammed the spike randomly into her abdomen, and she went solid again.

"Ebon, hurry!" I yelled as Lilith twisted in my grip. I risked a glance at him, trying to see what was holding him up. He was just—standing there, the spike hanging from his hand as he stared at me. Under the blood, his face was twisted with indecision. *"Ebon!"*

In one movement, he was next to me, his own weight bearing down on Lilith's chest, his face only inches from mine. Lilith redoubled her efforts, but between us we pinned her to the ground. As Ebon raised the stake over her heart, his pale, guilt-stricken eyes met mine. "I'm so sorry," he whispered—not to Lilith, but to me.

He drove the stake down.

"No!" I was thrown off Lilith as Van slammed between Ebon and myself, knocking us both aside. The stake skittered across the floor; with a shout of triumph, Lilith tore the other spike out of her side and erupted into silver mist. I looked up just in time to see her streak toward the window, curling out into the night air. In seconds, she was gone.

Ebon sprang to his feet, sheer murder in his face, but was met with an uppercut from Van that was powerful enough to send him staggering. The vampire hunter sprang for him, and I caught the glint of another stake in his hand. Desperately, I snatched at his leg. I managed to throw him off balance enough that he missed his swipe and planted the stake in Ebon's side rather than his heart.

"Van!" I clung with grim determination to his boot as he tried to shake me off. "Cut it out!"

Ebon staggered back, ripping the stake out of his flesh. With a last wild, stricken glance at me, he whirled, his body coming apart into dense gray vapor. The stake clattered to the ground. He poured out the same way Lilith had gone, instantly vanishing into the dark.

Van stopped trying to kick me, but I was so pissed off that I sank my teeth into his leg anyway. I instantly regretted it, both for the disgusting taste and for the fact that he booted me hard in the head. I let him go and rolled to my feet. "You *idiot*," I screamed at him, spitting blood. "You let her get away!"

"I *know*," he snapped, not looking any happier than I felt. He limped over to the bed, where Sarah had collapsed unconscious again. She moaned and stirred groggily at his touch. "You have to come with me," he told her. He picked up Brains's jar and shoved it into a pocket. "They'll be back, and the normal authorities can't handle them. I'm here to protect you—I'll get you to safety."

"Backpack," she mumbled. She looked shell-shocked, barely aware of what was going on. "Can't go without my backpack. . . ."

Van slung the indicated bag over his shoulder. "I've got it. Come on now, we've got to hurry." He lifted her up, cradling her in his arms. "And you have to come too," he added sourly, glaring in my direction.

"What sort of a vampire hunter are you?" I demanded as he shouldered the window open.

"A real one," he said, clambering over the sill. Sarah let out a muffled protest as he clipped her head against the window frame. "One that doesn't let any human get hurt."

"She was a *vampire*!"

"Yes," he said grimly. "Your sire. And you're effectively her sire." He jerked his chin down to indicate Sarah. "And she is human."

"Yes! So what?" I yelled. "What does that matter?"

"It matters, because"—he took a deep breath—"when you kill a vampire, its descendants die too." He looked me in the eye, his face set. "All of them."

Chapter 18

"Your call cannot be connected at the moment." The pleasant, automated voice echoed tinnily in the close confines of the van. "Please try again later."

"I *am* trying again later," I yelled at Ebon's iPhone in frustration. "I've been trying for hours! Mum, Dad, where *are* you?"

The only response was a shrill, continuous beep as the call automatically ended. I jabbed at the screen with my feet until I managed to hit the right button to shut the phone up. I was lucky that Ebon had picked a handset that could be operated with only my toes.

Of course, I wasn't *very* lucky, considering that my entire family was mysteriously missing and unreachable, while I myself was bound, hand and foot, in the back of a van being driven God-knew-where by a guy who hated my very nature.

When we'd finally escaped the hospital last night, we'd found Dad's car right where we'd left it, but my family had been nowhere in sight. There hadn't been time to work out where they'd gone, not with the alarms going off in the hospital and more police cars arriving; Van had shoved Sarah into the passenger seat of his white van, thrown me in the back, and taken off with his foot flat on the floor. I'd tried calling Dad on Ebon's iPhone, but only got the voice mail message. No one had answered at home either, nor on any of the family mobiles. I'd still been trying to reach someone, anyone, when the sun had come up and laid me out like a brick to the back of the head.

And I awakened to find myself wrapped in approximately two metric tons of silver-plated steel chains. I was going to *slaughter* Van when I finally got free.

"We've got to get out of here," I said to Brains, who was sulking at the bottom of its jar. Van had wrapped silver chains around that too and hung it from a ring set in the wall of the van. "Can you give me a hand?"

Brains pointedly swished its fins, looking about as sardonic as a fish could.

"Why couldn't Mum have done her experiment on a useful animal, like a monkey?" I swore as the van bounced over another pothole, and I lost my grip on the iPhone. It skittered across the floor and disappeared amid the piles of boxes on the other side. I strained against my chains, trying without success to stretch a leg out to reach it. Something about the silver stopped me from misting; it made my skin feel tight and tingly, a bit like licking a battery. There was no way I could wiggle out of them either. Van obviously knew how to restrain a vampire.

My eyes widened, and I would have face-palmed if I could. Van knew how to restrain an *ordinary* vampire. I braced my feet against the floor of the van, pulling against the chains with all my weight. Nothing. Closing my eyes, I tried to visualize superstrength flowing into my muscles, then flung myself forward again. Metal screeched in protest as the bolts securing the chains to the van started to pull free. I gathered myself for another attempt, blood pounding in my chest—

The van grumbled to a halt. I heard the front doors open, followed by booted footsteps tramping round to the back. I quickly slumped back to hide the weakened bolts and let my head loll down to my chest, pretending to be asleep.

The back door grated open. "Don't bother, vampire," Van growled as he climbed in. "I know what time someone as young as you arises." Then, in a much gentler tone that definitely wasn't aimed at me: "Are you *sure* you want to stay back here? I could get some pillows to make the front seat more comfortable—"

"No, I need to lie down." Sarah's voice sounded faint with exhaustion. "Please."

"I'll arrange things for you." Van's boot prodded me. I smelled leather and sweat as he leaned over me to check my bindings. "Hm. And find some more chains."

"You are such a dead man." Giving up my attempt at subterfuge, I opened my eyes. Sarah was sitting on the back of the van, her bare feet dangling. Her crumpled, blood-splattered pajamas swamped her waifish body. With her wide almond eyes and overall tragic air, she closely resembled Bambi after his mother was shot.

Poor kid. It was hard to believe that this frail little girl was the Superluminal of online fame, creator of awesomely clever vids featuring the hottest TV vampires. She looked more like she should still be playing with Barbies. Why couldn't Superluminal have turned out to be a kickass action heroine with her own combat boots?

"Hi, Sarah," I said, trying to sound as calm and in control as I could given that I was swamped under ten tons
of metal. "Don't worry, everything's going to be okay." I
offered her a friendly smile. She dropped her gaze, avoiding my eyes. Oops. Possibly I shouldn't have shown her
my teeth. Giving up on the futile attempt at reassurance, I
turned my attention on Van. "Hey, listen, you've got to let
me go. I can't reach any of my family on the phone—they
could be in trouble. I've got to get back there."

"I've been driving half the night. We're miles away."
Van was busy shifting aside some of the boxes that lined
the sides of the van, strapping them into new positions.
"Though I'm not about to tell you exactly where, given
that Elder Hakon could be listening in."

What with all Ebon's lies, I'd almost forgotten about
Lilith's initial claim that Hakon was my great-grandsire.
"So I really am descended from Hakon's Bloodline? Are
you sure?"

"Of course." Van sounded personally insulted, as if
I'd questioned his ability to read. "I could taste it."

"Huh. So Lilith was telling the truth about that." I
was starting to wonder if *everything* Ebon had said was
flat-out lies. "If she's descended from Hakon, I guess that
means she isn't really an ancient, evil vampire-goddess

either. Don't suppose you could taste who she really is, could you?"

Van shot me a look suggesting that now I was just being silly. "No. I just know she's your sire and Hakon's descendant." His surly expression smoothed into a slight, introspective frown as he folded down a long, narrow shelf, revealing it to be a simple bed with vampirically neat sheets. "I'm sure she's not in any of our databases," he muttered down at the covers, sounding like he was talking mainly to himself. "Odd. We're supposed to have records on Hakon's entire current Bloodline."

"Whoever she is, she'll be able to find me no matter where I am," I said. "You can't outrun her forever. But if you release me—"

"I *am* a fully trained vampire hunter," Van said icily. "I'm aware of the problem. But I'm not about to free you to go off and slaughter innocents."

"I want to *rescue* innocents, you moron. I thought you were all about protecting humans."

"I am." Van threw me his habitual glare, but I could see the worry lurking around the edges of his bravado. "I'll go back to look for your family myself, if they've been captured."

Okay, I had to admit, Van had his good points, and

they weren't just his torso and arms. Of course, his major bad point of treating me like an evil monster did kind of outweigh any positives. "Thanks. I do actually appreciate the offer. But I'm by far the better choice for any rescue mission."

"Right. You, the bloodthirsty, undead killer." Van's voice dripped sarcasm. "Give me three good reasons."

"I'm superstrong, can't be killed, and there is no one on this planet who cares more about my family's safety than I do," I said promptly.

Van blinked.

"Look," I said, taking advantage of his momentary loss for words. "When are you going to get it through your thick head that I'm just your average girl, only dead? An all-liquid diet and serious lack of tan don't make me a psychopath. You think I *wanted* to be a blood-drinking freak?"

Van looked at me oddly, as if seeing me for the first time. "Like me," he said so quietly I barely heard it. For a second I thought he might actually start behaving like a rational human being—but then his jaw set. "No. Vampires can't be trusted. I have to keep you secure and get you to a safe location." He glanced at Sarah. "Both of you."

"There are places that are safe from vampires?" Sarah sounded dubious. Even her voice was a weak, fluttery thing, like a butterfly.

"Many, in fact." Van's mouth quirked, which was the nearest he ever seemed to get to a smile. He helped Sarah up. She had to lean heavily on him to go the few steps to the bed. "It's not that difficult to keep vampires out, once you know their weaknesses. All you need to do is scatter a lot of objects around. You can always tell a hunter's house by the army of garden gnome statues covering the lawn." His expression turned glum again. "But in order to take you to a hunters' safe house, I'll have to call my uncle. My leader," he added at Sarah's puzzled look. He squared his shoulders and pulled his phone out of his pocket, looking about as enthusiastic as a kid contemplating a trip to the dentist. "Best get it over—" The phone buzzed in his hand. Van glanced down at the screen, and his eyebrows rose. "Well now. That changes things." He pocketed the phone again, looking much happier. "That was my employer—I texted her earlier to explain the situation. She's offered us a safe house and, as it happens, it's very near here."

Even when you're bound hand and foot with your family missing, there's always a way for the situation to get worse. "No way. I'm not going to the home of some-one who sent a hit man after me!"

"I wasn't offering you a choice," Van said with a pointed glance at my chains. "Anyway, I wasn't hired to hunt you. I'm contracted to stake Ebenezer Lee. I only ran into you because I was following him."

"I was some sort of two-for-one deal?" I wasn't sure whether to be relieved or insulted.

Van shrugged. "I couldn't miss the opportunity to end the unnatural existence of another monster." He tucked the sheet in carefully around Sarah and put her backpack at her feet. "Are you sure you're all right?" he asked, voice softening. For a six-feet-plus, leather-clad vampire hunter, at the moment he had a rather striking resemblance to a big, overprotective dog, bristling with eagerness to defend his owner. I could practically see his tail wagging.

"I'll be okay." Sarah rested her head against the wall, her eyes closing in exhaustion. "I've been getting these blackouts and dizzy spells all week."

"Do you need medicines?" Van ran a hand through his close-cropped red hair, frowning. "I could . . . hijack an ambulance, I suppose."

"You had a seriously disturbed upbringing," I told

him—and blinked. "Hang on. Sarah, you started to feel bad just now, and you've only been having this problem for the past few days?" She nodded. "That was when I, uh—" There was no non-crazy way to put it. "That was when I rose from the dead. I think you're blacking out whenever I tap my vampy powers too hard."

"I," Van growled, "am *definitely* keeping you chained up."

Unfortunately, it turned out that Van had a lot more bondage gear at his disposal, including a vampire-proof gag. I was reduced to trying to kill him with the sheer force of my glare as he triple-checked all my bindings. "All right, she's secure," he said at last. "If she moves, bang on the wall." With a last backward glance, Van left, shutting the door. A moment later, the van started up again.

"At *last*," Sarah muttered. I heard rustling sounds, and then the beam of a flashlight cut through the dimness. A moment later, she was at my side, the light playing over the fastenings of the gag. "Give me a sec . . . there." She tossed the gag aside, then bent over the locks securing the chain. "Hmm. This is going to be harder."

"Uh . . ." It was probably stupid to say this *before* I was free, but— "You do know I'm a vampire, right?"

"Of course I know you're a vampire." Sarah rattled

the chains, looking for any give. "Why do you think I'm trying to free you? I would have done it earlier, but it took forever to persuade that dhampir to let me back here. He only relented when I really did faint."

I gaped at her. "Van told you what he is?"

"No, I just guessed from the way his glove compartment is organized. Only vampires sort their change that way." Sarah sounded perfectly matter-of-fact. She frowned at me with a mixture of exasperation and concern, as if I was the helpless tweenager in need of protection. "We don't have time to do this the slow way. Mutual brain dump?"

"Huh?"

"I'll start," she said, charging straight over my bewilderment. "Hello, I'm Sarah Chana, otherwise known as Superluminal. When I was little, I met Lily in the hospital—I bumped into her when she was sneaking in to steal blood out of the blood banks. She felt sorry for me because I was a poor, sick orphan, and ever since then she's been like a secret fairy godmother, only with fangs. She always finds me, no matter what hospital or foster home they dump me in. Anyway, ever since meeting her I've been preparing to become a vampire. Lily said that after the transplant she'd finally be able to turn me—but then she disappeared, and I didn't see her again until last night when you guys burst in and tried to stake her. Now I need to find her." She sat back on her heels, looking at me expectantly. "Your turn."

"Uh . . . okay." I took a deep breath. "Hi. I'm Xanthe Jane Greene—JaneX. Don't use my first name. I'm a vampire. It is not really turning out as I imagined. I think you've got my heart, which is letting me drain your blood without me actually biting you. I have no idea how the heck any of this happened—Ebon said I was bitten by a really ancient, renegade vampire called Lilith, but I'm starting to seriously doubt that he's trustworthy. Um, anyway. I woke up dead last week and promptly had one guy turn up to kill me and another guy turn up to rescue me—except that now it seems he's the one who really wants to kill me, and the *other* guy is trying to save me, though possibly only to kill me later. My family's currently missing, and I need to find them. Uh . . . you really didn't know any of this? I mean, you sent me that IM, so I assumed—"

"You tripped my Google Alert. I keep an eye out for anything that might be vampiric activity, just in case." Her brown eyes narrowed as she studied me. "Lilith. Lily. Hmm. Well, she obviously *is* your sire. I've been waiting for years, and yet she vamps *you* first?"

I rattled my chains meaningfully. "From where I'm sitting, it's not really something to get jealous over."

Sarah looked levelly at me. "You're going to always be young, have superhuman strength and speed, never get sick, and basically have all the time in the world to do whatever you want. Explain to me why I shouldn't be jealous."

"Uh . . ." I had to admit, when she put it like *that* . . . "Okay. You totally should be jealous."

"Damn straight," she said, which in that butterfly-soft voice sounded as out of place as Cinderella breaking into rap. "I should resent you and bitch about you and leave you to the dhampir." She pulled a pair of bolt cutters out of her backpack. "But that would be *dumb*. Lean forward."

"I have to ask," I said, shifting as much as I could in my chains to give her access. "*Why* are you carrying bolt cutters?"

"I told you, I've been waiting to become a vampire." The jaws of the cutters squealed over metal as Sarah tried to snip through the chains. "I prepared an emergency kit, in case Lily had to take me away without advance notice." She jerked her chin at her backpack. "Stuff like my laptop, cash, fake IDs . . . that sort of thing. I always make sure to keep it handy."

"But . . . bolt cutters?"

"I might need to steal a bicycle. Or break into some-where to shelter from the sun, if I haven't got enough energy to mist. You never know." She leaned back again, slightly out of breath. "This isn't working—I planned on having vampiric strength if I needed to use these. Guess I should have packed that crowbar."

"Maybe we can call for help." I nodded in the direc-tion the phone had disappeared. "I had an iPhone, but it slid somewhere under there." I watched as she poked around under the bed shelf. "Anything?"

"Yes." She reemerged, brandishing a dog-eared paperback. "An alphabetized box of Buffy the Vampire Slayer romance novels."

"Huh. Who knew?" Fortunately, she'd also found the phone. "Great. I can't get in touch with my family at the moment, but maybe you've got someone you trust you could call?"

"Sure." Sarah started dialing as she spoke. "Good think I've got Lily's number memo—"

"Whoa, whoa!" I nearly gave myself whiplash jerking upright. "I kinda meant someone other than Lily."

Sarah cocked her head at me. "Why? What's wrong with Lily?"

"She did try to kill my friend, you know. That doesn't exactly fill me with confidence."

"Uh-huh. That would be the same friend who tried to kill *you*."

She had a point. "She also slaughtered a whole roomful of innocent people." Sarah looked at me blankly, as if that had no possible relevance. "Look, just not Lily, okay? You must have someone else you could call. A relative, maybe?" Sarah shook her head. "Uh, a friend? A foster parent? A social worker?" More head shakes. "Don't you know *anyone*?"

Sarah shrugged. "I don't bother to make friends with alive people. What would be the point?"

"Oookay. You are now officially even scarier than my little brother." Giving up on the idea of calling in the cavalry, I tested the chains again, tugging against the links she'd weakened with the bolt cutter. "I nearly got free myself earlier . . . I might still be able to break these, if I Hulk out enough." I bit my lip, eyeing her. "Um, there's no real good way to ask this, but do you mind if I kinda drain your blood?"

Sarah wrinkled her nose at me. "Actually, yes. I like my plan better."

"What plan is that?"

Sarah pulled a syringe out from her backpack with a flourish. "Next time the dhampir comes back here, I drug the hell out of him and take the key from his unconscious body."

My mouth hung open. I shut it. "Right. Is there anything you *haven't* got in there?"

"I wanted a portable power generator, but it was too bulky." She patted her backpack. "It's easy enough to steal drugs when you're a long-term hospital patient. I've got enough stuff to last years. For feeding," she explained, at my blank look. "For when I don't feel like killing people. I can knock them out or get them high before I bite them, and then they won't remember a thing."

"That's . . . very practical, I guess—what do you mean, *when* you don't feel like killing people?"

"Oh, I've got a shit list too," she assured me gleefully. "For when I do."

I made a mental note to never, ever piss Sarah off. "Fine, we'll try it—"

The van lurched, making us both fall back against the sides. A second later the engine cut off.

"Shit!" Sarah hissed, hiding both syringe and iPhone in the waistband of her pajamas. She scrabbled back onto the bed as Van's footsteps sounded round the side of the van, heading for the door. "Don't worry, I'll find an opportunity—" She cut herself off, collapsing into a totally convincing imitation of innocent slumber as the door squealed open.

Van frowned at me. "How did you get this off?" he asked, kicking the discarded gag to one side. He unhooked Brains and shoved the jar in a pocket, then knelt down to unshackle me from the wall.

"I'm a supervampire, remember?" I resisted the urge to bite him. He'd only taste awful. "You have no idea what powers I have. You better let me go, before it's too late."

Van's only response was a derisive snort. He heaved me up and shoved me toward the exit—unable to keep my balance, I fell out of the van in a clatter of chains, and found myself lying on the doorstep of an ordinary-looking town house. Van had backed the van up so close to the house, he'd practically parked the vehicle in the front hallway.

"Quickly now," I heard him say. A second later, he stepped over me, carrying Sarah in his arms. He kicked the door a couple of times in a distinctive rhythm, all the while glancing nervously around. "We have to get out of sight before we attract atten—"

The door swung open. And there, on the other side, smiling, was Lilith.

Chapter 19

Van yelped as Lilith, still smiling, clobbered him over the head. Sarah yelped as he dropped her. I yelped as they both fell on top of me.

"Sorry, darlings." Lilith fastidiously rolled Van's limp form over with the tip of her high-heeled shoe, excavating me from underneath his bulk. "Sarah dear, since you're down there anyway, would you be a sweetie and find the key for these chains? Xanthe here seems to be in quite a predicament."

In a few minutes, I was free. I occupied myself with fishing through Van's pockets to retrieve Brains. It gave me an excuse not to meet Lilith's eyes. I had no idea how to behave—last time we'd met, I'd tried to kill her, but here she was smiling away as if I was her best friend in the world. It didn't help that the heat of the Bloodline between us made me feel like a stupid schoolgirl standing next to a catwalk model.

Sarah had no such problem. "Lily!" she exclaimed, throwing her arms around the vampire. "How did you know where to come to rescue us? Did you kill the hunter's employer?"

Lilith—or Lily—threw back her head and laughed, her sharp black bob swinging. "Darling, I *am* the hunter's employer. Vampire hunters are always hired by vampires. Who else knows that we exist?" She prodded Van with her foot. "The hunters are just pest control—no one wants to be neck deep in baby vampires, so the Elders hire them to get rid of all the victims who spontaneously rise after death. Though personally I've always used a much cheaper way to avoid that problem—no one rises as a vampire if their heart has already been destroyed. And I must say, crunching people's rib cages when I've finished with them is so very *satisfying*. Like crushing the can after finishing a soda." Bending down, she picked up the unconscious Van by the scruff of his neck. Her lips pursed as she studied his slack face. "Hm. So that's how he turned out. Shame about the ginger hair." She turned away, carrying Van like a shopping bag. "But let's not loiter in the hallway. Come in, darlings."

Sarah followed her without hesitation, trusting as a puppy. I trailed after them, clutching Brains's jar against my chest like a teddy bear and feeling badly out of place. The house didn't help—knickknacks and lace doilies littered every surface of the battered furniture. Though someone—presumably Lily—had scrupulously straightened everything into precise alignment, the clutter still set my teeth on edge. The air held the faint aroma of boiled cabbage. It was not exactly how I'd pictured the lair of a mysterious vampire queen.

I ended up perched next to Sarah on a rock-hard, ancient sofa, watching as Lily manacled the still-unconscious Van to an old-fashioned cast-iron radiator with disturbingly practiced efficiency. "There now," she said, looking down at him with satisfaction. "All secure. Now, my dears, I think we all need a long chin-wag. But first, who would like a nice hot drink?"

For Sarah, this turned out to be tea. My own beverage, served in a martini glass, was lukewarm, thick, and crimson. "Uh," I said, holding the thin crystal stem as gingerly as I could. "I really don't think so."

Lily swirled her own glass. "You need to keep your strength up. It's lovely and fresh, I assure you." My gaze shot straight to the door that led to the as-yet-unseen kitchen. "Oh, you funny little thing. Not *that* fresh."

I set the glass of blood down on the coffee table, where Brains eyed it with interest through his jar. "Um. Look. You aren't really Lilith, are you?"

"Good Lord, no." Lily shook her head. "What an interesting story Ebenezer spun for you. No, I was turned in 1926. I'm the youngest of our Bloodline— well, until now, of course." She raised her glass to me. "Lillian Larkspur—Lily Lark, if you want my theatrical name. I practically grew up on the stage." She fogged, and for an instant a slim, blue-eyed young man lounged in her place. "Which has paid dividends in unexpected ways, as it turns out."

"I *told* you so," Sarah said to me impatiently before switching her attention back to Lily. "Why did you vamp my heart donor?"

"Because I had to, of course." Lily shivered back into her own form. "This is the closest I could get to making you a vampire, darling." She sighed, sitting back in her chair and crossing her long legs. "It was your heart, you see. You already had a hole in your heart. Pre-staked, as it were. If I'd tried to turn you in the normal fashion, you'd have expired on the spot, instantly."

"You mean this is it? I can't be a real vampire?" Sarah looked like a kid who'd unwrapped a birthday present and found socks. "You could have turned me after the heart transplant—" She stopped as Lily shook her head. "Oh. My own heart would still have been . . . gone."

"Exactly. No heart, no unlife." Lily pointed at me, making me jump. "And so Xanthe, I'm afraid, became our only option. We were lucky you had a donor that could be turned."

"So all of this was about Sarah?" I said. I didn't expect the universe to revolve around me or anything like that, but it wasn't a good feeling to find out that I was just a convenient body that had happened to be lying around. "You weren't trying to make some sort of supervamp?"

"I admit, it's a rather lovely side effect," Lily said with a rueful smile. "But no, it wasn't foremost in my mind. I was more concerned with saving my Sarah from a painful mortal existence." She sighed. "I'm not sure whether it's worked, mind. All blood-bonds work in both directions—I hoped that Sarah would be able to draw on your powers the same way you currently draw on her blood. We'll have to see."

I'd been in the wrong place at the wrong time. There was nothing about me that was special. I stared down at Brains, feeling oddly hollow. The fish gave me a glance of pure indifference, then went back to trying to unscrew the lid of the jar with its nose.

I'd always wanted to be normal. Now I just felt ordinary.

"Xanthe." I felt a touch on my hand, like a spark of electricity shooting through my veins. I looked up into Lily's face. Her eyes were warm with understanding and sympathy. "I *am* glad that it was you. Imagine if I'd had to turn some disgusting old man or a silly ninny. Ugh!" She gave a theatrical shudder. "But it was fate. Fate that of all people it was you, who loves all things vampire, on death's door after that horrible car crash, at the right place and time to let me save both you and my Sarah. You always wanted to become one of us, deep down, even when you didn't know we really existed. Secretly you *knew*. It was destiny, my darling, destiny that brought you to me. You're meant to be one of us."

My eyes were burning, but I couldn't blink, or the tears would overspill. My heart felt small and cold in my chest—no, not my chest, but Sarah's. The tightness in my throat was an echo of hers. I looked at her. She too was keeping her eyes very wide, unblinking, as if she could reabsorb the tears welling at their edges. There was nothing feigned about her fragility now.

She hadn't asked for any of this either. "Sucks, doesn't it," I said to her.

She made a funny noise, half sniff, half hiccup, and swiped the back of her hand across her eyes. "Massively."

"Oh, darling, don't despair." Lily leaned forward to pat her knee. "You're still with me, freed from those dreadful institutions, just as I promised. And we don't yet know how your link to Xanthe will affect you. You are linked into the Bloodline, even if I can't feel it." She hesitated, glancing at me. "You do, though, don't you, Xanthe?"

"Yeah." On impulse, I let my attention flow away down the link—and found myself looking at myself, through Sarah's eyes. Man, did I need a better haircut. I withdrew back to my own senses again. "It's as if she really was my vampiric childe, only . . . more so. You really can't feel it?"

Lily shook her head. "My link to you is a tad odd— as if there's a faint echo underneath it—but that's all. I

can find you perfectly well, but Sarah's invisible to me."
She tilted her head in Van's direction, with a slightly
aggrieved expression. "Annoying that the dhampir *could*
feel it, with his greater sensitivity, but at least Hakon's
in the dark. Count our blessings on that, my darlings,
because otherwise he would have kidnapped Sarah, or
worse, as soon as he felt the link."

I blinked, the word *kidnapped* hitting me like a bucket
of cold water in the face. "Crap!" How could I have
forgotten? I scrambled up off the sofa. "My family—"

"Is missing." Lily tapped her forehead meaningfully,
which I took to indicate that she'd been eavesdropping
on me earlier. "I know."

"Great, then I don't have to explain." I headed for
the door—but Lily got there ahead of me in a blur of
superspeed. She leaned against it, blocking my path.
"Lily, I mean it, I have to go!"

Her dark eyes regarded me soberly. "Darling, I'm
terribly sorry but, to be blunt, your family has either
escaped Ebenezer Lee and is perfectly safe, or he's
already slaughtered them like mice."

It took me a moment to realize who she meant. "*Ebon?*
Slaughter anyone? You have got to be joking."

"He tried to slaughter *you*," Sarah pointed out.

"He nearly staked Lily, and that's as good as a murder attempt on you as well."

"The man is half beast," Lily said. "Don't underestimate how dangerous and unpredictable he is—I should know, Hakon's had him hunting me for years now. Very clever of him and very annoying. You realize that we can sense when someone of our own Bloodline is nearby, even if they aren't our sire or childe?"

Remembering the weird fuzzy sensation I'd got in my head around Ebon's so-called "vampire hunters," I nodded.

"Well, as Ebenezer is completely unconnected to our Bloodline, I have no idea when he's around. I thought he'd followed me away from your grave, so I nearly died—metaphorically speaking—when I peeked down the Bloodline and saw that he'd doubled back to turn up at your house instead." She shook her head. "I can only assume that he worked out early on that he couldn't take you on in a fight, and fortunately you never left your family unguarded. Until . . . well, look what happened when you did."

It all sounded scarily plausible. I couldn't think of any time that Ebon had been alone with my family without me in the house as well. Had he just been waiting for an opportunity? His harmless geek act could be as much a lie as his French aristocrat persona. Look how he'd nearly killed Van several times over. Lily was right, he *was* savage.

I had the nagging feeling that I was forgetting something . . . something important, something that had happened in the hospital . . . but Lily was talking again, her voice washing away my doubts. "The important thing now, darling, is not to go charging off half-cocked. That would be playing right into Ebenezer's and Hakon's grubby paws." She put her hands on my shoulders, steering me back to the sofa. She sank back into her own chair, lounging with perfect ease. "But don't worry, darling. I've got a plan to help you get revenge."

"Revenge on . . . Ebon?" I said a bit dubiously. Something was still bothering me about the whole picture Lily had painted—

"Why settle for the servant when you can strike at the master?" Lily said, breaking my train of thought. "Think big, darling." She looked meaningfully from me to the unconscious Van. "Think . . . Hakon."

"Ohhh," Sarah said in tones of dawning enlightenment. "I get it."

I didn't. "I thought he was, like, an Elder or something. Isn't he going to be insanely powerful? Not to mention the fact that if we *did* manage to kill him, we'd all go poof too."

"Darling," Lily said, sounding rather like a kindly kindergarten teacher trying to explain the alphabet to the slowest kid in the class, "*you're* insanely powerful. And who said anything about killing?"

Uncrossing her long legs, Lily rose and went over to the sideboard. A red Louis Vuitton handbag perched on the cheap pine veneer, spectacularly out of place in the drab decor. Lily picked through the bag, pulling out first a very small and sleek mobile, followed by a very large and ugly gun. I flinched, but she put the gun down on the sideboard, delving again into the bag. "Voilà," she said, taking out a small metal canister. She tossed it to me. "You can simply pop him in there."

"Silver?" I said, feeling the way the metal tingled against my palms.

"Over a titanium alloy," Lily said. "Lightweight, durable, and practically unbreakable. The perfect thing for storing a vampire. Don't worry," she added, seeing how gingerly I was holding it. "It's not some priceless artifact. They're practically mass-produced."

I hefted the canister. It nestled neatly in my palm. "Um, I don't think he's going to fit."

"Oh, we don't need all of him," Lily said breezily. "Just his heart."

I stared at her, then back at the canister. "What am I supposed to do with the rest of him?"

Lily waved a hand airily. "Use your imagination, darling." She smiled in fond reminiscence. "I certainly had a jolly amusing time getting my own sire into one of those things."

"Vampires don't die as long as you leave the heart alone," Sarah said to me. "They can survive forever in one of those, but they can't regenerate unless someone frees them and gives them some blood." She had a slightly superior air, like a forum moderator lecturing some hapless newbie. "Most vampires secretly dream of locking up their own ancestors. It's the only way to be safe. Being an Elder vampire just means that you've got control over all your sires, at least as far back as you know."

"Precisely," Lily agreed. "I've had my own sire tucked away in a nice secure hidey-hole for, oh, about fifty years now. But I've never had the chance to take a crack at Hakon, given that I had no idea how to find him, and less idea how to wade through all his goons to reach him." She smiled like a cat with a mouthful of canary. "But now, thanks to the dhampir and Xanthe here, both of those problems are no more."

"I don't know about all this," I said slowly, struggling to find the right words. I felt like my brain was having to push my thoughts uphill, battling against Lily's cheerful certainty. "Even if I can get rid of Hakon, what do we do after that?"

"Why, darling, that's obvious." Lily's bloodred lips curved upward, and her dark eyes gleamed. "Whatever we want."

"Like take over the world!" Sarah said, bouncing on the edge of her seat with childish and distinctly disturbing enthusiasm.

"It's certainly a possibility," Lily said, far too seriously for comfort. "Though," she added, with a sour glance at Van, "the dhampir is much more intractable than I'd hoped. Honestly, the boy seems to think he's on some sort of personal crusade. I don't know what Quinns was thinking."

"Quinns?" Sarah frowned. "Who's Quinns?"

"Quincey Helsing, the hunters' Lord High Grand whatever," Lily said with a dismissive flick of her long fingers. "Silly name and title, but I thought he was a sensible enough man, even if not quite as practical as his sister was. I can't believe dear Quinns raised the boy to be quite so naive."

I gave up trying to think of objections to Lily's plan. It was obvious it had no flaws anyway. "I've talked to that guy," I said, remembering my brief phone encounter with the hunter leader. "He's Van's uncle. I think he might come looking for him."

"Oh, we'll tuck him up somewhere nice and snug with Sarah and me, where neither vampire nor hunter can find us," Lily said. "While you take care of Hakon." She yawned, covering her mouth daintily. "Pardon me. Getting close to sunrise." She rose, motioning us up as well. "Your Elder needs her beauty sleep, my darlings. I'll show you where you can bunk down."

I trailed silently after Lily and Sarah as the two of them bustled around happily, laying out sleeping bags and chattering about the relative merits of different exotic destinations. My stomach churned with worry over my family. Even with all of Lily's perfectly sensible arguments as to why it was a bad idea, I still couldn't help wanting to rush out and find them right away. But it was far too close to dawn now; I could feel a faint drowsiness settling over me.

Lily excused herself and disappeared down the hallway to her own room. Sarah lay back in her sleeping bag, crossing her arms behind her head. "Good thing I've trained myself to sleep days," she said. "You okay over there?"

"Yeah." I wriggled into my own sleeping bag. "I guess so . . . but does this all seem right to you?"

"What, the house?" Sarah sniffed. "No, it sucks. I always pictured Lily and me living somewhere much more—"

"No, not that." I stared up at the ceiling. "Only . . . there's still something bothering me about Lily's whole plan. I wish I could put my finger on it." My Bloodline link to Lily abruptly slackened, like the volume had been turned down. I guessed that she'd fallen asleep. It was like a noisy radio station had been switched off in my head; suddenly I could think again.

I sat bolt upright, nearly ripping the sleeping bag. "*That's it!*"

"What? What is it?" Sarah twisted to stare at me.

"The problem is that Lily is a stone-cold psycho killer!" I couldn't believe I'd managed to forget the sight of her slaughtering an entire room of innocent people. "I don't want to be her hit man. I certainly don't want to kill Ebon. And I sure as hell never wanted to be a vampire!"

"Why not?" Sarah sounded as puzzled as if I'd announced that I didn't want to win the lottery.

"Because I'm not *crazy*. What normal person thinks vampires even exist?" I replayed the conversation in my head, gob-smacked at the nonsense I'd swallowed whole. "Why the heck did all that sound so reasonable at the time?" I slapped myself on the forehead. "Of course. She's been putting the whammy on me. Using her influence as my sire."

"Well, *duh*," Sarah said in withering tones. "Of course. Otherwise you'd freak out, like you are now."

"You're okay with the fact that she goes around killing people?"

Sarah looked at me like I was a complete drooling idiot. "She's a *vampire*. Of course she has to kill people sometimes. It's no different from any predator hunting prey. You don't have hysterics over the fact that humans eat cows, do you?"

I decided not to try to get into an argument on comparative ethics with a psycho preteen who'd been raised by an undead murderer. "Okay, leaving that aside, don't you think it's a little too convenient that she 'accidentally'"—I made air quotes with my fingers—"came up with a way of creating a supervampire?" I frowned, something else occurring to me. "Not to mention Van just happening to be around right when she needs a dhampir in order to track down Hakon. There's no way that all this is only some nice way of saving your life. No offense."

"None taken." Sarah rolled her eyes. "Of course Lily must have planned it. She's *clever*. Killing two birds with one stone—helping me and herself at the same time. It's exactly what I'd do, if I was her." She frowned thoughtfully. "Except I think I would have done something to ensure your loyalty. As it is, you're way too attached to your family for anyone's good. That was kind of sloppy of her."

My indignant reply was cut off by an unexpected, loud ringing sound. Both Sarah and I jumped. She scrabbled in the pile of discarded clothes next to her sleeping bag, pulling out the vibrating iPhone. "Someone trying to call you?"

"My family!" I grabbed the phone. We both peered at the caller ID displayed on the screen.

HAKON

"Oh my God," I said. "This is Ebon's phone. He must be trying to contact Ebon."

"That's not possible!" Sarah's eyes were wide. "Lily told me Hakon's a Viking, he's something like a thousand years old. He's got to be asleep this close to sunrise." We both stared at the phone as if it was a land mine we'd just uncovered. "Should we answer it?"

"I can't, I don't speak Swedish!" The phone finally went dead, and I sagged in relief. "Good, he gave up. I hope he doesn't get suspicious."

"Come to think of it," Sarah said, her forehead furrowing, "Ebenezer would have to be asleep as well, given his age. Why would anyone be trying to phone him now?"

The phone chimed, nearly making me punt it through the wall. I peered down at the phone screen, trying to decipher the glowing icons. "Whoever it was, they've left a voice mail." I touched the PLAY command.

"Jane." Even from the tiny speaker, the recorded voice was unmistakable. "Call me back. Now."

It was Ebon.

Chapter 20

That can't be him," Sarah said, but even as she spoke, I was hitting the CALL BACK button. The phone barely rang before it was picked up at the other end.

"Jane?"

"What's the chorus you bomb out on every time?" I demanded.

There was the briefest pause, then, "Skullcrusher Mountain," Ebon said. "The falsetto is impossible, even on Easy."

"It's him," I said to Sarah, covering the phone's microphone briefly. I put the call on speakerphone so she could hear too. "You've got some nerve, Ebon."

"I know. There isn't time." His voice was flattened

by more than just the distortion of the phone line; he sounded bone-weary. "The drugs keeping me awake won't last long. Jane, I know the general gist of what Lily's been telling you—Hakon listened in as long as he could, relaying it to me. But I've had to wait until now to talk to you without her overhearing."

"Give me one good reason why I should listen to you," I said. "Mr. Lies-Through-His-Teeth-and-Tries-to-Murder-Me."

A long silence.

"You're supposed to say something." Ebon's voice was fainter, as if he was some distance from the handset.

I blinked. "Huh?"

"Not you!" Ebon snapped. Then, evidently not to me, "Please, I haven't got time. Say something. Anything."

"No way," said a boy's voice, shaking but determined. "You're trying to use us to lure her here!" He paused. "Oops."

It was Zack.

There was no way that could be a vampire imitating him. The iPhone glass cracked beneath my crushing fingers. "Ebon! If you've hurt him, if you've so much as *touched* him—"

"We're fine, we're all fine here." This time it was my dad's voice, filled with forced calm. It was exactly the same way he'd sounded when he'd had to tell us that Mum had collapsed with acute appendicitis; it had taken weeks before he'd admitted that she'd nearly died. Hearing that tone now made my throat tighten in dread. "Stay away from here."

"It's all under control," added my mum's voice.

"You are handcuffed to chairs and surrounded by hostile vampires!" Ebon practically wailed. "Will you all *please* be sensible?"

As usual, it seemed that fell to me. "I get it. Hostages. What do you want, Ebon?"

"It's not what I want, it's what Hakon wants." Ebon took a deep breath. "You. All of you. The dhampir, the girl, yourself . . . and Lily."

"No!" Sarah exclaimed. She reached for the phone, but I swung it out of her reach. *I'll handle it,* I mouthed, and she subsided, though her face was pale and set.

"If you all turn yourselves in, Hakon will release your family," Ebon said. "If you don't—"

"Don't do it, Xanthe," Mum interrupted. "Three for four is a bad deal. Stay away, and send help to—" Her words degenerated into a muffled mumble.

"I'm sorry, but I can't—*ow*—let you tell her—*ow*—where we are," Ebon said, evidently to Mum. "Would you please stop biting—*ow!*—me! I'm trying to help you all here!"

"It would have been a lot more helpful if maybe you hadn't kidnapped them in the first place," I snarled.

"I didn't! I swear I didn't, Jane."

"That's actually true, to be fair," Zack said. "A couple of big guys grabbed us not long after you went into the hospital. Ebon's been pretty cool." There was a momentary thoughtful pause. "Apart from the whole tying-us-up thing, of course. But he was very apologetic about it."

"Zack, stop telling your sister how nice the evil vampires are," Dad said firmly. "Don't you believe a word Ebenezer says, Jane." Seemed that Ebon had come clean with them about his real name and origin. "Not unless he offers you a show of good faith. Like releasing your brother."

"I told you, I can't do that," Ebon said wearily. "Jane, I promise I'll get your family out of this. Please trust me."

"Yeah, right." But I had to admit, there was something raw about Ebon's voice that made me wonder. It was a stark contrast to Lily's polished self-composure. "Ebon, let's say I do what you want." Sarah glanced sharply at me; I shook my head at her. "What happens then?"

"They'll kill Lily!" Sarah burst out. "They'll kill you, Jane, it's suicide!"

"No, Hakon's planning to imprison Lily, not stake her," Ebon said. "He wants you to work for him, Jane. He always has, that's been the whole point of all this."

"You don't want to do that, Xanthe," said Mum. "This Hakon is *not* an ethical employer."

Sarah grabbed my sleeve. "Listen to her, Jane. Lily's told me all about Hakon. He's pure evil."

And that was *Sarah* saying it. I rubbed at my face, trying to fight the sleepiness that clouded my thoughts. "I have to say, this really doesn't sound like a good deal, Ebon. I don't want to work for anyone."

"That's my girl," Dad said. "You stay safe."

"You all really aren't helping here, you know," Ebon said with a resigned sigh. I heard footsteps, and guessed that he was moving out of earshot from my family. "Jane, we're vampires. We can't help but be under the thumb of those older than us. You can accept that, or you can die."

"*Lily* escaped," Sarah said, lifting her chin proudly.

"For less than a hundred years," Ebon snapped.

"That's nothing. Even I'm almost twice as old as that, and most of the other vampires regard me as an infant. My own grandsire? She is eight *thousand* years old. To Hakon, Lily might as well have run away last afternoon. If it wasn't for this experiment of hers, he might have been content to let her run for another couple of centuries before getting around to disposing of her. Until now, he hasn't even made any real effort to find her."

"Apart from sending you after her," I pointed out.

Ebon laughed: a bitter, painful sound. "Me?" His farm boy accent thickened. "I'm a joke."

"You're from a different Bloodline. So you've escaped from your own sire."

"No, my Elder simply doesn't care where I am or whether I'm alive or dead. Why do you think I've been trying for over a century to get accepted by another Bloodline? It's hard, impossibly hard, to be a lone vampire. You're constantly dodging hunters sent by other lineages. The Bloodlines *hate* rogues. And on top of all that you still have to find food, shelter, money, all without officially existing. And everyone you ever knew is dead and everything keeps changing, utterly—" He broke off. When he spoke again, his voice was more composed, but quiet. "It's . . . very lonely."

"Oh, my heart just bleeds for you, guy who has my little brother tied to a chair." Despite my brave words, my unease was ballooning into full-scale panic. Ebon may have deceived me before, but I couldn't persuade myself that he was lying this time; the self-hatred and hopelessness in his voice were all too real.

"You have to turn yourself in, Jane." Ebon's words were starting to slur together, as if he was badly drunk. "By the deadline. Otherwise . . . otherwise, Hakon'll—"

"Ebon!" I was finding it hard to speak now myself. "Talk to me! What deadline?"

"Tomorrow night. Midnight," Ebon mumbled, barely audible. "Hakon's deadline. Surrender yourself and them, or he'll kill one of . . . one of your family. Jane, I'm sorry, so sorry . . . won't let him . . . I won't."

I stared at the dead phone, my mind struggling as if my thoughts had to swim uphill through syrup. Capture Lily. Turn her and Van and Sarah and myself in. Tomorrow, midnight. I couldn't *think*. There was no way I'd ever be able to take her down on my own, not when she could practically put me on my knees just with her smile. *Think*.

"Jane." Sarah grabbed my lax hands, squeezing them fiercely between her own. I could barely feel the pressure through my numb skin. "It's okay. I'll think of something, I'll make a plan while you're resting."

"Help me," I croaked, forcing myself upright. My feet were dead lumps of flesh; I lurched across the room like a zombie. "Living room—help me!"

I could feel the rising sun like the muzzle of a gun pressed to the back of my neck. By the time Sarah had supported me to the living room, my legs were dead from the hips down. A faint gray light filtered through the gap in the curtains; my vision blurred. Everything was too bright, like an overexposed photo.

"You." Van glared at me. His wrists were rubbed raw where he'd been trying to free himself. "By my mother's blood, I will stake you if it's the *last thing I do.*"

I'd never been so glad to see anyone before in my life. I tripped and sprawled, having to crawl the last few feet. Van twisted in his chains, as if he thought I was trying to attack him—but I reached past him.

"Jane, what are you doing?" Sarah yelled, swaying as I pulled strength from her in order to snap the chains binding Van to the radiator.

"No time." I grabbed Van's leather-clad shoulder, unable to stop myself from collapsing against him. "I need you," I said, up into his puzzled but still suspicious face. "Hakon's got my family. Get Lily. Help me!"

"What?"

I could *throttle* him for being so slow. "I'm hiring you, hunter!"

"What? No!" Sarah lunged for me. With a silent apology, I opened the blood-bond between us, deliberately drawing as much power as I could.

Sarah had just enough time to gasp, "Oh, you total cow," before she keeled over. Fresh energy roared through my veins as she toppled into a limp heap.

I shook my head, clawing for a few more minutes of consciousness. "Ebon called," I said to Van, my voice steadier. "He's got my family. Hakon's going to kill them unless I give myself up by tomorrow midnight."

Enlightenment dawned across Van's face. "And it's not only you he wants."

"Right. He wants Lily and Sarah and—" I stopped dead.

I was too late; Van had already worked it out. "And me," he finished neutrally.

I hesitated, then nodded.

"And you want me to secure your sire for you."

I nodded again, mute. We stared at each other, barely inches apart. His eyes were so green in the daylight.

They studied me, reading my desperation, and his own expression softened. I felt the rough calluses on his palm as he cupped my face in his hand, supporting my drooping head.

"I am a hunter," he said, his deep voice very quiet. "And I protect the innocent with my blood. You can trust me."

I closed my eyes for a second in relief, and then wished I hadn't, as I couldn't pry them open again. The dawn was beating on my skull like a hammer. Van's hand holding me up was so warm, so nice. I could float away.

"Jane." Van's voice drifted down from somewhere very far away. I forced my eyelids up for a fraction of a second. His intent face swam before me, his hair blazing like fire. "Just in case . . . don't surrender Sarah, but anything else you have to do to save your family . . . do it. Just do it."

I was falling back into my grave. Earth closed over my head.

His words followed me into the darkness. "If you have to, give me to the vampires."

Chapter 21

"**W**e," said a cold, curt voice, jolting me awake, "have got to talk."

"Bzuh?" My eyes were blurry with sleep, and my neck was killing me. I seemed to be lying full length and facedown on the carpet. I managed to lift my head a few inches and saw a row of tan blurs laid out inches from my nose. I blinked them into focus.

Scrabble tiles. Y, O, U, A, R, E, A, N, I, D, I, O, and T.

An instant migraine lit up my skull. Wincing, I reached for the tiles, intending to rearrange them into a logical order—and hesitated. Either they could go in alphabetical order, or numerical sequence, but not both at the same time. . . .

"Argh!" I clutched at my head. Any vampire couldn't help but be paralyzed with indecision over the impossible choice. This was far worse than mere paper clips. Glaring at the unholy things, I came to the obvious conclusion.

"VAN HELSING, I AM GOING TO *MURDER* YOU." My hands hovered helplessly over the tiles. "You jerk, we had a deal!"

"Not with me," someone said from somewhere above me. I looked up, squinting against the searing glare of the light. Sarah was sitting on the sofa, with Lily's gun in one hand and a seriously pissed-off expression on her face. Van was sprawled on the floor in front of her, limp as a dead fish.

"Things," Van said, his syllables slurring together drunkenly, "didn't go 'xactly as planned."

"No kidding," I said. Sarah was using him as an impromptu footstool. I tried pulling strength from her down the Bloodline, but it felt like trying to suck a thick milk shake through a thin straw—the pulse of power between us beat slow and sluggish. Looked like I wasn't going to be able to lay her out that easily. I tried to think of ignoring the Scrabble tiles and making a lunge for her, and had to squeeze my eyes shut against the bolt of pain. Opening them again, I nodded at Sarah's gun. "You know you can't actually kill me with that, right?"

"Yes." Sarah had the gun pointed rock-steady at my forehead. "But *think* how much fun I could have shooting you."

"Don't shoot her," Van mumbled. "'S a pretty nice vampire. Nice pretty vampire. Something." He hiccuped.

I stared at him, at least as best as I could while wrestling with the siren call of the Scrabble tiles. "What's up with him?"

"Drugged to the eyeballs." Sarah twitched the gun down to point at the back of Van's head. "And I'm pretty sure bullets would ruin *his* whole day. Now, do I have your attention?"

"Absolutely." I had no doubt that she'd do it too. She looked healthier, stronger, in the bright sunlight streaming through the window; it picked out the warm tones of her skin and turned her brown eyes to topaz—

Hang on. Sun?

"Wait a sec. It's day. And I'm awake." This was a bit of an overstatement—my dry eyes burned, and I felt as though someone was lightly and repeatedly bouncing bricks off my skull. "How?"

"I reckoned that if Ebenezer Lee could use drugs to stay awake, I could do the same to get you to wake up." Sarah waved an empty jar in one hand. "You have to be tapping my blood a little bit, all the time. So I loaded up with caffeine, in the hope that it would trickle down to you."

I squinted at her. The way that she seemed to be vibrating was not, in fact, just a trick of the light. "My God, how much did you drink?"

She brandished the empty jar again, her eyes bright and slightly crazed. "I don't know. I poured hot water straight into a full jar of instant. I had to eat it with a spoon."

Great. Not only was I being held at gunpoint—or rather, Scrabble tile–point—by a juvenile sociopath, she was a juvenile sociopath hopped up on enough caffeine to fuel an entire class of students through end-of-year exams. No wonder I was awake. I was amazed that Sarah wasn't *dead*. I looked down at my hands, which were shuffling tiles around of their own volition. Nope, alphabetical order wasn't any better. "Did you go through all this trouble to wake me up in order to yell at me?"

"No." Sarah leaned forward, shifting the gun so that she could rest her elbows on her knees. "This is the only way to be certain that no one is listening in. You can't give in to Hakon's demands. It's madness. Worse, it's stupid."

"They've got my family." My voice cracked on the word. "My family, Sarah!"

She held my gaze, unfaltering. "Lily is *my* family."

I pressed my lips together on the words *That's different.* It couldn't help.

"That's diff'rent," Van supplied helpfully. I winced as Sarah's eyes narrowed. "'S a vampire. Should be dead." He frowned as though wrestling with a deep conundrum. "Deader. More dead. Whatever."

"Um, ignore Van, he's got issues," I said hurriedly as Sarah looked like she might be contemplating taking out a kneecap or two. "He doesn't mean it personally. I mean, he'd kill *me* without a second thought."

"Not true," Van said, sounding hurt. "Feel sad abou' it after."

"Lily's all I have, Jane. I won't let you harm her." Sarah's face was fierce, uncompromising. "Anyway, Hakon's deal stinks. There's no way he's going to release your family, no matter what. You really believe he'd let go of such a good bargaining chip? He's going to keep your family locked up for the rest of their lives, so you'll be forced to do what he wants."

I bit my lip. I hated to admit it, but what she said made sense. "How can you be so sure?"

Sarah shrugged. "It's what *I'd* do, if I was him."

And Sarah was, let's face it, evil. I rubbed my forehead, fighting back both a Scrabble-induced migraine and a growing sense of despair. "It doesn't matter," I said, dropping my hand again. "Whether or not Hakon means to keep his word, I have to try. I can't leave my family."

"Of course you can't," Sarah said, sounding annoyed, as if I was insisting on stating the blatantly obvious. "They're your *family*. We have to rescue them."

"We?" I indicated the Scrabble tiles. "I thought you were trying to save Lily. Keep me here until past the deadline."

"Yeah, what a good idea." Sarah rolled her eyes. "I'll just royally piss off the unstoppable supervampire I'm psychically linked to, by causing the horrific deaths of her nearest and dearest. Now why didn't I think of that? Oh, yeah, because I'm not a drooling idiot." She gestured impatiently with the gun, making me flinch. "We're bound together now, for better or worse, and that means that our problems are shared. Now, are you going to stop flailing around like a noob and let me help? God knows you need someone to do your thinking for you. Truce?"

"Truce." I hesitated. "But what if the only way to save my family is to sell out Lily?"

"Let's put it this way." Sarah stuck the gun in her waistband and hopped off the sofa. "Don't. I won't be so nice to you next time." She swept up the Scrabble tiles, much to my relief. "Anyway, I came up with a plan. We know Ebenezer called from Hakon's office, so all we have to do is use the dhampir here," she kicked Van, "to locate Hakon using your blood. As long as we get there in daylight, we can walk in there and bust your family out while Hakon's goons are still sleeping."

I thought it over, searching for weaknesses. "You know, that actually sounds like a *good* plan."

"Yep," Van said. "Good plan. Very good plan." His tone turned tragic. "Won't work, o' course. Apart from that, 's perfect."

I looked at Sarah. "How long is he going to be like this?"

"Should wear off in an hour or two." She frowned down at him. "I hope. His over-sharing has been kind of tedious. I really didn't need to learn so much about his mommy issues."

I struggled to prop Van up against the sofa. He kept sliding down again, with a glazed look on his face. "Why won't the plan work, Van? I thought you could track anyone."

"Can. Anyone. Jus' need blood, can find ev'ry vampire of that Bloodline in abou' five hundred miles." Van seemed to mull this over for a moment. "Huh," he said, sounding surprised. "I'm awesome." Sarah snorted.

"Right," I said, struggling to keep my voice calm and soothing. "So what's the problem? You can use my blood to find Hakon."

Van shook his head doggedly. "'S not like looking up an address. Can't tell who's who, apart from t' vampire the blood came from." He started to slump sideways again, and I caught him. "And Hakon's Bloodline? Big. Lotsa vampires."

"How many?" I asked. "Twenty? Fifty? A hundred?"

"Thousands."

There was a small silence.

"Shit," Sarah supplied succinctly.

"But you can look through their eyes?" I asked Van. He grunted confirmation. "So trawl through them all until you find the ones who are looking at my family."

"Thousands o' vampires," Van repeated patiently.

"Take too long. Can't look all at once. Head would explode." He made a vague motion with his hands. "Boom."

"Small loss," Sarah muttered. "So you're useless, then."

"Yes," Van agreed woefully.

"If only we had a bit of Ebon's blood—" I stopped, memory flashing on the hospital fight. The blood running down Ebon's face where Lily had clawed him, and the way the crimson drops had scattered as he'd shaken his head, trying to clear his eyes . . . "Sarah! Get your pajamas!" She opened her mouth, obviously about to inquire if I'd gone completely bonkers, but I cut her off. "I think Ebon might have bled on them. Go look!"

Sarah's face lit up in understanding. She dashed away, returning a moment later brandishing the crumpled, stained pajamas like a battle flag. Spreading them out on the floor, we both pored over the striped fabric.

"There," I said, pointing to a spray of rust-brown stains. "Is that Ebon's, Van?"

He blinked blearily at it. "'S dried on."

"Well, lick it or something." Even drugged into La-La Land, Van could still muster a remarkably good glare. I didn't care; I was fully prepared to force-feed him the whole outfit in a sandwich, if required. "*Please*, Van."

"A'right," he said reluctantly. "For you. Since you're a freak."

"Gee, *thanks*," I said, closing his groping hand around the cloth. "What a compliment. I'm touched."

"Me too," he said, both voice and expression painfully earnest. "Never met 'nyone like me b'fore." His voice went muffled as he mashed the fabric against his face. "Didn't think ever would. . . . 'S not Hakon's flavor. Mus' be t' cat. Can try tracking him wi' it later, at dark." Letting the pajama top fall again, he leaned his head back on the sofa, closing his eyes. "Nap till then."

I jabbed him in the shoulder, making him wince. "No. Now, Van!"

"Better wait until he sobers up," Sarah said. "Don't want him sending us off in the wrong direction like a cheap GPS."

"Got to wait 'nyway," Van said. "Can't use Bloodlines during day. Vampires asleep."

I checked my own Bloodlines. Sure enough, they were a mere whisper, far too quiet to follow. I couldn't even sense Brains, who was barely two feet away, floating belly up in its jar on the coffee table. "Crap. That means we'll have to go at night. They'll all be awake."

263

I flexed my hands, thinking about what Lily had said. Despite everything, there was one thing I didn't think she'd been lying about. "Well, I am a supervamp. If it's a straight fight, I'm pretty sure I can take them. It's not like they can actually kill me."

Sarah rolled her eyes. "Yeah, and your whole family are invulnerable immortals too. Think, Jane. You can bet Hakon will be spying on you as often as he can. You wade in there, and he'll promptly put a bullet through your mum's skull. You can't ambush him."

"I can." Van perked up, like a dog hearing the word *walkies*. "Can I? Please?"

"You are currently captaining the good ship *Stupid* through the seas of Crazy," Sarah informed him. She shrugged, glancing at me. "On the other hand, we don't have anyone else."

I looked at his hopeful expression. "Van, no offense, but how many vampires have you actually staked?"

Van subjected this to deep consideration. "Including you?"

"No. I got better."

"Then . . ." Van's lips moved silently. He seemed to be counting. "None."

"Okay," Sarah said after a pause. "You suck."

"'S not my fault," Van protested. "M' uncle never let me go out. Too valuable. Had to run away to take this job. I'll show him. Protect t' innocents, like Mother did." With great dignity, he drew himself upright, squaring his shoulders in determination. "Fight all t' vamp'rs, 'cept Jane. Ha."

"Great," I said as Van toppled over like a felled tree, ending up face-planted into the carpet. "Van can't do it, I can't do it—"

"Don't even think about me," Sarah said, waving one hand to indicate her frail form. "Not only am I sick, I'm also not insane." She saw my gaze move to Brains. "Okay, *you* are insane."

"I wasn't seriously contemplating it." I rubbed my forehead. "It's got to be me. No one else stands a chance. Maybe . . . maybe if I keep my eyes shut?"

"Brilliant," Sarah said witheringly. "Not only are you going to fight vampires blind, you're going to advertise to Hakon that something is up. Don't you think he'll be a little suspicious when he can't see anything through your eyes?"

An idea burst in my mind like a firework. "Then we have to give him something to look at." Rolling Van over, I rifled through his pockets until I found his wallet. I hoped his credit card limit was high enough to get all the supplies we'd need. "Hey, Superluminal?"

Sarah blinked at my use of her online name. "What?"

I grinned at her. "I want you to make me a vid."

Chapter 22

I just don't want you to get hurt," I said. I fought down
a rush of embarrassment, avoiding eye contact. "I mean,
we didn't get off to the best of starts, but I've come to feel
that there's a real connection between us. I'd feel awful if
anything happened to you. So, because I care for you"—I
took a deep breath—"I have to let you go."

There was a pause. A couple of leaves fell into the
canal. Brains nosed at them, then looked back up at me.

"Are you even listening?" I waved my arms. "Go!
Shoo! Swim away!"

Brains turned in a circle, surveying the muddy waters
of the canal, then neatly jumped out of the water and
back into its jar.

I groaned, rubbing at my eyes. The sun was only barely under the horizon, and I still wasn't properly awake. It was far too early in the evening to be trying to wrangle a goldfish. "Look, you can't come with us. If things go badly, it could get messy. Violent."

Brains bounced up and down in its jar like an excited puppy. It snapped its toothless mouth viciously.

"No. You are a *fish*. It would be carnage." I dumped it back out into the canal again, and held the jar up-ended above my head. "Go on, I mean it! You have to leave, otherwise Hakon can use you to spy on us. You can find me later with the Bloodline if you really miss me too much. But for now, be free! Return to your ancestral spawning grounds, or whatever." Concentrating on the Bloodline between us, I tried a sort of mental push. "As your sire, I command you—*go home.*"

With one last disappointed glance at me, Brains flicked its tail, disappearing into the murky depths of the canal.

"Huh." From the wake I could see on the surface of the water, Brains could superspeed with the best of them. I stood up again, dusting the dirt off my knees, and set off back to the house. Behind me, there was a brief, startled quack, and the splash of a struggling bird being yanked underwater.

The sun had set properly by the time I'd made it back to the house. I suddenly felt much more alert and energetic. Van was outside, folding up a wheelchair he'd liberated from a nearby shopping center. "Hi," I said, jogging up to him. "Brains is gone. How long until things kick off?"

Van glanced at his watch, doing some mental calculations. "Under ten minutes until Lily wakes up, twenty-three minutes for Ebenezer. Hakon should rise in about forty minutes, though I can't be precise. I don't know his exact age."

"Great." I picked up a shopping bag from near Van's feet, checking the contents. Two iPods and two video headsets, all present and correct. "Looks like we're all ready then." I hesitated, looking at Van out of the corner of my eye. "How're you doing?"

"I'm fine." Van did not look fine. His skin was pale, and he was moving a bit gingerly, as if afraid the top of his head might fall off. He still managed to make the heavy wheelchair look like it was made of Styrofoam as he hoisted it without apparent effort into the back of his van. He jerked his chin in the direction of the shopping bag. "Better than my credit rating anyway.

Uncle's going to—" He cut himself off, his habitual stoic expression turning even more stony.

Van hadn't taken the news about his organization's real employers well. Of course, Sarah's cheerful greeting of "Hey, did you know you guys work for the vampires?" as soon as he'd sobered up hadn't been the gentlest of ways to break it to him. He'd been rather quiet and withdrawn ever since. Given that I was feeling self-conscious around him too—having him jump from mortal enemy to staunch ally in the space of a day was enough to give me mental whiplash—it made for some awkward conversations.

Or in this case, awkward silences. I fiddled with one of the video headsets, pretending to be deeply interested in the technical specifications. I'd felt more comfortable when Van had been trying to cut my head off. At least that had been straightforward. I sneaked a peek at him, and found that he was studying the health and safety instructions on the back of the wheelchair with the same sort of intent fascination I'd been giving to the headset. The silence lengthened.

I was barely five minutes from being plunged into a life-or-death situation where one mistake could mean the end of my family. I should have been dreading Lily waking up. Instead, I was starting to wonder if she'd rise earlier if I prodded her.

"So," Van and I said at the same time, just as the silence was reaching a painful volume. We both stopped again, with a little wave for the other to go first. Another awkward pause. "Um, so," we chorused in inadvertent unison again.

"For God's sake, will you two get a *room*?" Sarah snapped from the shadowed depths of van. "I'm sitting right here, you know."

"Sarah!" I yelped, spinning away from Van to glower at where she was sitting cross-legged next to the chain-wrapped, slumbering Lily. I'd always thought it might be nice to have a little sister rather than a brother, but I was rapidly changing my mind. Certain that my face was bright red, I forced myself to turn back to Van. "Sorry. Uh, what were you about to say?"

Van wasn't blushing, but he'd turned about as expressive as the average brick wall. "You first."

"Oh. Okay." I bit my lip, glancing back into the van. Sarah had gone back to watching Lily for any sign of movement. Her usual cocky expression slid away, leaving her looking young and anxious. As I watched, she gently brushed a stray lock of auburn hair away from Lily's slack face.

It had been a surprise to find that Lily hadn't been using her real appearance. Asleep, she was a stunning redhead, amazingly tall and curvaceous with strong, lean muscles. When she walked down the street, she must have stopped guys like a traffic light. I couldn't imagine why she preferred her more subdued, dark-and-elegant look.

Or maybe I could. "I was wondering something," I said to Van. "Do you know who your vampire parent was?"

"No," he said curtly. "I told you before. My mother was captured and raped by a vampire."

"Your mother?" I'd forgotten about that. It rather torpedoed my half-formed suspicion out of the water. "Your mum was human? Are you sure?"

Van treated me to a do-you-think-I-am-an-idiot variation of his infinitely adaptable glare. Reaching into his coat, he pulled out a well-worn leather photo wallet and flipped it open. "There," he said. "Hunter-General Lucy Helsing."

A short, tough-looking brunette grinned up at me from the photo, a crossbow in one hand and a toddler in the other. Baby Van stared owlishly at the camera, chewing on a stake that a redheaded guy was trying unsuccessfully to wrestle away. The family resemblance between all three faces was unmistakable. "That's your mum and . . . her brother? Your uncle?"

Van nodded. "She died a couple of months after this, on a hunt. My uncle took over. Both the business and me." He folded the wallet shut again with care, tucking it back into the pocket next to his heart. "Why?"

"Oh, uh. Not important," I said hastily. So much for that theory. "Anyway. What were you going to say?"

Van thrust his hands deep into the pockets of his coat, hunching his shoulders. "Wondered if you wanted to go hunt some vampires sometime," he muttered at the ground.

I blinked. "Uh, yeah. That's kinda what we're about to do. Well, hopefully we won't actually have to fight, but—"

"No," Van interrupted. "After this. When we're done."

"When we're done killing vampires, do I want to go kill some vampires?" My perplexed frown deepened. "Um, not really. I'm kind of hoping to get back to doing normal things. No offense."

"Oh." Van was now looking at his boots as if he'd just discovered they'd been made from the tanned skin of his favorite kitten. "Right." He glanced at his watch again. "It's time. I'll . . . go."

I stared after him as he beat a retreat to the driver's compartment of the van. "What the heck was that all about?"

"You," Sarah remarked behind me in tones of deep pity, "are *such* an idiot."

I replayed the conversation in my head . . . and face-palmed. Van had said "Go hunt some vampires" in exactly the same tones a normal guy might say "Go see a movie." And I'd totally brushed him off. The guy who was risking everything to help me, and who coincidentally also had abs you could grate cheese with. "Oh, crap."

"Forget your love life and get back here," Sarah ordered. "Lily's waking up."

Reluctantly, I clambered into the van, reaching Sarah just as Lily's head lifted. I caught a glimpse of her hazel eyes as they fluttered open—and then they were black once more, filled with such raw anger that I flinched. But the expression was gone so fast I could almost believe I'd imagined it. Her sharp, elegant face set in emotionless lines, totally neutral as she looked down at the silver chains binding her. Her gaze flicked to me, then settled on Sarah. *"Et tu, Brute?"* she murmured.

Sarah looked stricken. "Lily, it's not what you think."

"Ebon called," I said, cutting over the top of her. "Hakon's holding my family hostage. He'll kill them unless we turn ourselves in." The van floor vibrated beneath us as Van started the engine, letting it idle in neutral.

"I see." Lily's shoulders twitched as she tested her chains. She looked back at me, and I felt the Bloodline between us surge like the tide coming in. "Xanthe darling, I do understand how you must—"

"Cut it out," I said through gritted teeth. The mental image of my family in danger was enough to counteract the worst of Lily's influence, but I still couldn't help but feel sorry for her. I was being an ungrateful child to even think of putting her at risk, when she'd given me the gift of unending life and power—"I *said*, cut it out, or I swear I really will turn you over to Hakon!"

"You will not," Sarah said indignantly. "Don't worry, Lily. No one's turning in anyone."

"But we're going to make Hakon think we are." I pulled Ebon's iPhone out of my pocket, switching on its video camera. "Sarah, move back a little, you're in the shot. Lily, you said you were an actress, right?"

Lily looked in bemusement from me to the phone I was pointing at her. At least she'd stopped trying to beat my brain flat with her influence. "Yes?"

I pressed the RECORD button. "Act captured."

It took a few hissed prompts of stage direction from Sarah to get Lily looking appropriately murderous, but I got a good ten minutes of footage before Van beeped the horn, indicating that Ebon was about to wake up. I saved the new video alongside the one that Sarah had taken of me earlier, and tossed her the phone. "You got enough there to do your thing?"

Sarah plugged the phone into her laptop, downloading the files. "Should do." The phone rang in her hand; she disconnected the cable and flipped it back to me. "I think that's for you. And now," she muttered, crouching over her keyboard with a ferocious scowl, "for the world's fastest and sloppiest vid."

Lily's general air of bafflement increased as Sarah began to key in commands at a breakneck pace. "What—" she started.

"No time!" HAKON, said the phone's screen. I took the call. "Ebon?"

"Jane," said Ebon's voice, sleep-blurred and rough. "Did you get her?"

"Yeah, she's captured. And Sarah's got Van at gunpoint, forcing him to drive us." Lily looked sharply at me. I put my finger over my lips. "Where are we meeting you?"

"It'll be somewhere in Croydon. I'll check exactly where Hakon wants you to go—he's not awake yet. As soon as he's up and has confirmed the capture, I'll call you back. Don't let her out of your sight, Jane." There was a pause. "And thank you." The line went dead.

"Xanthe, my darling," Lily said slowly. "What *are* you doing?"

"Making Hakon think that we're doing exactly what he wants." Picking up the second video headset and iPod, I went over to her. "Here's one we made earlier." I put the headset on her nose, and pressed PLAY on the video loaded into the connected iPod.

Lily's mouth made an O shape of understanding as she watched the video. "I *see*. And so will Hakon."

"Exactly." I turned to Sarah, my fingertips twitching nervously. "How's it going? Anything we can do to help?"

"Yes," Sarah snapped. The glow of the screen lit her delicate face from below, showing her intently focused expression. "If you're an expert in video-editing software, you can clip for me. Otherwise, everyone can shut up. I'm trying to *concentrate* here!"

The minutes crawled by. I kept a nervous eye on the iPhone clock, mentally counting down the time until Hakon would wake up. Sarah crouched over her laptop like a concert pianist. I checked through her eyes and was dizzied by frames of video leaping and jumping in arcane patterns. Her fingers flicked commands faster than I could follow.

Van honked the horn again, giving us our three-minute warning that Hakon was about to wake up. Just as I was starting to sweat about how close Sarah was cutting it, she sat back. "There! I've stretched it to two hours of footage, looping perfectly." She slid iPod and headset across to me, then dashed over to Lily to adjust her own headset. "That should—"

Her voice cut off, replaced by the recorded drone of the van as I shoved the video headset's earbuds in. On the screens in front of my eyes, Lily appeared, glaring.

"Wow." I couldn't even hear my own voice over the video's sound. There was nothing to tell that I wasn't looking at the real Lily. I switched perspective, hijacking Sarah's senses. Through her eyes, I could see both Lily and myself, our heads swathed in hardware.

The phone rang.

Sarah picked it up. "This is Sarah," she said. It was

weird hearing her voice through her ears rather than my own; it sounded deeper and stronger. "Jane's in back, busy watching Lily."

"I know!" Ebon sounded ecstatic. "Hakon's confirmed the capture. He says to tell Jane it's a most satisfying sight. Meet us at the Croydon Travelodge. Room 301."

"See you there." Sarah turned the phone off. She cracked her knuckles, shaking out her hands. "Ow. I think I have blisters." She crawled over to Lily and started undoing the chains.

I got to my own feet, watching Lily carefully through Sarah's eyes. Lily's shoulders and back tensed as she fumbled free of the last of her restraints, and my own muscles coiled—but with a quick, blind glance in my direction, she relaxed back into her usual attitude of studied languor. I guessed she must have sensed my readiness to deck her if she tried anything. Her long fingers brushed her headset in exploratory fashion. "I'll assume all is well," she said, speaking too loud. "But whatever you're planning—and I'm presuming it's some sort of rescue—I'm not going to be much use until we can all take these things off."

"It's okay—" Sarah started, then scowled as she realized that of course Lily couldn't hear her through the headphones. She caught up one of the vampire's hands instead, giving it a reassuring squeeze, then guided her out of the van.

"Ah, so I'm to stay here," Lily said as Sarah pushed her up the garden path. I still wasn't thrilled about this, personally, but Sarah had flat-out refused to help at all if we took Lily into danger with us. "Excellent. Xanthe, I'm monitoring you—if I see your view change, I'll know it's safe to come to your aid." She entered the house, then popped her head back out to add, "But this tape is going to get excruciatingly monotonous. Would you mind hurrying as much as possible, darlings?"

I waited until Sarah had returned before banging on the wall. "Van!"

He appeared at the back of the van. "I'm ready." He clutched a bottle containing the world's worst cocktail— a shot of vodka, orange juice, and the shredded remnants of Sarah's nightshirt. Van had insisted on the vodka. "Now?"

"Do it."

Van threw back the drink. For a nasty moment I thought it was going to come back up, but, with a slightly sick expression, Van swallowed manfully. His green eyes unfocused.

"Found him." He pointed off through the wall; Sarah hastily marked the direction with a piece of tape. Van's head tilted, forehead furrowing in concentration. "Ebenezer is standing next to your family in what looks like a . . . warehouse, I think. Two other vampires are there too, talking with him. They're . . . they're Hakon's Bloodline, Jane; they're speaking Swedish. Can't understand it. Ebenezer seems upset by something, but they're calm. There's a large van behind them. Blue, yellow trim. Can't read the license plates." He held up a hand to forestall interruptions, as both Sarah and I opened our mouths to ask questions. "Wait, now they're opening up the van doors. Ebenezer is helping your family inside—they're handcuffed, but they look unharmed. He's . . . no, he's not getting in. He's closing the doors. The Scandinavian vampires have gone round to the front of the van—I think they've got in, I can't see them anymore. The taillights have come on."

I frowned. "Are they actually taking my family to the place they said? I thought they'd go back on the deal."

"They will," Sarah said. "In some way, they will."

"They have," Van interrupted. "The van hasn't moved. Ebenezer's opened the doors up again. Your family is getting out. I don't know what Ebenezer's expression is—there aren't any other viewpoints to look through—but your parents look . . . upset. The van's driving off without them."

Sarah looked at me, giving me an interesting view of my own expression of dawning enlightenment. "What was all that about?"

"They *are* going back on the deal," I said, pieces falling into place in my head. "Just in case Van was looking through the Scandinavian bloodline, they staged it to look like they were driving off with my parents. But they aren't taking them there at all. They've left them with Ebon—but they don't know we can see him."

"I think Ebenezer's taking them back deeper into the warehouse," Van said. "They're in a room, a depot, racks of shelves. Boxes. Different sizes. Letters on them. They're—" He shook his head. "I'm losing it. The blood's nearly run dry. I think they're going through a door—STAFF ONLY—it's gone." His eyes refocused. "That's all I can do."

Sarah let out her breath. "Well, we got a direction," she said, despondent. "But that could have been anywhere, from the description."

"What did the boxes say?" I demanded. "Think, Van!"

"I couldn't read proper words; it was gibberish!" He

struggled, brows knotting as he tried to piece it together. "I saw . . . it looked like . . . Hopen? And . . . Komplement. Billy, that was the only real word. I'm sorry, Jane, Sarah, I tried . . ." He trailed off, looking from Sarah to me. "What?"

"There's only one place that names things like that," Sarah whispered. She spun to face me. "And there's one in Croydon."

Through Sarah's eyes, I saw my own jaw drop open. "And it's even Scandinavian," I said. "They're in IKEA."

Chapter 23

Despite all our plans on how to get into IKEA— I'd proposed trying a staff-only entrance, Van wanted to climb the sides of the building to find a ventilation shaft, and Sarah was in favor of shooting the security guards and stealing their uniforms—in the end we walked in the front door.

"Open until midnight?" Sarah muttered as we rode the elevator down to the warehouse area. Her hands nervously toyed with Lily's gun, hidden under the blanket over her legs. "No wonder Hakon is using this as his hideout. Who desperately needs to buy shelving in the middle of the night?"

"Those of us who only wake up at night," I said,

pushing her wheelchair out as the doors opened. A passing late-night shopper did a double take at my video glasses; I ducked my head, feeling horribly conspicuous. Despite the anxious churning in my stomach, I couldn't help slowing down as we passed a mouth-watering display of innovative storage solutions. "And you have to admit, the shelves *are* awesome."

Sarah looked from me to Van—who was also eyeing the unit with a wistful expression—and sighed in exasperation. "Snap out of it, you two," she said, deliberately turning her head away from the enthralling cupboards so that I lost sight of them. "Try raptly contemplating a store map instead." My point of view swung as she looked around the cavernous depot, with its towering racks of plain brown boxes. "How're we going to find where they're storing Billy and Komplement?"

"Easy. Van, how big were the boxes you saw?" I poked Sarah to turn to look at him, and saw the dimensions he sketched in the air. "Great. Then . . . Sarah, look around again?" I considered the shelves nearby. "Okay. We want to go that way."

Sarah followed the line of my pointing finger. "How do you know?"

"Because I'm a vampire," I said. I shrugged as we

started off down the row. "Believe me, if you were a hyperacute OCD sufferer with supernaturally sharp senses, the organization system would be obvious to you—"

Van grabbed my shoulder, yanking me back before I could step into the aisle. He tapped his forehead in warning. His internal radar must have picked up a vampire, courtesy of the bit of my blood he'd drunk while we were in the parking lot. I could feel a sort of white-noise hum, like a detuned radio, over my own Bloodlines. Someone related to me was approaching.

"—so irritating that the signs don't tell you that the last piece you need is out of stock before you've collected everything else," a woman's frazzled voice was saying in the next aisle. "Who on earth would want to buy the wardrobe body and shelves without the door?"

"Love, don't worry about putting it back where it came from. Dump it anywhere so we can leave," a man said, sounding fed up.

"Excuse me, madam," said a third voice. Sarah peeked through a gap in the boxes, and I saw a big, blond guy stalking toward a middle-aged couple. Sarah's breath drew in as she read his name tag—HELLO MY NAME IS SVEN HAKONSSON—and she ducked back down into the shadows. "What are you doing?"

"About time!" said the first man. His voice rose in indignation. "I've been looking for a member of staff— all on a bloody tea break, were you? I want to make a complaint—"

"One moment, sir. Madam, I said *what* are you *doing*?"

"I'm putting these boxes back. We decided we don't want them after all—"

"You're putting them in the *wrong place*." Hello-my-name-is-Sven's voice dropped into a low, venomous snarl that sent a chill up my spine.

"Look, mate, you can't talk to my wife like that! I demand to speak to your manager!"

There was a moment's pause. "Certainly," said the vampire blandly. "Quick, look over there!"

"Wh—?"

I heard two muffled thumps in quick succession, followed by a rustle. Sarah risked a quick peek round the corner. The vampire had loaded the limp forms of the shoppers into their own shopping cart, and was covering it with a tarpaulin. Whistling, he strode briskly off, pushing the cart in front of him.

It was my turn to grab Van's arm. His muscles were bunched with outrage. "No!" I whispered. "They're only unconscious, I can hear them breathing. Follow him!"

We shadowed Sven through the maze, Van keeping us two aisles behind and out of sight. The trail ended at a plain, handleless door marked STAFF ONLY. Sarah started to push at it, but Van caught her hand, shaking his head warningly.

" . . . a whole store to choose from, and you bring back this," a woman was saying inside, sounding aggravated. "You know I hate O-negative."

"They deserved it," Sven replied. "Anyway, it makes a good seasoning."

"Yeah, well, *you're* not the one who has to glamour them. A glass of O-negative is like drinking neat Tabasco."

"So submit the application form to kill them instead. Hakon will approve it. We're well under the fatality quota for the quarter."

"We are? I missed the last newsletter." The woman sounded happier. "Well, stash them over there for now; we'll process them later. The boss wants us upstairs. Did you see that memo . . . ?" Her voice trailed away into the distance as the two of them left.

Van put his palm on the door, pushing, but it didn't move. "There's no handle on this side," he muttered.

"Let me try." I misted, slipped under the door, and

re-formed on the other side. Thankfully, the video headset stayed with me, like my clothes had; unfortunately, being separated from Sarah left me blind. The now-familiar video of Lily glared at me as I fumbled for the door handle. "Great," I said as the door opened and Sarah's eyes gave me a view of myself standing there. "Let's move—" Then I stopped as I saw what was in the rest of the room.

"Well," Sarah said after a second of collective appalled silence, "I think we've just discovered why shopping here always seems to take so long."

Banks of white, coffin-sized cubbies lined the walls. Each one had a pair of manacles hanging at the top, and an empty blood donation bag at the bottom, tubing neatly coiled. A rack of hypodermic needles gleamed in the center of the room, next to a scrubbed steel operating table and a humming refrigerator. The whole setup looked horribly efficient, like a factory production line. Each of the cubicles was precisely identical.

"The Blüd System," Sarah read from a sheet of paper taped to the side of the nearest cabinet. She examined the pictorial operating instructions far more closely than I would have liked. "Huh. Now there's something that's not in the catalogue."

Van made a low growl deep in his chest. The shopping cart full of unfortunate shoppers was parked in the corner; he pulled the tarpaulin off, then shoved the cart out the door. "I hope someone finds them," he muttered.

I swallowed hard, trying to ignore the scent of blood hanging enticingly in the air. "It's the best we can do for now. Anyway, I think we've found the right place. Which way?"

Van's eyes went vague for a second, then he shook his head. "I can't see your family using any of the nearby vampires. Everyone of your Bloodline seems to be congregating in a room upstairs." A slightly bemused expression crossed his face. "Someone's switched on a PowerPoint presentation about building workplace team morale."

"Let's hope it's really long and boring." As I spoke, I pushed Sarah across the horrible room, wishing that she would stop looking with interest at the blood-draining equipment. The door on the other side led to a long, featureless white corridor, and a staircase off to the left. Assuming that Hello-my-name-is-Sven and friend had gone up that way, I picked the corridor instead, desperately praying that Hakon had left Ebon somewhere down here to guard my family alone. We hastened past various innocuous, perfectly ordinary offices and meeting rooms.

A door opened ahead. Out of it stepped a familiar white-blond figure, with a quick glance left and right. His pale blue eyes widened in astonishment as he saw us.

I vaulted over the wheelchair in a blur of superspeed, abruptly getting a view of my own back as I lunged for Ebon. I slammed into him so hard we were both knocked off our feet, sliding back into the room he'd just left. I grappled blindly with him, trying to pin him down. Sarah was still out in the corridor, so I had no way to see what I was doing—

"No!" Hands closed over my wrist. I jerked away, twisting to strike at whoever was attacking me, and came perilously close to knocking my little brother's head off his shoulders.

"Zack!" I yelled, pulling my blow at the last second. Thankfully, Sarah had entered the room just in time for me to realize who was attacking me. But the effort made me lose my grip on Ebon; he heaved, twisting, and I was flung to one side. I bounced to my feet, only to find that Zack had flung himself between us. "Zack, get out of the way!"

"No!" Zack wailed. He spread his arms wide, shielding the groggy Ebon. "You can't kill him! He's a *Victorian!*"

Chapter 24

Sarah, and me through her, stared at my little brother. His face was dirty and tracked with snot and tears, but he seemed unharmed and rational. Apart from the fact that he was determinedly shielding the vampire who'd kidnapped him. How fast could Stockholm syndrome set in?

"Xanthe!" Mum grabbed my shoulders, pulling me into a bone-crushing hug. It lasted barely a second—then she thrust me to arm's length, shaking me hard enough to rattle the video glasses. "What are you doing here? We told you to stay away!"

Zack's defiant gaze had slid to focus on something over my—no, Sarah's—shoulder. His eyes widened.

"Janie, look out!"

I dropped in a rolling dive, as Sarah spun her wheelchair in a sharp, practiced motion—but we found ourselves looking at nothing more threatening than Van, who had sprouted a crossbow and was trying to aim at Ebon without also skewering Zack.

Unfortunately, my surprise acrobatics made him jerk the crossbow, instinctively tracking my motion.

"YOU!" roared my dad, snatching up his plastic chair and lunging at the vampire hunter. My mum was only a second behind him, wielding a ream of printer paper. To his credit, in the face of this outraged parental assault, Van dropped his crossbow and simply cowered.

"Mum! Dad! No!" I yelled as Dad cracked Van over the head with the chair. "He's here to help *rescue* you!" I grabbed my dad's impromptu weapon as he raised it for another swing, while Sarah charged her wheelchair into Mum, knocking her back. "Stop it!"

"But that's the vampire hunter guy," Zack protested. He was still hovering protectively in front of Ebon, who was leaning against the wall and looking as if he had not yet caught up with current events.

"Yes, but he's on our side now." At least, he was on my side. I wasn't sure what side Zack was on. "Mum,

Dad, this is Van Helsing—really," I added, as three sets of eyebrows shot up. Even though he was still reeling from being battered with tasteful furniture, Van managed a resigned sigh. "And this is Sarah. She's—uh." How best to put it? "She's sort of the protégé of Lily, my vampire sire. And she's also the person who received my heart after I died but before I became a vampire, but when I rose from the dead my heart became a vampire heart, so now we've got this sort of psychic-bond thing where I feed off her blood and can use her eyes and ears, which is how I'm able to see and hear you now even though I'm wearing this headset."

When you said it really fast, it almost made sense.

My family, as one, boggled.

"Hi," Sarah said with the briefest of glances around at them all. "Jane, can you info dump later? I remind you we've still got dozens of vampires above our heads. Kill the freak, so we can get out of here."

For a second I thought she meant Zack. He spread himself even wider in front of Ebon. "You can't hurt him. He's an endangered species!"

"Vampires are not endangered." Van's tone made it clear that it was his life's work to rectify this regrettable situation.

"No, not that," Zack said dismissively. "He's a Victorian!"

"Brainwashed," Van muttered.

"Crazy," Sarah proclaimed.

"Steampunk," I corrected with a sigh. "Zack, just because he knows how to make frock coats or whatever—"

"He's so awesome, Janie! He went to the *Great Exhibition*." Zack's entire face was alight with enthusiasm. "And he worked in a proper factory, and was a subscription member to save up for railway trips, and he saw Brunel, and—"

"And, in case it escaped your notice," I interrupted, "he kidnapped you."

Dad cleared his throat. "Actually, he didn't."

"I told you, Jane," Ebon croaked. He put his hands on Zack's shoulders and bodily moved my protesting brother aside. "It wasn't my idea to capture your family. I've been trying to free them."

"It's true." Dad held up his left arm, displaying a snapped set of manacles.

"Mr. Lee seems to have had a change of heart regarding his current employer," Mum said.

I stared at Ebon through Sarah. He had his hands in the air, but was otherwise totally ignoring Van and his crossbow. His head turned to look straight at me, which put him in profile to my current line of sight. What I could see of his face bore a curiously calm, resigned expression. "But why?"

"*Jane!*" Sarah deliberately turned her eyes away from Ebon, treating me to a view of the storage units lining the room. "Either shoot him or decide to trust him for now, but let's move!"

"I vote for the former," Van said. Zack emitted a howl of protest and tried to tackle Ebon to the ground, bodyguard style.

I made up my mind. "All right—*no!*" I yelped, as Van's finger tightened on the trigger. "I mean, all right, we won't kill him." For one thing, my little brother would have made my unlife a living hell. "Don't make me regret this later, Ebon."

Ebon, with Zack still clinging to his waist like a squirrel trying to climb a greased tree, bowed solemnly. "My thanks," he said, dropping his hands and gently disentangling himself from Zack. "I can but hope that there *is* a later." He cocked his head, studying my video apparatus. "That, by the way, is most ingenious."

"Thanks. Seems to be working so far. Lily's wearing one too. Did you have a plan for getting out of here?"

Ebon nodded. "There is a fire exit down the corridor, which leads to the car park." His mouth quirked ruefully. "After that, I confess my plans were somewhat nebulous."

"We'll work on that. Van, vampire update?"

"Still gathered up above us. If we hurry—" Van broke off in mid-sentence, his head snapping up toward the ceiling. Utter horror filled his face. "Jane! The vents!"

Everyone looked up. A thick, silvery mist was starting to trickle through the ventilation grills set in the ceiling. A very familiar type of mist.

"*Run!*" I yelled, ripping off the video glasses as the first vampire solidified. The abrupt return of my own senses made me stagger, momentarily perplexed by being back behind my own eyeballs. My head felt full of wasps. Vampires were condensing like raindrops, falling ceaselessly from the ceiling. Unfamiliar hands grabbed me; I reflexively punched straight into the vampire's chest, crushing his heart, and felt the hands dissolve again as he died.

Superspeed rushed through my veins. I whirled, ducking another vampire and ripping out her heart too. A weight crashed down onto me as a vampire resolidified right on my shoulders; but I'd barely started to stagger before Van had shot a bolt directly into its chest. Ebon lunged past me, hurling two vampires away from my family.

I pulled everything I could down the Bloodline—no time to consider Sarah now—making myself faster, stronger, tougher. Even the other vampires seemed slow to me now. I dodged blows that would have taken my head off, and returned them with punches that sent my opponents hurtling through walls. Someone managed to get a stake through my chest; I ignored it and killed another vampire.

We were doomed from the start, of course.

There were too many of them. I caught a glimpse of Ebon vanishing under a wave of vampires piling onto him like a rugby scrum. Van kept smoothly reloading, firing, reloading, eyes tight shut the entire time—but then his left hand was empty, and in the second it took him to reach under his coat for more ammunition, they had him. He went down too, and now there were even more vampires surrounding me. I whirled, ready to fight them all—

And put my hands in the air. "I surrender."

Vampires had my family. Two of them held my struggling parents without any effort at all. Another had Zack's arm twisted viciously up behind his back, immobilizing him. No one held onto Sarah—they didn't need to. She sprawled in her wheelchair like a puppet with cut strings, motionless.

The room suddenly seemed very quiet. Hakon's vampires ringed me, out of arm's length. I could hear the thunder of my family's hearts, Zack's helpless sobs of pain.

Every vampire in the room looked up, all at the same instant, like dogs hearing their master's whistle. Even I did it.

Something was coming down the Bloodline. I could feel it slipping closer, stalking down my veins. Something huge, and dark, and silent, and old . . .

Mist swirled down from the vents, and solidified. And there, unmistakably, stood Hakon.

Chapter 25

He was a kid. Just a tiny kid. No more than seven or eight, small face very solemn, his golden hair as neat as if he were about to pose for a school photo. The stark whiteness of his perfectly tailored silk shirt and trousers gave an illusion of warmth to his pallid skin. He looked perfectly innocent—except that no child ever stood so still.

"You again," Mum said to Hakon, scowling aggressively even though her voice wobbled. "Don't you dare—"

"Silence," Hakon said mildly, and my mum shut up instantly. *That* scared me more than any mere display of power. Zack had gone still as a frightened rabbit, huge eyes fixed on Hakon. Dad tried to step between him and the Elder, only to hiss in pain as the vampire holding him jerked him back.

Hakon stretched on his toes, peering up into my face. His blue eyes transfixed me: bright, curious, and utterly merciless. Oh, we were so very dead. I couldn't help glancing from him to the discarded video headset by my feet. How had he known . . . ?

As if reading my thoughts, one corner of Hakon's mouth curved upward. He pointed to the ceiling of the room.

I followed the line of his finger and groaned, suddenly feeling incredibly dumb. We'd spent all that time worrying about the supernatural threat, when all he'd needed to see us were—"Security cameras."

Hakon's tight, thin-lipped smile sat very oddly on his little-boy face. "Do not think me a displaced relic, Xanthe Jane Greene, a piece of history transported into a strange modern world." Even his voice was just a kid's voice, high and clear. "I have traveled through one thousand years—one day at a time."

I heard a muffled curse off to one side, followed by scuffling sounds. Hakon glanced that way. "Ah," he said, turning. There was something unnatural about the way he went from perfectly still to motion to perfectly still again. It made it seem as though he hadn't really moved. "Yes. Let me see also the hunters' secret knife, their treacherous feeder of ravens. Bring him out."

Three vampires hauled Van into view. Apart from a bloody nose and an expression of deep disgust, he seemed fine. Hakon looked him up and down, head cocked, while Van attempted to ignite the Elder vampire through the sheer force of his glare.

"There is no mistaking your parentage," Hakon said at last, sounding mildly aggrieved. "And how Lily managed *that* without my knowledge, I will be most eager to discover." Both Van and myself blinked, as Hakon turned to one of his vampires. "Disarm him. Carefully, but miss nothing." The goon set about what quickly proved to be a lengthy task. Van had weapons in places I hadn't even imagined. It was a miracle he'd been able to walk at all.

"And what of the lioness's grandson?" Hakon swiveled precisely on his heels to face the other pile of vampires, the motion so clipped and fast it looked robotic. "Where is my cat?"

One at a time, the vampires gingerly disentangled themselves. They stood up, separating to reveal——nothing.

Hakon's angelic face never changed. He glanced at two of his people, a mere flick of the eyes. They dissolved into mist, swirling briefly around the room like a whirlwind before streaming upward into the air vents.

High up on one of the shelving units behind Hakon, the tiniest flicker of motion caught my attention. It was a flash of something slinking across the top of the unit: a slender, sand-colored shape, hard to see against the beige walls and ceiling. A pair of triangular ears poked over the edge of the upper shelf.

Ebon? With a mighty effort, I kept my gaze fixed on Hakon. Out of the very corner of my eye, I saw the ears flatten out of sight again.

Hakon had gone back to studying me. He wrapped one small hand around the stake through my chest. Without any effort, he pulled it out and tilted his head to watch as my bones and skin knitted back together. "Now, that may be the most interesting thing I have encountered for centuries."

So Ebon had been right. Hakon really *was* curious about me. Which meant . . . I had something to bargain with.

I took a deep breath, shoving my fear aside. "I *am* interesting," I said. "The invulnerability, the shared senses, the way I don't need any other blood . . ." Oh yeah. He was definitely interested. "I can tell you everything you need to know. I'll help you. But first—" Hakon's eyes narrowed, and I gulped, feeling that gathering of power down the Bloodline like thunderclouds massing on the horizon. "But first you have to let my family go."

"That I cannot do, Xanthe Jane Greene."

"You don't need them as hostages to control me. Look, I'm not stupid." I jerked my head to indicate Hakon's descendants, and the situation in general. "I can't fight you, and I can't run. So I'm giving up. Surrendering. Let my family go, and I'm yours."

"Me too," Van said staunchly. I could have kissed him.

"Again I tell you, I cannot." Hakon turned to address my parents. "What will you do, should I accept your daughter's bargain? Will you take your remaining child and retreat peacefully, never again to trouble me nor mine?"

"Like hell," Mum snarled.

"*Janet*," Dad said. "Sir, of course we would. *Wouldn't we*, honey?"

"What—oh." Mum paused. "Yes. Yes, we would. Of course." I winced.

Hakon wasn't fooled either. "You see, Xanthe Jane

304

Greene," he said. "Loyalty binds both ways, like blood. I cannot release your family while you remain, for they would be wolves on my trail forevermore. And while mortal lives are brief, blood feuds are heirlooms, handed down. I do not care to have a stake planted through me by your brother's daughter's son. So." He held out one hand, palm up. "Let me make you a different offer."

"What sort of offer?" I said suspiciously.

"The same that I make all my vassals. You and your family will be under my protection. I shall provide for you shelter, food, a stipend. Your family shall live in one of my towns. They shall not be free to leave, true, but I will allow you to visit them, as it pleases me. None but I shall have power over them; no vampire will touch them, save at my command. You will serve me whole-heartedly and well, and in return they shall be safe."

There was a small silence. Zack looked at me, "Huh?" practically hovering above his head. My mum was shaking her head, looking grim. Dad opened his mouth, but I made a small gesture at him, silently pleading him to let me handle the talking. "Serve you doing what?" I said to Hakon.

Hakon tilted his head a little. "Do you know what binds vampires, Xanthe Jane Greene?" He pointed at my parents. "Humans? They are so blind, they don't even realize we are among them." His finger swung toward Van. "The hunters? Laughable pawns, easily bribed. So, what is the only thing that keeps us in check?"

I got the feeling he didn't mean paper clips and Scrabble tiles. "What?"

"Other vampires," Hakon said softly. "Delicate webs of alliances and pacts, enforcing rules to divide the human herd between us. The only thing that keeps us Elders in check is other Elders."

"Jane, he wants you to be his assassin," Van said. He did not look at all happy, though it was difficult to tell whether this was due to Hakon's proposal, or the fact that he was now down to his underwear. The vampire searching him was eyeing his boots speculatively. "He wants to rule the vampire world." His searcher pulled a hidden knife out of the sole of Van's shoe, sighed, and started undoing the laces.

"Yes," Hakon said, perfectly calm. He spread his hands. "Would that be such a terrible thing, Xanthe Jane Greene? I follow the old ways, of loyalty and oaths. My vassals will attest that I am a just lord. And," he shrugged slightly, "what evil have you seen me do?"

I stared at him—so small, so fragile, so harmless.

My mind flashed on the white, waiting ranks of blood-collection cubicles. I thought of the undercurrent of fear in Ebon's voice, whenever he'd spoken of Hakon.

I wondered what Sven had meant, when he'd casually mentioned a quota for killing people.

"Okay," I croaked, past the dryness in my throat.

"You swear your oath to me, for now and all time?"

I swallowed. "Yeah."

"Xanthe," Mum said, just as Dad said, "Baby Jane, are you sure?"

"My decision," I said to them, then, to Hakon, "Okay. I'll do it."

"Swear loyalty and obedience to me then, Xanthe Jane Greene," Hakon said. "On your blood, and on the blood of your family, and on the blood of your gods, swear it."

"I swear loyalty and obedience to you, on . . ." My mind had gone blank. "On, um, all those things, and stuff."

Who cared? It was only words, after all. Hakon might believe in blood oaths and loyalty and all that crap, but *I* wasn't some thousand-year-old baby barbarian. I'd swear whatever he wanted—and then double-cross him the instant his back was turned.

"I accept your fealty, and give you my protection in return." Hakon gave me a small, solemn bow. "I will reward loyalty with loyalty, and obedience with honor, and treachery . . ." He straightened, tilting his chin up to look me straight in the eye—and all my half-formed thoughts of rebellion dropped dead.

"And treachery," Hakon said softly in his sweet, childish voice, "I will meet not with death, but life eternal. For should you betray me, I shall turn your family myself. And then I shall torture them, daily, for one thousand years, until they are nothing more than mad husks that have only ever known pain." A bright smile lit his face, and he reached out to pat my hand. "Of course, it shall not come to that. Now, your first task shall be to snare my wayward granddaughter. For too long Lily has evaded me. You shall catch her, and her long torment shall begin at last."

"Not so fast," said Sarah's cold, hard voice. She sat upright in her wheelchair, glaring at us all. "You didn't cut any deals with *me*."

Her loaded gun, reversed, pointed straight at her own heart.

Chapter 26

N obody move," Sarah ordered as vampires bristled in her direction. "One twitch, and I kill myself *and* your precious supervamp, little boy. Then you can kiss all your grand plans good-bye."

Hakon made a tiny, downward motion with one hand, and all of his vampires subsided again. His pale eyebrows rose. "Can you not control your soul's vessel, Xanthe Jane Greene?"

"Uh—" I eyed Sarah. Her finger was white on the trigger; there wasn't even a millimeter of slack. There was no way I could suck her unconscious fast enough. "Actually, no."

"Don't you *dare* ignore me!" Sarah yelled at Hakon.

He said nothing in return. His own gaze was focused on the gun, and his face had lost a little of its eerie calm. He moved to the side, circling Sarah. Her eyes swiveled, but she couldn't keep him in view without turning her wheelchair, which she couldn't do without both hands. He was now standing nearly behind Sarah, where she couldn't possibly turn to aim at him before he could get out of the way; his vampires relaxed slightly.

Sarah's eyes rolled, as if trying to see through the back of her head—then, quite suddenly, fixed on me. "Keep an eye on him for me, okay, Jane?" she said, seemingly casual.

I stared at her. She had a weird, abstracted look, her eyes not actually focusing on me. It reminded me of Van's expression when he was using the Bloodlines.

"I said to keep an eye on *him*," Sarah repeated, through gritted teeth. "Not me."

Was she using *my* senses now? I flicked my attention to Hakon, who was watching Sarah carefully; out of the corner of my eye, I saw Sarah give me the tiniest nod. She *was*.

Which probably meant that she'd sense any motion I made even before I started to make it. Wonderful.

"Girl, don't be silly," my mum said. "These theatrics

won't help." She seemed more baffled than worried. I had a horrible suspicion that she hadn't really understood the whole heart thing.

"It's all right, Sarah," Dad said much more soothingly. He was the closest to her; he took a cautious step in her direction, hands raised in the air. The vampire who'd been holding him had let go, obviously far more worried by the crazy girl with the gun than the unarmed middle-aged painter. "We're all going to be okay. Everything's fine."

"For you all, yes!" Sarah pressed the muzzle of the gun harder against her chest. Dad stopped dead. "You're all *so happy* to sign up with the bad guys. Well, I'm not." Her angry eyes met mine, focusing properly this time. "And I will die before I let you sell out Lily!"

"I'm sure Hakon will let her swear loyalty too," I said rather desperately.

"No," Hakon said flatly. "I shall not. I do not accept the fealty of kin-betrayers. I will chain and cage the she-wolf if I must, but she will not sit at my hearth."

"Like Lily would want to, you little bastard," Sarah snarled. "Now listen. Either you let us all walk out of here, or I end this, right now."

"Such loyalty," Hakon said with a shake of his head.

"And yet, so misplaced. Tell me, vassal's vessel, where is your Lily now? Xanthe Jane Greene, perhaps you would look through your sire's eyes?"

In all the excitement, I'd completely forgotten about Lily. For an instant, my hopes soared. Lily was clever and powerful; she could rescue us. Surely, she wouldn't abandon Sarah . . .

On the other hand, from Hakon's smug expression, I was willing to bet that Lily was not, in fact, rushing to our aid.

I peeked up the Bloodline. The endless loop of myself no longer played in front of Lily's eyes; she'd removed her goggles and headphones. Instead, she was looking out through a car windshield, rain splattering the glass as she drove. I saw a motorway sign flash past, indicating that she was heading north.

"She's running away," I told Sarah.

"Good," she said fiercely. "I'm glad. Lily's going to get away, and one day, little boy, she's going to come back and then *she'll* be the Elder! Hope you've memorized some good books, because you're going to be spending ten thousand years in silver." She took a deep breath. "I'm sorry, Jane."

"No!" Van exclaimed, muscles bunching—but he

didn't dare move toward her.

"Sarah, please, I'm begging you," I gabbled, frantic as her face went very calm. "My family—"

"I'm sorry," she repeated. "But we did make a deal."

"Before you so nobly sacrifice yourself for your liege," Hakon said, somehow managing to *not* sound totally sarcastic, "there is one thing I feel you should know. It was not your father, Sarah Chana."

Everyone except Sarah looked at him in confusion. I had no idea what was going on—but I could feel the blood draining from Sarah's face, and the catch of her breath in her throat.

"Suck sunlight, bastard," Sarah spat, though her voice shook. "I was there."

"Yes, you were." Hakon clasped his hands behind his back, like a kid at a school recital. "You saw. You saw your father draw his gun, at the culmination of that terrible fight. You saw him shoot your mother, four times, and then escape into the night. Yes, you saw. *Do not*," he said suddenly, forcefully, as Sarah's hand trembled on the trigger. "You will not die of hearing this, Sarah Chana—you will live. Because I tell you that he did not kill her. You saw only what you were supposed to see. *Exactly* what you were supposed to see." He paused.

"Lily is a very gifted shape-shifter."

"You're lying!" Sarah shouted. "You're just trying to stop me—"

"I also saw it. I also was there," he interrupted. "I have ten thousand eyes through which to see, but there are some that interest me more than others. And Lily is *very* interesting. I gave her free rein, letting her run, in order to see what she would do. I snatched glimpses through her eyes, slowly putting together a picture of her intentions. I watched as she acquired a sudden fascination with medical records. I watched as she found someone with a certain condition. And I watched as she took steps to ensure that you would be bound to her. It was not your father who shot your mother, Sarah Chana. It was Lily. Your father was already dead."

Sarah had gone whiter than Hakon. She shook her head in mute denial.

"She stripped away every person you loved, so that she alone could take that role. She has been planning this"—Hakon gestured from Sarah to Van to myself—"for some time." His head cocked. "Did you not find it a little too much of a coincidence, Xanthe Jane Greene, Sarah Chana? A girl who loves vampires, in need of a heart transplant . . . and a girl who loves vampires, able to donate her heart? Did it never occur to you what a *convenient* car crash that was, Xanthe Jane Greene?"

I wasn't sure which one of us was making our heart stutter now. Blood pounded in my head.

Dad was staring at me in horror. "The police never found the driver of the other car," he whispered.

"It all fits," Mum said slowly. "It does fit together."

Sarah's wild eyes met my own. "Lily? Are you there?" Tears spilled down her cheeks, but she still held the gun steady. "Jane, is she listening?"

I realized what she wanted, and tuned into the Bloodline. Immediately, I heard Lily's voice: "I'm listening." She spoke to no one, alone in the car she drove. "Jane, please. You must tell her it isn't true, any of it."

"Sure," I said reflexively. "Sarah, Lily says Hakon's lying." I kicked myself the instant the words left my mouth. *Damn* my desire to do whatever Lily said. If I'd lied, said that Lily had confessed, maybe I could have got Sarah to put the gun down.

Small chance of that now. Sarah's whole face brightened with desperate hope. "Lily? It is all lies, isn't it? You—you didn't . . . you wouldn't."

"Of course I didn't," Lily said soothingly. "Hakon's a monster, you know that. He's saying whatever he can

315

think up in order to make you join him. Sarah, my poor darling, I do love you. You must know that."

Her voice was so gentle and warm that I couldn't help but repeat her words. Sarah glowed in response, her trembling lip firming again. Hakon let out a small, disappointed sigh, shaking his head as though despairing of our gullibility. I didn't know who to believe anymore. What Hakon had said all made sense, but Lily sounded so sincere, so loving. . . .

"Sarah, I'm so very proud of you," Lily continued, with me dutifully relaying the words for her. "You've been so brave. Now, listen. I need you to be brave one last time."

Sarah nodded, filled with renewed determination. "Anything."

"You realize what terrible things Hakon would do with an invulnerable vampire. You can't allow that to happen. So." Lily sighed delicately. "Pull the trigger, darling."

"'Allow that to happen,'" I repeated. "'So'—*what*?" I stopped dead. "I'm not saying that!"

"She wants me to do it, doesn't she?" Sarah took a deep breath. "She's right. Lily, I'll make you proud!"

"Nonononono!" I yelped, waving my hands. "Wait,

316

she's—she's saying something else, something real important!" Sarah's finger stopped with the trigger half-pulled. "She—she says to drop the gun immediately or she'll never forgive you! Um, she says to surrender for now, and she'll find a way to rescue you soon! She's gonna come back, really!"

Sarah looked at me pityingly. "Lily would never say that."

"Really! I swear!" I gabbled as she lifted her chin and closed her eyes. "She really, *really* wants you to live!"

"No I don't," said Lily. "I need her to kill you both. I'm sorry, Xanthe darling, but you really are too dangerous to me in Hakon's hands."

I yanked my attention back from the Bloodline, savagely wishing I could take an ax to it. "Sarah, no, listen, *listen*. You're right. Lily *does* want you to do it. Don't you see, that means *Hakon's* right!"

Sarah's eyes opened again. She looked at me suspiciously. "What do you mean?"

"Listen. Lily wants you to kill yourself so that I'll die too, and then Hakon won't be able to use me against her, right? She'd rather you die than she be put in danger." I gulped for air. "That's not love. I'm sorry, but Hakon's right. She's playing us all."

"But . . . but . . ." The certainty had slid off Sarah's face. Her eyes flicked over my parents, Zack. "Your dad was ready to leave *you*."

"Sarah," Dad said very gently. "I was lying through my teeth."

"We would never leave Jane in danger," said Mum fiercely. "*Never.* We'll always protect her."

"But . . . what if it didn't make any sense to?"

Dad shrugged. "That's family," he said simply. "It doesn't have to make sense."

"Sarah," I said as her desperate gaze fixed on me again. "I'm really sorry. But this isn't right. If Lily would let you do this to yourself, then she doesn't love you." I took a cautious step toward her. "I don't think she ever has. Don't do it." Another step. The point of Sarah's gun was shaking. "Don't kill yourself for someone who doesn't deserve it."

Sarah lowered her hand, just a fraction. "If it's true . . ." she whispered. "My dad, my mum . . . I do remember them, I *do*." The muzzle of the gun dropped another millimeter. "If she did kill them . . . if she did, then I want, I want . . ."

"I should want revenge, were I you," Hakon observed.

I froze in mid-step.

I was terrified. Utterly terrified. But I looked at Mum, Dad, Zack—one last, long look—and I knew what I had to do.

"Yes," I said to Sarah, "you *should* want revenge. I want revenge too." I stared hard at her, willing her to understand. "I want to *end* this, all of it. You know?"

Sarah looked at me as if I'd started barking. "What?"

Crap. "I mean, try to see it from my perspective," I said desperately. "We can both get what we want. Lily killed your family, so you want justice. While I'd do anything to keep my family safe. *Anything.* Look at it through my eyes, and you'll see what I mean."

I wasn't looking at Sarah anymore. I was looking at Hakon. Hakon, standing out of her line of sight, off to one side and slightly behind; a twitch of the gun away, if only she could see.

"*Oh,*" Sarah gasped. She fell silent for a second. My heart thundered in her chest. I felt her swallow, hard.

"Okay," Sarah said softly.

I threw the Bloodline wide, as wide as I could—not drawing on the link, but opening it. I could feel the weight of the gun and the burn of fatigue in her shoulder. I could see my own face through her eyes—crap, I'd thought I was doing a better job of not looking scared shitless. And at the same time I could see Hakon, and I could see Sarah seeing me seeing Hakon, and I was Sarah and Sarah was me.

Together, we aimed. Together, we pulled the trigger. And together, we shot Hakon straight through his heart.

Chapter 27

It didn't hurt. It didn't feel like anything at all. In fact, being dead was just like being undead.

I looked down at myself. I seemed not to have vaporized.

Neither had Sarah, for that matter.

Holy crap. I really was unkillable. Our mystic soul-bond thing had protected us from the death of my great-grandsire. . . .

And it seemed to have protected every other vampire in the room, because they too had failed to go poof.

And so had Hakon.

Oh, *shit*.

"Xanthe Jane Greene," Hakon said, standing up again.

He cast me a very disappointed look over the scorched hole in the center of his shirt. The bullet didn't seem to have penetrated very far. He brushed at the fabric as if clearing away spilled crumbs, and the flattened bullet clattered to the floor. "Really, now." He undid shirt buttons as he spoke, letting the garment drop open. "Do you truly believe I would have shown myself if there was any way you could possibly harm me?"

Body armor covered him from his throat downward, disappearing into the waistband of his trousers. Rounded, perfectly smooth, overlapping plates protected his chest. It looked hi-tech enough to be the hull of a spaceship. He could probably take a bazooka to the chest without even getting a bruise.

"I am over one thousand years old," Hakon repeated, meeting my eyes. Though his face was smooth and his voice calm as ever, what I could feel down the Bloodline turned my spine to jelly. "Did you really think that I would be careless?"

"Actually," Zack piped up unexpectedly. Like my parents, he'd managed to slip out of his distracted captor's grasp. "Yeah." And with a sharp, sudden movement, he kicked the neatly arranged pile of Van's weapons.

Paper clips, stakes, grains of rice—they all went

flying. The vampires standing nearby all reflexively leaped after them, leaving my family completely unguarded.

"No!" Hakon shrieked—but my dad had already joined Zack in kicking at the pile, sending more vampires haring off after the bouncing items like Labradors after balls. Mum grabbed a pot of pens off one of the shelves, scattering them on the floor. Two vampires cracked their heads together as they dived for the same ballpoint.

Like all the rest, I was helplessly sucked down to the floor. "Run!" I yelled, even as I frantically gathered up grains of rice one at a time. "Quick, go!"

"Xanthe Jane Greene," snarled a childish voice, and I looked up to find myself nose to nose with Hakon. He too was on his hands and knees, picking up rice as fast as he could—though unlike me, he seemed compelled to immediately lay them down again in a neat grid pattern. Despite his controlled, precise movements, his face was as furious as any kid pitching a tantrum in a supermarket. "I will count this as a betrayal."

"You do that," I said to him. It didn't matter. My family was going to *escape*.

But there were too many vampires, moving too fast. Already the stakes were all gone, and the paper clips wouldn't last much longer. Mum and Dad seized more office supplies, but with a sick feeling I realized that they possibly couldn't disarray things faster than Hakon's vampires could pick them up. And I was *helping* Hakon's goons, unable to stop my traitor hands from picking up rice.

With a squeal of tortured metal, an entire shelving unit peeled away from the wall. I caught a glimpse of Ebon crouched on the top shelf, riding it down with his frock coat flapping and his eyes determinedly screwed shut—and then, with an almighty crash, the shelves hit the ground, squashing two vampires and sending a blizzard of paper into the air.

"That was *alphabetized!*" a vampire howled in agony. The room erupted into a mad brawl. A sliding vampire clutching a handful of highlighters bowled Hakon head over heels. It was pure, wonderful chaos.

"Run!" I yelled again. "Don't wait for me—"

"Don't be daft," Mum said into my ear. Before I knew what was happening, hands hoisted me up by my elbows. "And stop struggling!"

I closed my eyes against the siren lure of the spilled rice. I couldn't have walked away from it of my own free will . . . but I could go limp, letting my parents pull me away. My heels dragged against the carpet as they swept me along; I heard another door slam and felt cold air on my face. I risked cracking open an eye. We were out under the night sky, clattering down the metal treads of the fire escape. Zack was supporting Sarah; Van, wearing the expression of a man who couldn't quite believe what he was doing, had a groggy Ebon slung over one shoulder.

"I'm okay now," I said, getting my own feet under me as we reached the bottom of the stairs. Across the dark expanse of the car park, I could see our white van glowing under a streetlight like a beacon of safety.

Surrounded by the dark forms of at least twenty vampires.

"We're cut off." I whirled, desperately searching for an escape route. Already I could hear shouts in Swedish at the top of the fire escape.

"Look out!" Sarah yelled, pointing off to the side. A glowing ball of silver mist had shot around the far corner of the building and was arcing toward us like a falling star. Van dropped into a combat crouch, even though the only weapon he had was a slightly stunned Ebon. Dad and I tripped over each other, him trying to step protectively in front of me just as I tried to step in front of *him*.

The mist coalesced in front of my face into a small, glowing, and unmistakably fishy form.

"Brains?" Openmouthed, I put out a tentative hand, my fingers passing straight through an ethereal fin. The goldfish bobbed up and down in the air, then looked back the way it had come. Its glow brightened.

A white van skidded around the corner with a screech of tires. For a second I thought it was Van's, but as it spun to a halt in front of us, I saw it had pink flower decals emblazoned across the sides. Black lettering underneath proudly proclaimed: Q'S GARDEN SERVICES.

"Oh." Van dropped Ebon with a thump. After all his stoicism in the face of renegade psychopaths, ancient vampires, and my family, he finally looked properly horrified. *"No."*

The driver's-side door opened. A redheaded man leaned out, narrow green eyes seeking out first Van, then flicking over the rest of us. His lean, weathered face didn't betray even a hint of surprise.

"Little fish told me you might need a lift," said Hunter-General Quincey Helsing.

Chapter 28

"Found the fish at your house," Quinns said when it was his turn for explanations, some time and quite a long story later. He'd dropped the partition between the front and back of the van so that we could talk; Van and Sarah were squashed into the passenger seat, while the rest of us were crammed into the back between boxes of equipment.

Turned out, Quinns really was a gardener. Unlike Van's small arsenal of crossbows and axes, there was nothing in Quinns's van that looked in any way unusual. Just ordinary gardening equipment: shovels, stakes, seeds.

In other words, Quinns was armed to the teeth with

anti-vampire weapons. Ebon and I were both sitting a bit gingerly.

"Yes, but how did you find our house in the first place?" I had the urge to throttle the Hunter-General until he coughed up more than half a dozen words at a time. Getting information out of Quinns was turning out to be harder than getting sense out of Zack.

"Your phone call." Quinns shrugged. "Tracked you from that."

"How?" I said dubiously. "Magic?"

"Google," Quinns said dryly. "Had your first name, enough clues. Found a blog post by a girl named Lorraine." He shifted gear, taking a roundabout at twice the speed limit. "Got full name, then address. Then found the fish. Rest you know."

"You really did go home," I said to the goldfish, now resting smugly in a jar between my knees. Mum and Dad sat on either side of me, holding on to my hands as though they'd never let go again. I didn't want them to. "*Good*, Brains. I'll buy you a . . ." What *did* you buy an undead evil goldfish? ". . . coffin fish-tank ornament. To lurk in." The goldfish waggled its tail in contentment.

"Insisted I follow it." Quinns rubbed absently at a red bite mark on the side of his neck. "Thankfully."

Van crossed his arms over his bare chest, scowling out the side window. Quinns had found him a pair of leather trousers—usually used for protection when pruning rose-bushes, apparently—but didn't have a spare shirt. As Van was a good deal stockier and more muscular than his lean, rangy uncle, said trousers were practically skin tight. A bad part of my mind whispered that I really had to find an excuse to walk behind him sometime soon. "I had it under control," he muttered.

"Mmm," Quinns murmured with a sideways glance at him. "Evidently." Van slumped farther down in the passenger seat.

Ebon cleared his throat. He leaned forward a little, careful not to disturb Zack, who was tucked up under his arm, dozing. "Not to wish to appear ungrateful for the rescue, Hunter-General, but I must ask you as to your future intentions. I am well aware that your organization hires out to the Elders, and I know something of some of your recent dealings. Were you not in the employ of Hakon?"

Quinns looked at him in the rearview mirror, his eyes flat and unfriendly. "Weren't *you*?"

"Ah." Ebon went faintly pink. "I found that I had certain feelings that meant I could not continue in his service."

"Are you in love with Jane?" Sarah twisted round in the front passenger seat to peer at him with interest.

"Sarah!" I yelped. I was horribly aware of my parents on either side of me. Ahead, Van's shoulders had gone tense.

"Well, it would explain things," she said matter-of-factly. "Are you?"

Ebon looked aghast. "No!"

There was a pause.

"Oh," I said after a moment. It came out a little more coldly than I'd intended.

"Ah, that is, I mean no offense," he stuttered, blushing even harder now. "You are very delightful, Jane, and I, er, hold great affection for you, truly, but . . ." He sighed. "Forgive me for mentioning a lady's age, but . . . you are fifteen. I am nearly two hundred years old. It does put certain limits on our association."

"So if it's not Jane," Sarah said, frowning, "why are you doing this?"

He sighed again. "Truly? It was Zack."

This time the pause was rather longer, and when my dad spoke his tone was downright arctic. "Excuse me?"

"I could not help but find myself beguiled," Ebon started, and then noticed the expressions on all our faces. "Good heavens, not like *that!*" He looked down at Zack's sleeping face, and tenderness stole across his own features. "He delights in my era," Ebon said softly. "I have met very few who do. It was one of the darkest periods in vampire history, thanks to the efforts of Lord Hunter-General Abraham Stoker—"

"Wait, *Bram* Stoker?" I interrupted. "As in *Dracula*? Bram Stoker was a *vampire hunter*?"

"And dhampir. Best general we ever had," Van said reverently. Then, in much more his normal surly growl, he added, "And now we're all stuck with the idiotic Dracula names in his honor. We could have just put up a damn statue." Quinns cast him a sardonic look.

"Yes, Stoker was the last known dhampir," Ebon said. He tilted his head in Van's direction. "Until now. Anyway, it was not a good time for vampires." His mouth quirked. "Plus, the fashion for cluttered interior decor meant the Elders could not leave their own barren rooms. I somewhat suspect that's the source of Hakon's current obsession with making minimalism fashionable worldwide." He sighed, his expression turning wistful. "Regardless, it was *my* time, and sometimes I long for it fiercely. To be able to share that feeling with someone is a rare thing. And then . . . then there were the rest of you." Ebon's pale eyes met each of ours in turn, steadily.

"You knew what I was and yet welcomed me in. I have not know such kindness since . . . for a very long time."

There was yet another awkward silence.

"Er," Dad said. "I threatened you with a paintbrush."

"And I grilled you on French history," Mum added, sounding uncharacteristically sheepish.

"Indeed," Ebon said with a grin that made his face suddenly boyish. "And that was still the warmest welcome I have received in over a century. Tragic, am I not?" He hesitated, the smile sliding away, leaving him looking still young, but now vulnerable. "Please. May I stay?"

"Yes," I said, just as Van muttered, "No," and Quinns said, "Maybe."

"Yes," I repeated firmly. "Ebon's one of us."

Quinns kept his eyes on the road. "Don't like vampires much."

"Wow, we've got something in common then. But in case you hadn't noticed, *I'm* a vampire."

"Yes," Quinns agreed, voice flat.

A chill went down my back. I realized that Quinns hadn't yet denied that he worked for the Elders. Seemed that I wasn't the only one to have that thought, as the atmosphere in the van was suddenly very tense. My parents looked at each other, then, as one, at Quinns. My dad's hand surreptitiously drifted down to the handle of a nearby shovel, while Mum palmed a pruning hook. "I think," Dad said, "we'd better talk about what you intend to do with us."

"We're going to protect you," Van said instantly. "All of you. *Aren't we,* Uncle?"

The Hunter-General said nothing for a long moment. What I could see of his face was perfectly expressionless. I was beginning to understand where Van got it from.

"Maybe," Quinns said at last. "Depends."

"On what?" everyone said at once, voices overlapping. Sarah was eyeing Quinns as if she really wished she still had Lily's gun, while Van looked poised to push his uncle out the side door. Ebon had gone very, very still, his lip curled to show the barest hint of fang. Both my parents' hands were white on their makeshift weapons.

Quinns seemed remarkably unfazed for a man on the verge of being murdered at least five times over. "On what you're doing." His eyes met mine in the rearview mirror. "Lily."

It took me a second to catch his meaning. "You think she's monitoring us? Hang on, I'll check." I focused inward. My attention flowed away up the Bloodline, pulling me across space. . . .

"—one moment," Lily was saying into a mobile phone. I felt the hard impact of her high heels hitting concrete as she paced back and forth in front of a motorway service station. "I've got another call coming in." She moved the phone a little way from her ear, addressing thin air. "Why, hello, Quincey darling. Long time no see."

Evidently, Quinns had guessed right. "Um," I said to him. "She's saying hi to you, actually. Says it's been a while."

"Not long enough," Quinns growled, the first sign of real emotion I'd seen from him so far.

"Why, Quincey, I'm hurt," Lily purred. "Is that any way to talk to family?"

"Oh my God," I said, pieces falling into place. "You really are Van's mum. And Quinns is actually his dad, right?"

The van lurched, throwing me into Mum's side, as Quinns jerked hard on the steering wheel. Lily whooped with laughter. "Oh, Xanthe darling," she gasped, wiping her eyes. "Grant me *some* modicum of good taste."

Van stared at Quinns. "*You're* my father?"

"No!" Quinns snapped. "Don't be ridiculous."

"Of course he isn't," Lily said cheerfully. "I am."

"Uh . . . what?" I said. I held one finger up at Van in a "wait a sec" gesture.

"Dear Lucy Helsing," Lily said with what sounded awfully like genuine fondness. "We did have some good times. Jolly fine girl. Ever so practical too. I needed a dhampir, but I could hardly carry a baby myself for nine months without Hakon finding out about it. So Lucy and I came to a little mutually beneficial agreement." She took a long drag on her cigarette, and added, "You were never quite so keen on the deal, were you, Quincey dear? Should have guessed you'd end up keeping the boy to yourself."

"So the hunters did collude with you in creating the dhampir," said a clear, cold voice from Lily's phone. Ice ran through my veins. Hakon. "You are a foolish child, Lily. You know nothing of history, so blithely tempting the hunters with such a weapon again."

"*I* had him perfectly under my control," Lily retorted. "Until *you* blundered in."

I jumped as Sarah prodded me in the shoulder. "What's going on?" she said impatiently. "What's Lily doing?" Her face bore a strange, half-hungry, half-apprehensive expression.

"Uh, telling Hakon all about how she did a deal with Van's mum," I said, distracted. "And that she's his father. Van's, I mean, not Hakon's."

"What?" Van looked like he'd been whacked upside the head with a brick.

Quinns let out a long, resigned sigh. "It's true."

We all stared at him.

"Shape-shifter," said Quinns. This appeared to be all the explanation he felt was necessary.

"Lily can turn into anyone," I said to my puzzled parents. I remembered the male appearance she'd briefly assumed. "Including guys. Guess it's quite a, um, complete transformation."

"Why didn't you *tell* me?" Van demanded of his uncle. His voice shook with barely controlled anger and shock. "Why? You lied!"

"Didn't," Quinns said, sharp as a knife blade. "Not about the important things, that Lucy loved you, vampires took her, you had to hide." His voice calmed again. "Needed you to hate them. Afraid you might not, might have been curious about Lily, if you knew the truth. Had to stop you from going to her."

Van digested this. "Oh."

"Didn't go so well," added Quinns with a sour twist to his mouth.

Lily made a low, throaty laugh. "All I had to do was snap my fingers"—she clicked her varnished nails in demonstration—"and the boy came running. Poor Quincey. You should know by now that I always get what I want."

"You didn't this time," I said to her. "We got away. You lost."

"Really?" Lily flicked ash off her cigarette. "Always have a plan B, darling." She turned back to her phone. "Speaking of which . . . Hakon?"

"I am more minded to simply hunt you down like the rabid dog you are, Lily, and so end the threat of both you and your progeny," Hakon snarled. "You have released the whirlwind upon us. If another Bloodline brings Xanthe Jane to heel first—"

"And they will do so, if you don't accept my proposal," Lily interrupted. "You send a single one of your thugs after me, Hakon, and I'm taking this deal straight to another Elder. I'm the only one who can easily find our dear Xanthe Jane, but *anyone* with a large enough force could use my information to recapture her. And once one has Jane, her parents will surrender, which gives one the key to controlling Jane . . . a neat circle. Any Elder would offer me protection in return for such power. Maybe I'll call up, oh, say, to pick a name completely at random, Ilmari." I felt a smug, vicious smile curve Lily's lips at Hakon's sharp intake of breath. "My, what *do* you think an Elder like him would do with someone of Jane's potency, hmm?"

A pause, then Hakon spat out a long stream of archaic Swedish.

"Why, thank you," Lily said, her smile widening. "I'll assume that was a lovely compliment." She ground her cigarette butt daintily under one heel. "Let me make it crystal clear for you, little boy. You can shake off your silly cultural baggage, hold your nose, and work with me, or you can watch your empire burn. Now, should I start calling round and inviting the highest bid, or do we have a deal?"

A much longer pause. Then, "Deal," Hakon said, sounding as though the word were being pulled out of him on barbed wire. "Alliance between us, as long as your progeny lives. And, Xanthe Jane Greene?"

"Yeah?" I said, fighting down a shudder at the leashed rage in Hakon's voice.

"Tell Quincey Helsing I know his plan for the dhampir. And I shall make sure every Bloodline in existence knows too." Lily's phone clicked as Hakon hung up.

"Goodness, now there's a poor loser," Lily observed, snapping her phone shut. "Still listening, Xanthe darling? Really now. I should start running, if I were you."

I pulled back from the connection, feeling like I'd been for a dip in a rancid pond. "Uh, I don't think Hakon's real pleased with you," I told Quinns. "He said something about knowing what you're up to with Van, and that he'd tell all the other vampires too. He sounded like it was a really big deal."

Quinns let out his breath. "Over a hundred years of secrecy," he said rather grimly. "Thrown away." He glared, narrow-eyed, at Van. "You are *very* grounded."

"Secrecy?" Ebon said, frowning. "Hunter-General, all vampires are quite aware that your group became corrupt after Stoker's death. It is hardly a secret that you are vampire minions rather than vampire hunters."

"What we wanted you to think," Quinns said. "Had to, or you would have wiped us out after Stoker. Really, we are vampire hunters. Always have been. But we're not hunting vampires."

"Want to be a little *more* cryptic?" Sarah snapped.

"Being accurate." Quinns shrugged one shoulder. "Not hunting vampires. Hunting *a* vampire. That's the secret."

"Only one vampire?" I frowned. Quinns didn't strike me as a personal vendetta kind of guy. "Which one?"

"The first."

There was a pause, while we all contemplated that.

"That's . . . an admirably logical plan," my mum said at last.

"Thanks." Quinns drove in silence for a moment. "Slow, hard work, though. Got to stay low, appease the vampires, keep researching. Lucy didn't like it. Kept looking for shortcuts, like creating a dhampir." He shook his head. "Warned Lucy that Lily had to be playing her. Didn't listen. Like you," he added, cocking an eyebrow at Van. "Impatient."

"While you're sitting around researching, people are getting hurt," Van muttered.

"People always getting hurt." It sounded like a well-worn and long-running argument. "Bigger picture." Quinns sighed in exasperation. "Doesn't matter now. Cover blown. Traded for a handful of humans and a couple of teenage vampires. Ha." Van glared.

"Wrong," I said. Crap, it was contagious. Too much time in Quinns's company, and we'd all just be grunting at each other.

"Oh?" Quinns said, neutral.

"Wrong," I repeated. "Traded for"—I swung my finger to point at Van, Ebon, and Sarah in turn—"a supernaturally good fighter that no one can hide from, a shape-shifting spy who's been close to one of your greatest enemies, and a budding evil genius who thinks more like a vampire than the vampires do. And me," I added. "The world's only unkillable supervamp." I sat back, folding my arms and ignoring the way everyone except Quinns was staring at me. I glared at the back of the Hunter-General's head. "If you can't defeat the bad guys with *that* lot, then you seriously suck."

"Baby Jane," my dad said slowly. "What are you doing?"

"Angling for a job, I think," Quinns said, a hint of amusement in his level voice. Nonetheless, his eyes were thoughtful, serious, as he studied me in the mirror. "We'll have a conflict of interests eventually, you know."

My God, a complete sentence. I must have seriously impressed him. "I know," I agreed. "But until then, we can help each other out." I paused. "I warn you, I'm not coming cheap though."

Quinns's mouth quirked. "Suspected not."

"You've got to take care of my family. And Sarah. Ebon too, if he wants. Keep them safe, hidden from the vampires." I frowned, thinking. "And I want a credit card. Unlimited. I'm going to be doing a lot of traveling, and there's no way I'm sleeping in sewers. Not to mention all the new clothes and stuff I'll need."

Mum gripped my arm. "But you're staying with

us, Xanthe. You need—"

"I need to keep away," I said, swallowing the lump in my throat. "Mum, Dad, Lily's working with Hakon, and she can always find me. Until I've captured her, I can't be in the same place as you." I squeezed her hand. "It won't be forever. I promise. And we'll still be able to talk." I looked at Sarah. "You okay to stay with them?"

"The 'evil genius' has always been more into directing minions from her dark fortress rather than getting her own hands dirty," Sarah said dryly. Turning to my parents, she gestured at her forehead. "We're linked together. You'll be able to check up on her whenever you want." She flashed me a wicked grin. "Don't worry. There's nothing she can hide from me."

"So," I said to Quinns. "Deal?"

His face cracked in a slow smile. "Deal."

I sank back against the side of the van, feeling the tension ease from my muscles. My hands found my parents' again. I knew that soon I'd have to leave, but I could enjoy this moment of peace for a little while longer.

Funding, a purpose, and my family safe. What more could a teenage vampire fangirl want?

Well . . . maybe one more thing.

"Hey, Van," I said. "Want to go hunt some vampires?"

Acknowledgments

There are a vast horde of people without whom this book would not exist, but I must personally thank a few in particular:

First, enormous thanks to my agent, the redoubtable Nephele Tempest, for finding the perfect home for the manuscript. And second, to my amazing editor, Erica Sussman, and her equally amazing assistant, Tyler Infinger, for their sterling work removing the suck and adding the awesome.

To my copyeditors, for earnestly debating the correct spelling of "noob."

Special thanks to Claudia Smith, whose professional translating skills kept me from veering uncontrollably between English and American. And to Eljas Oksanen, whose book this is (and who, assuming the publication dates don't change, now owes me one shiny Euro for *just* beating him into print).

To the rest of the Jade Cats—Rob Mathews, Joe McDonnell, James Donnithorne-Tait, David Till, and Diego Virasoro—for starting me off down this path in the first place. May the muppetry never end!

To the Ricepaper gang, especially Yoon Ha Lee and Nancy Sauer, for the comradeship and critiques.

To the fine folk who run NaNoWriMo, without whom I would probably still be working on chapter three.

To all my friends at LiveJournal, for the virtual support and encouragement over the years. We may never meet in the flesh, but you are the finest collection of disembodied pixels I know.

Heartfelt thanks to my mother, June Keeble, who on many occasions was literally left holding the baby while I frantically wrote to meet the deadline. Mum, the next book's definitely for you (and I apologize in advance for the subject matter).

And last but by no means least, all my love and gratitude to my husband, Tim, who took me vampire hunting in IKEA.